Reckoning

· The Dominion Saga: Book Two ·

S.J. WEST

LIST OF BOOKS IN THE WATCHER SERIES

The Watchers Trilogy

Cursed

Blessed

Forgiven

The Watcher Chronicles

Broken

Kindred

Oblivion

Ascension

Caylin's Story

Timeless

Devoted

Aiden's Story

The Alternate Earth Series (A Jess and Mason Bonus Adventure)

Cataclysm

Uprising

Judgment

The Redemption Series

Malcolm

Anna

Lucifer

Redemption

The Dominion Series

Awakening

Reckoning

Enduring (2016)

OTHER BOOKS BY S.J. WEST

The Harvest of Light Trilogy

Harvester

Hope

Dawn

The Vankara Saga

Vankara

Dragon Alliance

War of Atonement

CHAPTER ONE
(Malcolm's Point of View)

Life rarely leads you down a straight path, and it's often the curves and hills you have to traverse that end up being the most interesting parts of the journey. To be honest, I could do without any more detours. I realize now how foolish I was to believe Anna and I could live out the rest of our lives together in peace. I had hoped when my father sent the War Angels to us, that it meant the responsibility of handling Helena's shenanigans would fall on their shoulders more than ours. After living on Earth for so long, I thought I might have earned the right to live out the rest of my life with Anna and our children like normal people.

Obviously, I was wrong.

I grab my sword from its spot beside our bed and phase back down to the living room to rejoin the others. When I arrive, Jess and Mason are speaking with Desmond, Brutus, and Andre while Vala is comforting a distraught Luna. Our resident hellhound has remained a constant by Lucas' side for as long as she's been with us. If someone had told me even a year ago that I would care so much about a hellhound, I would have told them they were insane. Against all probability and rules of logic, I do care about her, and I know she won't be the same until Anna and Lucas are safely home.

I notice Anna's War Angel guards haven't made it back yet. I advised them all to go home and wash off the blood they were covered in from the fight with the rebellion angels at the beach house. I'm sure the home I built for her is now drenched red with blood, but I can't worry about that right now. All I can think about is my wife and son being trapped in Hell with Helena. Getting them back overshadows everything else.

"I'm glad to see the three of you here already," I tell my fellow Watchers. "There are things that each of you need to handle while we're searching for Anna and Lucas. Brutus, I need you to take care of the Cirrun refugees, just as we discussed. Andre, there's bound to be some political fallout from the hellspawn attack. You need to deal with any questions the other cloud cities have about what happened there. Handle it the best you can without letting them find out what's actually going on. Desmond, I need you to keep an eye on Catherine and find out how she intends to use this latest development to her advantage. The election will have to be postponed now, of course, and it gives her more time to rally supporters to her side. All of you need to do whatever you can to make sure Anna doesn't return home to find that she's lost her throne before the election even has a chance to take place."

Brutus opens his mouth and looks like he's about to argue against my orders. I hold my right hand up, palm forward, to stop him before he can utter a single word.

"I need you all *here*," I say before he can protest that they should be going with me to Hell. "With so many of us gone, I need people I can trust to take care of things. The three of you are the only ones I have complete faith in to handle whatever might happen while we're in Hell."

Desmond is about to say something, but Andre places a restraining hand on his arm and says, "We'll protect Cirrus for you, Malcolm. Right now, all you need to worry about is finding Anna and Lucas and bringing everyone home safely."

I have to look away from Andre's earnest expression because all I can think is that I've already failed my family. It's probably painfully obvious to everyone that the babies don't feel as though I can keep them safe on Earth. With the rebellion angels determined to kill them and their mother, Liam and Liana seem to believe their psychotic 'Aunt' Helena is more capable of protecting them than I am. Perhaps she is, since no one is allowed to phase into Hell without her permission. The rebellion angels would be foolish to enter her domain through a fissure, which is exactly what we're about to attempt. Helena has complete autonomy inside her home. The only hope we have of succeeding there is if Anna can somehow find a way to keep her preoccupied with something else while we try to find her. If she can keep Helena distracted, she won't be watching our every move, and we might have a fighting chance to reach them.

"Malcolm…" Jess places a comforting hand on my arm and squeezes it lightly. I look into her eyes and know she understands the thoughts going through my mind without me even having to say them out loud. "We'll bring them back home. Don't doubt that."

"I don't," I tell her.

We either come back with them or we don't come back at all is what I'm thinking, but I don't say it.

As I look at Jess and Mason, I notice for the first time that they're wearing the same clothing they wore when we went to alternate Earth. She's dressed in the maroon leather outfit JoJo made her while we were there, while he's wearing his black one. There's only one thing missing.

"I'll be right back," I say before phasing back up to my bedroom to retrieve something. When I return, I hand Jess the sword that was originally hers. "You might need this," I tell her. "I don't think Anna will mind you borrowing it."

She smiles as she accepts the sword sheathed in its baldric. It's strange to think about how many years have passed since she first retrieved Jophiel's sword from the Garden of Eden. A long line of descendants has used it to protect this world, but only Jess has the distinction of being the one who pulled it from the Tree of Knowledge.

"Hello, old friend," she croons as she holds the sheath with one hand, gripping the hilt of the sword and pulling it out. "I've missed you."

"I think I have the perfect thing for you, Mason," Brutus says before phasing, only to return a few seconds later holding a well-crafted long sword. He still forges weapons on occasion, and I know the sword he hands Mason will be able to cut through anything Helena places in our path.

"Malcolm," Vala says as she walks over to me, "is there anything I can do to help?"

"Just take care of Luna for Lucas," I tell her. "I have a feeling he'll need her when he gets back."

Vala nods. "I can do that."

After hearing her name, Luna comes up to me and gently paws at one of my legs, as if she wants to tell me something. I bend down on one knee in front of her and pet the sensitive spot between the ears.

"I'll bring them back home," I pledge to her.

Luna whines and paws at me again. All I can do is assume she expects me to keep my promise.

As I stand back up, Anna's War Angels phase into the room. I know exactly fifteen minutes have passed since I last saw them. It was the amount of time I gave them to prepare for our trip into the bowels of Hell, and angel punctuality is practically infallible. All of them are dressed like me: shirtless, and only wearing black leather pants and boots; a weapon in their hand. Blood's a lot easier to wipe off if you're not wearing something that will absorb it easily. Like me, they expect Helena to throw a few obstacles in our way. There isn't a shred of doubt in my mind that we'll end up having to fight our way to Anna and Lucas. To be honest, I welcome the challenge. Perhaps it will help me get rid of some of my rage before I see my family again.

Not long after each War Angel was born in Heaven, they had to select a weapon that was an expression of their fighting style. For a War Angel, battle is like breathing to regular people. Their class of angel was specifically made to end the rebellion Lucifer started, and many of them felt like their lives were pointless after the war was won. I knew they all treasured the opportunity God gave them to live here on Earth and to be afforded the chance to forge a different sort of life for themselves. Selfishly, I'm thankful they're the ones who will be going into Hell with me. I couldn't have selected a better fighting force to stand by my side and help me rescue my family.

"We're ready when you are, Malcolm," Ethan, the commander of the War Angels, tells me, hefting the black and gold great sword he uses in his hand.

I turn to look at Mason. "I suppose Jered isn't back yet with the traitor."

Mason lifts a disapproving eyebrow at me. "No, he hasn't returned with Slade, and I think you need to curb that attitude of yours towards him.

He doesn't have to help you, Malcolm. Yet he's willing to risk his life to do so."

"He'll come with us whether I want him to or not," I say, having mixed feelings about Slade's involvement in this mission. My father told me I should try to find a way to be sympathetic to him, but I'm finding it impossible to change my mind about him. "Slade cares about Anna. He'll come for her sake, not mine."

Alex, the War Angel assigned to this part of the down-world, walks into the room carrying his silver morning star and dressed like the rest of us.

"Are you sure you want to come with us, Alex?" I ask. "It's all right if you would rather stay here."

He's always been a rather shy angel, even when I knew him during the war. When Anna returned from her trip to Heaven to seek advice from Lucifer about Helena, she learned that Amalie and Alex spent a great deal of time together there. Her mother was able to help him work through his issues and learn how to verbally express himself to others more easily. I guess I should have noticed the difference in him when he first came to Earth, but honestly, I wasn't around him enough to note the change.

"Unless you have a specific objection to me coming, I want to help you get Anna and Lucas back," he tells me.

"No, I don't have any objections to you joining us," I say as I look around the room at the group going to Hell with me. "I just want to make sure everyone here understands what we're going to be facing there. Helena won't make it easy for any of us while we're in her domain, and I'm not just talking about throwing demonic creatures at us to fight. She'll dig deep into all of our memories and try to use what she finds against us. I'm sure we all have secrets that we don't want others to learn about, but after this trip I have a feeling we'll know more about each other than we may want to. I hope you're all prepared for that to happen."

"We'll deal with whatever she tries to do to us," Cade assures me confidently.

"Out of all of us, you may be the one she focuses on the most," I tell him. "You won't be able to hide anything from her while we're there. She'll know every thought and feeling you have about her, so watch yourself."

Cade nods, fully understanding my advice to him.

I still can't understand how someone as pure of heart as Cade is Helena's soul mate. It's the ultimate irony. He couldn't be more dissimilar to her if he tried. When the dice were rolled to pair up souls, he definitely lost. I feel sorry for him, but there isn't anything I can do to change his fate. He'll have to figure out a way to deal with his feelings for her and live with them the best he can.

Jered phases just inside the entryway to the room with Slade standing by his side. Slade automatically lifts his gaze to meet mine, and I know exactly what he sees in my eyes for him: utter loathing.

It's not only the fact that he betrayed us that causes me to hate him; he also used Caylin's sense of decency to end his miserable life after we found out what he did. I hate weakness, and I hate the fact that he played on Caylin's caring nature to end his own suffering on Earth. He shouldn't have used her like that. Although, I suppose he got what he deserved during his time in Hell. I have zero pity for whatever he might have endured while he was there. As far as I'm concerned, he earned it.

Slade is shirtless and wearing a ratty pair of brown trousers that are smeared with black smudge marks, just like the ones staining his bare skin. I stationed him on Saturn to oversee the mining colony there because it was the farthest off-world site Cirrus controlled. I had heard that he often went down to the mines to work, but this was the first time I had seen any evidence to support those reports. Slade looks even more muscular than I remember, but he no longer has the large black tribal tattoo on his shoulder like he did the first time he lived on Earth. Back in the day, it was what he used to cover up his hellhound bite. To truly feel his torture in Hell, Lucifer gave him a new body there after he died, minus the tattoo. He holds a large mining pick in a firm grip by his side. I have to assume it's his weapon of choice to bring to Hell.

Mason walks up to him, extending his hand in greeting.

"It's good to see you again, Slade," Mason says. "Thank you for coming to help us."

Slade cracks a small smile and shakes his hand. "Jered told me you and Jess were back, but I guess I didn't really believe it until now. It's good to see you both, too."

"We should go," I say abruptly, not wanting to waste any more time since there's nothing else we need to wait on. "Where exactly is the fissure you came through?" I ask Slade curtly.

The only reason we need him here is because he came through an opening when he escaped Hell. Only those who have spent a great deal of time there can see the tears in the veil between Earth and Hell. Twenty other Watchers who sold their souls to Lucifer came through it with Slade, but I haven't welcomed them back with open arms either. They all have a lot to atone for, and I just don't have the patience to deal with their issues. Desmond was placed in charge of taking care of them. To my way of thinking, the less contact I have with them the better.

"It's in the desert where your first fight with the hellspawn took place," Slade tells me. "If we all hold hands, I can phase us to it."

Sheathing our weapons we gather into a large circle and hold hands so he can phase us directly to the spot.

Once we're there, I look around, but all I see is a multitude of sand dunes.

"Where is it?" I ask sharply, failing to hide the contempt I feel towards him and knowing he's the only one of us who can actually see the opening between the veils.

Slade looks over his shoulder to the dune right behind him. "It's there," he says before looking back at us all. "I can't promise that we'll find Anna and Lucas once we're inside. You all need to be prepared for the possibility that we won't."

"We will find them," I say, unable to prevent the growl in my voice. "And if you're going to have that kind of attitude about this mission, maybe you shouldn't stay with us after we go inside."

"I'm just trying to be realistic about the situation, Malcolm, that doesn't mean I won't do everything I can to help," Slade tells me. "If you thought outer space was infinite, Hell is even more so. If Helena doesn't want us to find your family, we won't. Anna may be the only one who can convince Helena to let her go."

"I don't intend to give her a choice in the matter," I tell him, fully determined to do whatever it takes to get Anna and Lucas back.

"Why don't we get going?" Jess suggests, putting an end to my argument with Slade. "I assume, since you're the only one who can see the fissure, you'll need to lead us into it."

"Yes," Slade says, diverting his gaze away from me to look at her. "Once we're inside, I'll be able to see the other fissures available to us in case we need to make a quick escape."

"We're not all cowards like you," I tell him, placing an emphasis on the last word. "We won't need an escape route."

Slade narrows his eyes on me. "You don't know what we'll need until we're in there."

"I know I won't be running away."

"Ok, boys," Jess says, looking between the two of us with her hands on her hips, "let's stay focused and remember why we're here. If the two of you want to have a pissing match later on, be my guest, but right now I'm more interested in finding Anna and Lucas than worrying about either of your egos."

"Have I mentioned how much I've missed you?" Jered tells Jess, a wry grin on his face.

"Of course you missed me," Jess replies with a small, unassuming shrug of her shoulders. "No one else can put Malcolm in his place as effectively as me and not get pummeled while doing it."

"Hmph!" I narrow my eyes at Jess to warn her that she's treading on thin ice with my patience. She winks at me with that little mischievous smile of hers, and I instantly realize she's right. However, I'm not about to own up to that small weakness where she's concerned.

“Let’s get going before Slade loses his nerve,” I say gruffly, getting the last jab in while I can.

Slade wisely chooses to ignore me. He leads us all inside, and I end up being the last one who enters Hell.

We walk into what looks like a narrow tunnel drilled through the center of a mountain. It’s just tall enough for me to not hit my head on the ceiling, and barely wide enough for us to stand two abreast. I realize the space is partially real and partially illusion. Hell is similar to Heaven in that regard. Almost anything you can dream up is possible here, if you’re the one in control. All Helena has to do is imagine something into being.

There’s an almost overwhelming sulfuric stench emanating from somewhere ahead of us.

“Where exactly will this tunnel take us?” I ask Slade. “I assume that smell is coming from wherever it is you escaped from the last time you were here.”

“Yes, it is,” he answers, looking uncomfortable in our surroundings. “I was hoping the location of things might have shifted around by now, but apparently they haven’t. I suppose that could work in our favor, though. I won’t have to guess where we’re going as much.”

“Where does this lead?” I ask again, promptly losing what little patience I have where Slade is concerned.

The dread that suddenly appears on his face tells me I won’t like the answer.

“The leviathan pits,” he informs me. “If we’re lucky, they’ll still be asleep. Helena keeps them all in hibernation mode to make sure they remain calm. Otherwise, they get agitated and try to escape.”

"Escape to where?" Ethan asks.

"Other levels of Hell," Slade answers. "As long as everyone keeps quiet while we're in there, we should be able to walk through their chamber without waking them."

"And what's waiting for us on the other side of the leviathan pits?" Jess asks.

"I don't know for sure," he admits. "But if things haven't changed since the last time I was here, I think I can take us to an empty chamber. It's used as a staging area for the souls Helena feeds to the leviathans. She only does that every once in a while, though. Hopefully, today isn't a feeding day. Make sure all of you watch your step as we walk through. The pathways between the leviathan pits are extremely narrow, and if you fall into one of them there's no way we can get you back out, since none of us can phase while we're in here."

Without saying another word, Slade turns around and starts walking down the tunnel. As we follow him into the leviathans' chamber, I can't help but think that we're making a colossal mistake trusting him to lead us around Hell. Who knows what being tortured down here for over a thousand years did to him mentally? He healed from his physical wounds quickly enough, but there are some things that can't be mended with just the passage of time. Yet, even if he is thoroughly off his rocker, I know Slade will never betray Anna. I may have lost my ability to tell a truth from a lie the first time I drank human blood, but I know without that angelic power that he will protect Anna with his life, if it comes down to that. Perhaps he feels guilt over betraying Caylin, and he wants to make reparations for it with the descendent he was originally meant to protect. He did glow to Caylin's eyes at one time. His desire to help her was real, even if we all assumed it was only so he could follow through with Lucifer's orders for him. Whatever his real motivation is, it's only known to him. As long as he helps me find my family, I really don't care why he's helping us.

As I approach the end of the tunnel we're in, the putrid smell inside the leviathans' chamber is practically suffocating. I have to keep myself from gagging on the foul air entering my lungs. The area itself is massive in scale, but so are the leviathans. The room is circular, with a circumference of at least a mile. The pits where the leviathans are sleeping are hexagonal in shape, making the floor of the chamber resemble the honeycomb structure of a beehive. I had hoped I would never have to see these particular creatures of Hell again after witnessing them in action on alternate Earth. Talk about bringing Hell to Earth. I try not to think about that time in my life too much. It has forever left a scar inside me.

The path between each of the leviathan cells is barely wide enough to fit both of my feet side by side. Zane is directly in front of me. I watch as he misjudges a step. His foot slides into one of the cells, grazing the top of the sleeping leviathan we're passing. The creature stirs slightly and groans in its sleep, but his trespass barely disturbs its slumber. Zane slowly lifts his foot out of the cell and looks back at me, shaking his head at his own clumsiness.

When we're close to the center of the chamber, I hear the low snarl of an animal come from directly behind me. I quickly look over my shoulder and see a hellhound standing at the entrance to the tunnel we just came through. Its pristine white fur is ablaze with the illusion of fire that reflects against its black eyes, causing them to be lit with a preternatural glow. As the hound continues to stare at me, it bares its teeth, growling even louder.

Before long, its snarl is joined by a multitude of them. I look around the chamber and see at least twenty hellhounds standing around the perimeter of the room. Each of them is guarding a tunnel leading out of the area, including the one we were originally headed for. As if by some predetermined cue, all of the them begin to run towards us.

Being left with no other choice, we all begin to run down the only pathway that leads to a tunnel not being guarded by a hound. After living with the pain of a hellhound bite for a thousand years, I sure as hell don't want to have to go through that experience again. In the back of my mind, I know this new development can only mean one thing.

Helena knows we're here, and she's using the hellhounds to herd us exactly where she wants us to go.

That's fine by me. We knew we couldn't hide from her forever. This is her domain, after all, and she has full control over what happens in Hell.

Slade is the first one to exit the leviathan chamber and make it to the area Helena is forcing us to enter. I take a deep breath as I run through the entryway. As soon as I see what's waiting for us, I know Helena is presenting us with her first challenge.

Game on…

CHAPTER TWO
(Anna's Point of View)

I feel betrayed by my own children. As I hold Lucas close to my side and stare at Helena's mocking smile, I can't help but wonder why Liam and Liana continue to go against my will, phasing us to her. She seems to believe it's because they feel safer in her presence. I guess I can understand that to a degree, but something about that explanation just doesn't sit well with me. I sense they're trying to accomplish a particular task involving Helena, and then I remind myself that they're just babies. How can they be thinking anything, much less strategizing a secret agenda? I refuse to believe our children think Malcolm and I are incapable of keeping them safe. If the babies are, in fact, cognizant of what's going on around them and thinking well beyond their age, they must know their father and I will do whatever it takes to keep them protected.

Even though the most probable explanation sounds impossible, I believe the babies have brought us here for a specific purpose. I simply don't know what it is yet.

"Do you like the décor I chose?" Helena asks me with a tilt of her head as she considers the furnishings in the room.

"A little too Goth for my taste, if this is supposed to be a nursery," I tell her truthfully as I consider the black-painted wood bed, cribs, and black and silver damask wallpaper. "It looks like you're going to have a funeral in here. Or is that the point of all the black? Are you planning to kill my children yourself, Helena?"

She giggles, making my skin crawl from the unnatural sound. “Oh, Anna, you are too much sometimes; so dramatic. You continuously think the worst of me. How are we ever going to develop a sisterly bond if you refuse to trust me? I only want to keep your little cherubs safe, nothing else. Haven’t I done enough to prove that to you yet?”

“You’ve lost your mind if you think I’ll ever trust you, Helena, and I don’t believe for a second that your plans for them are anything but selfish.”

Her smile slowly fades, as if I’ve made her angry by my statements. It’s the truth as I see it. I’m not about to lie to her just to stroke her ego.

“Oh,” she says, lifting her chin up a notch in righteous indignation, “I see how you are. You can forgive our father for the most depraved transgressions against humanity, but me you automatically place into the category of the unredeemable.”

“Are you seeking redemption?” I ask, not even sure that would work in Helena’s case, considering who and what she is.

“Not really,” she says with a carefree shrug of one shoulder. “I’ve done nothing to be sorry for. I am what I am because of the way Lucifer treated me. He made me the same way he made you, but I was never allowed to have the advantages you did.”

“And what advantages do you believe he gave to me and not to you?”

“His respect and love.”

“Are those things you wanted from him?” My question is a leading one. I’m curious to know if love is an emotion Helena can actually feel. Considering the fact that Cade is her soul mate, it seems plausible that even the personification of Hell is capable of feeling such an emotion. Could that be the reason God allowed (what seems like a travesty against the whole concept of soul mates) such a paring to occur? Maybe her connection to Cade wasn't only meant to teach her a lesson, but to also show the rest of us that she is capable of more than just hate.

Helena carefully contemplates her answer before replying, "It's a moot point. Lucifer never cared for me the way he did you. That's just a fact."

"I did receive his love in the end, but you were able to spend more time with him than I was," I counter.

She looks at me like I'm the one who has lost her mind.

"Are you serious?" she asks incredulously. "You spent more time with him than I could ever dream of spending."

It takes me a moment, but I finally understand what she's referring to.

"I don't remember the time he and I spent together in Heaven when I was Seraphina."

"Seraphina?" Lucas asks, looking up at me in confusion. "What do you mean, Mommy? Who is she?"

I hear Helena snap her fingers. Lucas instantly closes his eyes and falls asleep against my side.

"Why did you do that?" I ask tersely, finding it difficult in my pregnant state to keep Lucas from sliding to the floor now that he's unconscious.

"I didn't feel like having him interrupt us with a million and one questions about your angelic past life," she says with a roll of her eyes. "I don't have the patience for that sort of thing."

"He's a child. Children are naturally inquisitive. That's how they learn things."

"I don't really care what the reason is behind it. I would rather he slept while the grown-ups talk."

"You could at least help me get him into bed if you're going to be this way."

Helena huffs, "Very well."

She snaps her fingers a second time, and Lucas is instantly transported from my arms onto the top of the large four-poster bed in the room.

"Am I right in guessing that you haven't told him who he really is yet either?"

"He doesn't need to know about that," I say, turning my attention back to her. "And I would appreciate it if you never told him."

Helena tilts her head and smiles coquettishly at me. "Are you asking me for a favor, sweet sister?"

"I'm asking you to do the decent thing for once in your life."

"And who says telling him the truth isn't the right thing to do? Doesn't he deserve to know about his own past? He should be proud of who he was and know how much he sacrificed to save the lives of the people he loved."

"Lucas has his own life to live," I tell her. "Let him live it without the burden of knowing what happened before."

"Whatever," she says with a dismissive wave of her hand. "I don't really care about all of that anyway." Helena captures my full attention as she gazes at me intently. "What I do care about is this missing time you seem to have from your life as Seraphina. Can you honestly not remember anything? Not a single moment?"

"No. I don't remember that life. All I know is what God showed me when He finally explained my true relationship to Lucifer."

Her eyelids lower and a sly smile stretches her lips. "Would you like to see more of that life?"

Her question catches me off-guard.

"See more of it?" I ask, feeling as though I've just stepped into a well-laid trap.

"It's a simple enough question, Anna. Please try to keep up. I'm asking if you want to see more about your life as Seraphina."

"And how exactly would you be able to show me that?"

"Have you already forgotten that I have all of Lucifer's memories in here?" she says, tapping her right temple with her index finger. "I have every little thing he did stored inside my mind. I would be willing to share some of his memories with you, if you want."

"What does that do for you?" I ask, knowing Helena never does anything to help others unless she gets something in return. There has to be an angle to her seemingly-generous offer that I'm missing.

"Do I have to have an ulterior motive to do something nice for you?"

"Yes," I say without hesitation.

"Ye of so little faith, Anna." Helena shakes her head at me in disappointment.

"Oh, I have plenty of faith that you don't do things for other people if it doesn't benefit you in some way. So, what is it? Is there something from my life as Seraphina that you think will hurt me?"

"I just thought it would be a nice way for us to pass the time together. Who knows how long you'll be…"

Helena abruptly stops speaking and closes her eyes; she tilts her head to the right as if she's trying very hard to listen to something in particular.

"Those sneaky little devils," she says with a smile, sounding impressed.

"Who are you talking about?" I ask, curious to know what has her so intrigued.

She opens her eyes and looks directly at me. "It seems as if your husband is trying to rescue you, Anna."

My heart leaps inside my chest with excitement and newfound hope. I pray the babies allow their father to take us home when he finds us. Maybe this will finally prove to them that we are more than capable of keeping them safe.

"Why did you say they were sneaky?"

"I've prevented anyone from phasing here, but they've found a way through one of the fissures I left open," Helena tells me. "My, my, your husband has brought quite a formidable force with him to find you. He must love you a great deal."

"Is Cade with him?" I closely watch her reaction to my question, but she gives nothing away with her impassive expression.

"All of your War Angel guards are with him," she replies smoothly, not singling Cade out in any way. "Jered is with him and…" Her lips form a pleased smile. "Well, guess who decided to come back to me? My dearest Watcher pet, Slade. I do so miss my playtime with him." Helena's brows converge, as she looks confused by something else she senses. "There seem to be two other souls with him, but I can't quite place them. How interesting…"

"Is that unusual for you?"

"Very," she says, excited by this new development. "I'm sorry, Anna, but this little tête-à-tête of ours will have to be postponed. It seems I have some new toys to amuse myself with for a little while."

"What are you going to do to them?" I ask. Helena's apparent elation only fills my heart with dread.

"Play with them, of course," she replies with a devious smile.

Malcolm has to know that Helena has complete control over what happens in her domain. How does he plan to outwit her long enough to find me? I try to think if there's any way I can help him. Maybe if I can keep her distracted with something else, it will aid Malcolm's search for us. It suddenly dawns on me that she's already given me the key to keeping her preoccupied.

"Is torturing them more important than spending time with me?" I ask her. "I thought you were going to show me my life as Seraphina."

Helena laughs. "Oh please, don't think I can't see straight through your ploy, Anna. You're under the misguided perception that I can't do two things at once. This is my home, and you all have to abide by my rules while you're here."

"And what are the rules?"

"That I can do anything I want and you're at my mercy."

"Doesn't seem very sporting of you. I thought you would at least make things more interesting for yourself."

Helena narrows her eyes at me while she crosses her arms over her chest. "Are you suggesting we make this a game where the others actually have a chance to win your freedom? Interesting…"

"Are you up for it?" I challenge. "Throw your worst at Malcolm and the others, but if they survive it you have to let us all go."

"And what happens if they can't handle my trials? What do I get in return?"

"What do you want?"

"Your first-born child."

I let out a small laugh because her request sounds like something only an arch villain in a movie would ask for, but Helena stares at me with a stone-cold look.

"You can't be serious," I say in disbelief. "I'm not going to wager the life of one of my children on some sadistic game you devise."

"All right," Helena says, considering my objection. "What if I let you help formulate the rules of the game? I'll even allow for the possibility that Malcolm and the others can win it. I won't do anything to stack the chips in my favor, as it were."

"I'm not doing this with you," I tell her resolutely. "I refuse to wager the life of one of my children. You'll have to come up with something else that you want."

Helena lifts her right hand up with the pads of her middle finger and thumb pressed together like she's about to snap them.

"With one thought, I can kill them all in an instant," she says, a hard edge to her voice. The look in her eyes tells me that she's close to fulfilling her statement and that I shouldn't take it as a bluff. "Give me a reason to keep them alive, Anna, or be the reason your husband and friends die."

Helena doesn't make idle threats, and I know she'll do exactly what she says.

"So if I refuse your offer, you'll kill them? But if I agree to play your game, you'll give them a fighting chance to save me and my children?" I ask just to clarify the terms Helena is setting into place.

"That's about the gist of it, Sister. How confident are you that Malcolm can defeat what I set in his path?"

"I have total faith in my husband," I tell her with conviction.

"Then you have the chance to win everything your little heart desires, Anna. If you have that much confidence in him, then you're really not risking anything, are you?"

"It isn't right to gamble the life of a child," I tell her, attempting to make her see how outrageous her demand is.

"But you don't think you'll lose!" Helena says, throwing her hands up into the air in exasperation. "According to you, Malcolm will win. You have everything to gain in this scenario. Or, do you really have as much confidence in your husband as you protest? Seems to me that, if you did, you would make the wager in a heartbeat, and not have any doubts about the outcome. Poor Malcolm, does he know you don't trust him?"

"I trust him with my life."

"But apparently you don't trust him with your children's lives. It's no wonder they keep coming to me. They must sense your doubt in Malcolm's ability to keep them safe. It's quite pitiful really."

I know what Helena is trying to do. She's trying to goad me into making a rash decision. But she did make some good points. Do I doubt Malcolm? I don't think so, but why am I hesitating to make this deal with her if I'm confident he can save us?

"Will you really kill them all if I refuse to play your game?" I ask.

"If that threat helps ease your guilt about gambling away one of your children, then yes, Anna. Either play or they all die. You really don't have much of a choice."

I realize, in a weird sort of way, Helena is attempting to ease the burden of responsibility from my shoulders. Only she would consider the threat of mass murder a kindness.

"Then I'll play your game," I tell her, placing a protective hand on my belly, as if such an action will shield the lives of my babies from her. "And Malcolm will win it to save us."

Helena smiles as if she's already won, and I realize I've made a deal with a new kind of devil.

CHAPTER THREE
(Malcolm's Point of View)

As soon as I step inside the next chamber, I feel a wave of intense heat ram into my body like a physical entity. I quickly turn to look behind me to make sure the hellhounds aren't following us inside. I soon discover that the entryway I just passed through no longer exists. The interior of the cavernous space Helena's minions herded us into is composed of a glossy black rock, which resembles marble. The rock is alive with red-orange flames dancing across its surface in a random pattern, yet the blaze doesn't actually seem to be burning anything; only producing a wellspring of heat. The pyrotechnics seem to be more for show than posing any real threat to our lives. Besides us, the space is empty.

"Well, this is certainly anticlimactic," Jered quips as he looks around the room. I notice him tighten his grip on the hilt of his sword. He knows as well as I do that it's only a matter of time before Helena throws something at us that we'll have to fight.

"She didn't lead us in here for no reason," Cade says assuredly.

"Maybe she's trying to figure out what to do with us," Gideon suggests, resting the steel shaft of his large silver-etched war hammer over his right shoulder. "I doubt she planned ahead for our visit."

"Let's see if we can find a way out of here," I say as I begin to walk around the perimeter of the room.

It doesn't take us long to figure out there isn't any way to escape.

"Looks like we'll just have to wait for her to decide to show up," Jess says as we all gather in the middle of the room to form a large circle.

Without warning, Helena appears in the center of our group. A single shaft of white light from some unknown source shines down from the direction of the ceiling to illuminate her. She's wearing a red dress, but I only take time to make note of the color.

"Where is my family?" I demand as I stride up to her, determined to get an answer one way or another.

"They're safe," she informs me coolly, looking me up and down in an appraising manner. She meets my steely gaze with one of her own. "I would never harm them, Malcolm. You should know that about me by now. If I wanted them dead, I would have had them killed ages ago."

"Then give them back to me," I order.

"You make it sound like I'm the one who brought them here in the first place. I'll have you know that it was the babies' decision to come to me. I had nothing to do with their unexpected arrival."

"I'm fully aware of that fact," I growl, "but you're the one preventing them from leaving."

"True, I have suspended the ability for angels to simply phase into my home, but that was just a precautionary measure to prevent the rebellion angels from phasing here to kill Anna and your precious little cherubs. Though, I'm sure even someone as dense as you was able to figure that much out on your own."

"Anna doesn't want to be here. That much I know for a fact," I say confidently.

"No, she doesn't," Helena concedes with an exasperated sigh, "and she seems to have a great deal of faith in your ability to rescue her. I, on the other hand, have very little confidence in you."

"You say that like I care what your opinion of me is. I assure you that I don't."

She grins tightlipped at me but doesn't make a reply. Instead, she allows her gaze to travel over my shoulder to the people standing directly behind me.

"Well, well, well," Helena says as she scowls at Jess and Mason, "I wondered why I couldn't identify your souls. What an unwelcome surprise. Did God kick you out of Heaven? Were you disrupting its tranquility with your incessant need for matches and marshmallows?"

"We came to help Malcolm," Jess tells her, unaffected by her barbs. "Since you're a complete psycho, we thought he could use all the help he could get to deal with your unique type of crazy."

"I see spending time in Heaven hasn't curbed that smart mouth of yours, Jess," Helena retorts. "You don't know the joy I felt when you died, and I finally got Lucifer back. I would have danced on your grave if I'd been corporeal back then. I can't say it was very smart of you to come here, though. What makes you think I'll ever let you leave?"

A corner of Jess' mouth quirks up in a sardonic smile. "And here I thought Lucifer had the worst God complex I'd ever seen. You're even worse than he was because you actually think you are a god."

"Lucifer never had the gumption to harness real power," Helena says scathingly. "He was too short-sighted to take what he needed to succeed, and too afraid to do anything that might make him completely lose his soul."

Jess cocks her head as she looks at Helena. "What is it that you want to succeed at doing, Helena? What exactly is your end game here?"

"Funny you should mention a game," she says, looking back at me with an excited twinkle in her eyes. "Do you love your family enough to play a game with me to get them back, Malcolm? I sure hope so, because Anna has already agreed to my terms. I would hate to have to go back and tell her that you weren't up for the challenge."

I look over at Cade. "Is she telling me the truth? Did Anna make a deal with her?"

For the first time, Helena lets her eyes travel to where he is standing, and meets the steady gaze he's had on her since she phased into the room. The connection between them is undeniable; even I can feel it as they look at one another. I thought it wasn't possible for me to feel sorry for Cade any more than I do concerning his plight with Helena, but seeing them together like this makes me realize just how hopeless his predicament is.

"Yes, she's telling you the truth about Anna," he answers, never taking his eyes off his soul mate. It's not his intimate connection to her that I'm relying on, but his angelic ability to know when someone is lying. "Why can't you just let them go, Helena?" he pleads.

"What would be the fun in that?" she asks, shaking her head at Cade as if she pities him. "You won't survive this unscathed. If I were you, I would leave now before it's too late."

"It's already too late for me," Cade tells her, and I know he isn't just talking about the sadistic game Helena is about to force us to play in her realm.

Helena doesn't make a reply. She turns away from Cade and looks back at me.

"Do you accept the terms Anna and I have agreed upon?"

"What exactly are the terms?" I ask.

"To play the game, that's not something you need to know. If you trust your wife, then you know she did her best to negotiate on your behalf."

I look over at Cade to see if he can confirm what Helena is telling us. He nods his head once, letting me know I can trust what she's said so far to be the truth.

"I'll do whatever needs to be done to get them back," I state.

I trust that Anna has already weighed all the options and decided this is the best course of action for us. She knows I'll conquer any challenge Helena places before me.

"Wonderful," she says with a genuine smile. "I wish I'd had more time to prepare for this opportunity. I'm afraid your first challenge won't be very imaginative, but I promise to come up with some more interesting obstacles as we go along."

"What type of tests can we expect?" Ethan asks.

Helena takes two steps closer to Ethan. I see him flinch and close his eyes, as if he's experiencing a great deal of pain.

She casts her gaze around all of us, only Jess and Mason don't seem affected by what she's doing. When she looks back at me, I feel a sensation similar to the first time I traveled to Hell to beg Anna to come home and abandon her efforts to torture Levi to death. I know Helena is using her powers to delve into my guilt, teasing out memories I would rather keep buried. The pain isn't debilitating, and I know she's being gentle for some reason. She isn't using her full power to feed on our guilt, only learn from it.

"Ahh," she says with a pleased grin, "I almost forgot about that one, Malcolm."

"I have thousands of things that I regret doing during my life. You're going to have to be a little more specific than that if you want me to figure out which one in particular you're referring to."

"Oh, don't worry that pretty little head of yours about it. You'll be reminded soon enough," she says mockingly, "but for now let's put this game into terms even you can understand."

Helena lifts her right hand and snaps her fingers.

The room's illusion of flaming walls suddenly crumbles away like ashes in the wind, revealing a barren landscape. The sky above us crackles with lightning, infusing the air with the smell of ozone and the promise of a rainstorm that will never come. The parched earth beneath our feet adds a sense of desolation, which seems to be the way Helena wants us to feel. Far in the distance, I see a black version of the palace in Cirrus.

"I'm going to be kind and tell you exactly what you need to do," she tells us in a benevolent tone. "Make your way to the castle. If you can all make it to Anna within 24 hours, I'll let her and Lucas leave with you."

"Just out of curiosity," Mason says, "what happens if we don't make it there in time? What do you win if we lose?"

"What's at stake here is between my sister and me."

"It doesn't matter what Anna wagered," I tell Mason. "We won't fail."

"That's what Anna seems to believe, too, but, unfortunately for her, she doesn't know all the things that I do."

"And what is it that you think you know?" Jered asks.

"Oh, I know everything," she says with a lilt of pure glee in her voice. "Many of you have quite a few secrets that you've been hiding from each other. I can't wait to share them to see just how strong your friendships really are."

"There's nothing you can show us that will tear us apart," Cade assures her.

"I suggest you keep that confident outlook, dear heart, because you're going to need it when you find out the things I know."

"Why don't you get on with it, Helena," I say, becoming more irate with every passing second. "The sooner you start this game of yours, the sooner I can get my family away from you."

"As you wish," she says. "Like I said earlier, we're going to start off with something simple. All of you, except Jess of course, seem to share a common thread of guilt about the war in Heaven."

"What we did back then had to be done," Ethan informs her. "We had no choice."

"Yes, yes," Helena says, sounding bored, "I know the story. You War Angels were made specifically to ensure that Lucifer would lose the war. Yada, yada, yada. Talk about the Almighty stacking the deck against my father. Lucifer should have known he didn't have a chance of defeating an army designed by God Himself. It was his arrogance in thinking he could win that cost him everything in the end. Even though you all understood what was expected of you, none of you came out of the war unscathed. Some of you," Helena looks pointedly at Xander, "seem to still have nightmares about the lives you took back then. Is it true that when an angel dies in Heaven, they're dead forever?"

No one says anything because we all tried to forget that consequence. It was true. The energy of the angelic dead in Heaven returned to the universe to be used to make something else. Any angel who died during the war met a true death, and wasn't given the opportunity to have an afterlife. That was one of the major reasons the war affected us all so deeply. We had to kill to protect God's realm, but in doing so we doomed thousands of souls to nonexistence.

"You know it's true," Xander replies curtly, reverting to anger to protect his heart and his sanity.

I've always known that his bad attitude was a coping mechanism for his guilt. He was one of the most proficient fighters in Heaven during the war. He was good at what he did, and being a killing machine never sat well with him. I'm glad it doesn't, but there has to be a point where you let go of your guilt over things that were beyond your control. Xander hasn't come to terms with that fact yet, and it's the main reason I give him so much slack when it comes to his whoring and drinking. I assume he'll reach rock-bottom at some point and realize that his actions are only damaging his soul even more than it already is. Once he decides to leave the path leading him to his own self-destruction, all he can do is go up from there.

"Well, luckily for you the same rule doesn't apply here," Helena says. "Perhaps, in my small way, I can actually help you face the demons that continue to haunt your dreams."

A hundred yards in front of us a mirror image of our own group suddenly appears. It takes me a moment to adjust to what I'm seeing.

"Yes, you are seeing what you think you are," Helena says, giggling at her own mischief. "Oh, if only all of you could see the expressions on your faces right now. What better way to work through your own self-loathing than to literally fight yourselves? This should save you all years of therapy. Enjoy!"

She disappears, and our doppelgangers raise their weapons as they silently charge us.

We only have time to react as they attack. When my double reaches me, I raise my sword sideways, just over my head to block the downward strike of his blade. Helena's version of me isn't a very good fighter, and I experience a moment of vanity because I feel insulted by my doppelganger's lack of skill with a sword. I easily run him through with my blade and watch him vanish from sight in a puff of black smoke. All of us end up killing our mirror images rather quickly, which immediately sets off a warning inside my head.

"Something's wrong. That was too easy," Xander says, voicing my own thoughts.

"Yes, it was," Jess replies, raising her sword with both hands and assuming a defensive stance. "Here comes wave two."

I follow Jess' gaze and see that another set of our doppelgangers has appeared exactly where the first ones did. As they begin to charge, I have a bad feeling I know what Helena's plans are for us now.

As soon as we dispatch our mirror images, new ones spawn and attack. We seem to be trapped in an infinite loop, and I begin to wonder if Helena will ever stop this particular test of our stamina. I assume she's trying to not only wear us down physically, but mentally as well. How many times can someone kill themselves before they break? I don't know how long we battle ourselves, but after killing the five-hundredth me, I begin to lose count.

Eventually our doubles stop spawning, and most of us are breathing hard from the exertion. I look over at Jess and see that she and Mason aren't even sweating. When she was alive, I always worried over her since she was human, but in this situation, I guess it's only myself I need to be concerned about.

Jess catches me looking at her and says, "That won't be the end of it, Malcolm. She's just getting started."

I nod. "I know." I look out to the black castle in the distance. "And we're not stopping until we get to Anna and Lucas."

I start to walk forward. The first step I take makes our surroundings change again, and this time we find ourselves standing in a green meadow covered in a multitude of wild flowers. There's a small pond in the middle of the scene with a majestic weeping willow standing beside it. The sudden change to our setting is jarring, to say the least.

"What a lovely spot," I hear Helena comment.

I turn around to find her standing behind us.

"And what exactly are you going to make us fight here?" I ask her. "Hay fever?"

She laughs. "Oh, nothing that provincial. I just thought you could all use a moment to relax and get to know each other a little bit better." Helena directs her gaze in Alex's direction. "You remember this place well, don't you, Alex?"

His shoulders stiffen at being addressed. Reluctantly, he says, "Yes. I remember it."

"Sweet, motherly Amalie," Helena croons. "All those days you spent here together, and all that pining for what you could never have."

Underneath the weeping willow by the pond, we suddenly see Amalie and Alex appear. Of course it's only an illusion, but if someone didn't know any better they would mistake them for being real.

They're lying on their sides, facing one another on a white quilt. Amalie is dressed in a light blue dress with a white flower print around the edges of the skirt. An open book lies between them, and they each have their heads propped up on one bent arm. I don't need Helena to tell me what Alex's secret is. It's plainly written on his face as he watches Amalie.

"Poor Alex and his unrequited love for Lucifer's bitch of a wife," Helena says scornfully.

I look over at Alex and see his face contort with unmitigated fury. I'm not sure if he's angry about Helena showing us his true feelings for Amalie or her derogatory reference to Anna's mother. Either way, I know it's not good.

"She's baiting you, Alex, don't let her," I warn him in an attempt to bring him back to his senses. I know firsthand how dangerous it can be to allow your temper to take control of you, and in a place like Hell the smallest spark of anger can ignite into an inferno of rage before you realize what's happened.

"She has no right to speak about Amalie like that," he says in a low menacing voice.

"Still have the hots for her, eh?" Helena mocks. "Why don't we all watch what happens on this day together? When I first started delving into your memories, I have to admit I became a bit bored with what I found there. But when I came across this little gem, well, I discovered just how pathetic you actually are, Alex."

“Helena, don’t do this,” Cade pleads, taking a step towards her. “It’s not right.”

For a split second, I see her hateful expression soften after hearing Cade’s words, but maybe it was just wishful thinking on my part.

“Right or wrong,” she tells him with a stern expression, “it’s the truth, and the sooner you come to terms with who I really am, the better off we’ll both be.”

“Ok, now,” I hear the vision of Amalie say, drawing my attention back to the scene, “let’s see where we left off the last time.” She begins to flip through the pages of the book as a warm heavenly breeze blows through her hair, causing her brown tresses to float around her shoulders as she concentrates on her task.

We all watch as a mixture of emotions plays across memory-Alex’s face as he continues to gaze at Amalie. It’s painfully obvious from the yearning in his eyes that he’s in love with her. Either on impulse or finally giving into a long-held desire, he leans his body forward over the book and kisses her on the lips. She’s shocked for a moment as her eyes go wide, but she quickly comes to her senses and pushes him away from her.

“Alex,” she says, breathless with surprise and confusion, “what are you doing? Why would you do that?”

“I love you,” he confesses, opening his heart to her in a moment of vulnerability. “I’ve been in love with you for a very long time now, Amalie.”

She hastily sits up and automatically begins to shake her head at Alex. “No. You have to stop. I don’t love you in that way, and I never will.”

He sits up, too. “Why? Is it because of your feelings for Lucifer? You’ll never see him again, Amalie. Why waste an eternity longing for someone you can never have?” he questions. The earnest expression on Alex’s face tells us all that he hopes to convince her that he’s right.

“It’s not just my feelings for Lucifer,” she tells him on the verge of tears. “I love you, too, Alex, but only as a friend. If I’ve led you on in any way, I’m sorry. All I’ve ever wanted to do is help you learn how to express your thoughts to others better, and we’ve worked so hard to accomplish that. It’s taken a long time and a lot of hard work, but you’re finally able to tell people exactly what you’re thinking and feeling.”

“You make it sound like you see yourself as my mother, Amalie,” he says disdainfully.

Amalie remains silent, and we can all tell that’s exactly the way she feels about him. I know this is a fact because of my discussion with Anna after her visit with Lucifer and her mother. Apparently, Alex misunderstood the love she showed him, and this is the first time he realizes the truth for himself. As I watch the light of love fade from his eyes, a new understanding seems to take its place and everything he thought he knew up until this moment is forever changed.

“I don’t want to lose you as a friend,” Amalie says desperately, holding her hand out to Alex for him to take. “Please, don’t be angry with me…”

He looks at her outstretched hand with a sense of longing, but instead of accepting her offer of friendship, he phases.

“Poor Alex.” Helena’s words may have been sympathetic, but the way she said them was anything but. “There you were opening your itty bitty heart to Amalie, and she crushed it like a bug because she could never allow herself to love anyone except Lucifer. I might have felt bad for you if it wasn't for that pathetic look you gave her at the end."

"At least he can love someone else," Jered says, sticking up for Alex. "Can you, Helena?"

Unfazed by his question, she immediately turns her sights on him.

"You're a fine one to talk, Jered. At least Alex had the gumption to tell the woman he loves how he felt. You, on the other hand, decided to take the coward's way out. Why don't we all take a trip down memory lane, and see what you could have had if you had only been man enough to fight for it?"

I have a bad feeling I know exactly what Helena plans to show Jered. I just hope his heart is strong enough to take it.

CHAPTER FOUR

The setting around us changes once again to the inside of my New Orleans home not long after it was constructed. The world was on the cusp of war. We had done everything within our power to put an end to the petty bickering between the feuding economic classes, but humans can be stubborn creatures. After those who could afford to build and live in the cloud cities finally left the surface, fighting amongst the clans left in the down-world reached a fever pitch. We Watchers knew there was nothing we could do to stop the war, so we simply tried to help where we could. If the people in the cloud cities hadn't fled, I believe we could have prevented the nuclear holocaust that followed their departure. With no one trying to find a peaceful resolution to the disputes, a mad dash for power ensued among those left behind. They did this through the bloodiest combat in human history, and it ended in an all-out nuclear conflict. Besides the war in Heaven and the loss of loved ones during my time on Earth, the years during and after the Great War were some of the worst in my life.

The day Helena has decided to depict is actually from one of my own memories, and I know exactly why she's showing it to us. All I hope is that Jered can forgive me for what he's about to see me do in it.

"Riley! You're going to be late for your own wedding!" I hear myself grumble as I walk into the living room. My memory of her materializes in the living room and we see her as she was, sitting in front of the fireplace, clad in her wedding dress.

She looks away from the flames of the fire that seem to have her hypnotized and watches me as I walk over to her. She doesn't look like a bride should on her wedding day. There is no happiness in her eyes, only turmoil.

"What's wrong?" I ask her. "Are you having second thoughts about marrying him? If you are, I can throw Ollie out onto the street right now. I don't have a problem with doing that."

Riley begins to cry. I only stand there for a moment before I sit on the floor next to her and bring her into my arms.

"I don't know what to do, Uncle Malcolm," Riley sobs as she leans against me for comfort. "I'm so confused right now."

"Confused about what exactly?" I ask, resting my cheek against the top of her head and holding her close to make her feel safe.

"Jered," Riley confesses to me in a whisper.

I had known for days that she was interested in Jered. He had been away on a mission for most of her life, only meeting her for the first time when he came to celebrate her nuptials to Ollie. I knew they weren't soul mates, but most people don't need that once in a lifetime connection to fall in love with one another.

"You've only known him for a few days," I try to reason, even though I knew Jered's feelings paralleled Riley's. "Ollie has been in your life since your sixteenth birthday party. I seem to remember you telling me then that you were going to marry him one day, and here we are, five years later, with your fiancé patiently waiting for you at the altar."

"How can I marry him when I have feelings for Jered? What am I supposed to do, Uncle Malcolm?"

I let Riley cry a little while longer. I could have told her to follow her heart, but I didn't.

Instead, I tell her, "Jered has a mission to accomplish. You know that, Riley."

"But what if I'm the one you've all been waiting for?" she says, leaning back to look up at me with slightly swollen eyes.

"You're not," I say confidently.

We all knew early on that Riley wouldn't be the descendent we were waiting for. There was too much chaos among the humans to keep Lucifer occupied and happy. He was having a party on Earth. Why would he try to destroy it now? No, it was decided by all of us that the descendant we were waiting for probably wouldn't be born for many generations to come. The world would have to heal, and that process would take a lot of time. The thought depressed us all, but it was simply the way things were. I knew that if Riley went to Jered that night, he would abandon our mission in order to live out his life with her as a human. It was selfish of me to deny him such happiness, but I knew I needed him to stay with us and not get distracted by love.

"Ollie loves you," I tell her. "He has loved you since the moment he saw you. I know I was hard on him in the beginning, but I had to make sure he was strong enough to be a good husband for you. The life he's signing up for won't be an easy one, but he loves you enough to stand by your side no matter what. He passed all the tests I threw at him and never complained that they were too hard. Don't toss away his love for you like an afterthought. That's not the type of person you are."

Riley stopped crying then, and I knew my words were enough to convince her to go through with her wedding to Ollie that night.

Helena stops the scene and looks over at Jered.

"I know this is a rhetorical question, but for the sake of the others, did you know Malcolm convinced the woman you loved to marry another man?"

His eyes never waver from the image of Riley as he says, "No. I didn't."

"Too bad really," Helena sighs, mimicking regret. "It seems like she really loved you. If Malcolm hadn't persuaded her to stay true to her fiancé, I would bet my soul that she would have run straight to you instead. But, then again, you fled that night, didn't you? What happened, Jered? Did the possibility of someone loving you so absolutely make you feel like a scared little school boy?"

"I didn't deserve her love," Jered answers, lifting his gaze from Riley's tear-streaked face to meet Helena's mocking one. "Malcolm did the right thing. Ollie was the better man for her. I couldn't have made her as happy as he did."

"But you'll never really know that for certain, will you? You loved her, but you never worked up the nerve to admit it to her. It was certainly a missed opportunity, but it wasn't the biggest regret in your life, was it?"

Helena and Jered stare at one another in silence. Finally, Jered says, "Go ahead and show it. I don't think it will be a big surprise to anyone here what it is."

She grins. "No. I think I have a better way to reveal your guilt. Besides, I have something else I need to tend to right now."

The illusion of my home in New Orleans falls away as a thick fog rolls in, making it hard for us to see each other much less figure out where we are in relation to the castle we're trying to reach.

"I know, you're all thinking that this isn't very fair of me," I hear Helena say, even though I can't see her. "Consider this a real test of your bond to Anna, Malcolm."

"What do you mean by that?" I demand.

"Oh, I'm going to show your wife some things that might distress her enough to set off that pesky ability for soul mates to find one another, no matter where they are. Now, you still won't be able to phase to her, but you might be able to figure out what direction she's in through this fog. I don't want you to get bored, though." Just as she says these words, a multitude of howls the likes of which I haven't heard in hundreds of years fills the air.

"Watcher children," I hear Mason say with immense dread and a small measure of surprise.

It's been a long time since we've had to deal with the cursed children of the Watchers. It shouldn't come as a shock that some of them earned a place in Hell for the atrocities they committed while they were still alive, but I don't think any of us totally blame them for their tragic fate either. They didn't ask to be born to Watchers, and their damnation lies squarely on our shoulders. We were the ones who sinned against God, while their only crime was being born to parents who had fallen from His grace.

"Ta-ta for now," Helena tells us from somewhere in the fog. "I hope you enjoy your reunion, Jered."

It's only then that I realize Helena is still testing him. As the howls of the dead children of the Watchers sound again, even closer this time, I know we'll recognize at least one in their midst.

"Your son is out there, isn't he?" I ask Jered. I can barely see him through the dense fog, even though he's standing only three feet away from me.

He doesn't reply right away. He continues to listen to the piercing howls that seem to be getting closer and closer.

Finally, he looks over at me and says in a detached voice, "Yes. He's here. I can sense him."

It's been years since I thought about Jered's son, but I'm sure Silas has been in his father's thoughts every day since his death. I see Mason and Jess come to stand on either side of Jered, both looking concerned over what our friend will ultimately have to face here.

He looks over at Mason and says, "I've tried to put the night he died behind me, but it always returns to haunt me in my dreams."

Mason places a comforting hand on his shoulder, and I can see the strength of the bond between them that was forged out of a shared guilt.

"You've done a lot to atone for what you did in your past," Mason tells him. "Don't let Helena drag you back down by using your son against you."

"But I failed Silas the worst way a father can, Mason. I forced him go to Mama Lynn's house that night to feed my own ego and need for revenge against you. If I hadn't, you wouldn't have had to kill him. He lost his chance at salvation because of me. I'm the one who led him into the darkness, and he's suffered because of my mistakes all this time. That's something I will never be able to forgive myself for doing. I should have been a better father and protected him, even from myself." Jered looks at me. "I wish I had protected Silas like you did Sebastian. You never let him participate in our stupid games. If I had been stronger, Silas wouldn't be here right now."

"If there is one thing that I've learned in my life," I tell him, "it's that you can never change the past, no matter how much you might want to. Helena showed you my memory of Riley for a reason. She knew it was something I came to regret doing later on. At the time, I thought it was the best thing for everyone involved, but in retrospect, maybe I should have encouraged Riley to follow her heart and seek you out that night. If I had, you might have led a very different life."

Jered shakes his head at me. "No. You did the right thing for the both of us. If she had come to me and professed her feelings, I wouldn't have been strong enough to turn her away. Our life together wouldn't have been what she deserved, and I would have missed this opportunity to save Silas."

"And how exactly do you plan to do that?" Jess asks, sounding suspicious of his plan to free his son from Helena's domain.

"I'll make a deal with her."

"What kind of deal?" Jess presses for a more specific answer.

"The kind that she won't be able to pass up."

"Absolutely not," I say, walking over to stand in front of him because I know exactly what he's planning. "I won't allow you to trade in your own soul so she'll release his. That's what you're intending to do, isn't it? What makes you think it will work this time?"

Jered looks at me in surprise. "What do you mean by 'this time'?"

"Did you really believe Lucifer wouldn't taunt me about your attempts to make a deal with him for Silas?" I ask. "I've known you've been trying to save your son by bartering your own soul for years now. Lucifer used to tease me that it was only a matter of time before he wore you down and forced you to give him the location of the princes in order to save your son."

"You knew about that all this time?" Jered asks in confusion. "Yet you never said anything to me about it? Why? Why did you continue to trust me when you knew I might betray you at any moment?"

"Why do you think it took me so long to finally trust you? After a few hundred years, you proved to me that you would never betray our mission or me. You had countless opportunities to be disloyal to us, yet you never were. You stayed true to our cause and never wavered in your dedication to fulfil your promise to Caylin all those years ago. She had faith in you when others didn't, especially me. I tried to remember that after she passed away, but it still took me a long time to see you the way she did. I know now that once given, your loyalty is steadfast, even when others try to knock you down."

"That was something you attempted to do yourself, and quite often, if memory serves me well," Jered quips good-naturedly.

"I had to test you," I tell him. "Granted, I've never tested anyone's loyalty for as long as I did yours, but even I came to the conclusion that you were someone who would always stay true to his word and never fail in a mission. The only thing I've seen you fail at is forgiving yourself for what happened to Silas."

"That's something I'll never be able forgive myself for," he confesses. "He's my son, Malcolm. I should have shielded him from what we were, but instead I chose to drag him down with me. He never wanted to kill, but I made him become a murderer. I'm the one who turned him into a monster, because that's what *I* was. I never even considered the possibility that we wouldn't share the same fate. It took losing him to open my eyes and make me face who I had become. His death saved me, but maybe I didn't deserve mercy."

"*Mercy…*" a gravelly voice says from somewhere close by in the fog. "Mercy is for the weak."

We all hold our weapons at the ready, prepared to face whatever new threat is about to present itself.

The head of a Watcher child pokes through the thick fog in front of us, giving the illusion that it's floating in the air. Its elongated snout, large pointy ears, and hollow black eyes harken back to a time that I would just as soon forget. On Earth, the children of the Watchers weren't able to speak, but it seems the same rules don't apply in Hell. The Watcher child stares at us all until it finally settles a steady gaze on Jered.

"Hello, Father," Silas says. "You've finally found me after all these years."

"I never gave up hope that I would," Jered tells him earnestly.

"There was a time I wanted you to rescue me from this place and take me back home," Silas admits. "Unfortunately for you, I no longer care to leave. I've found my place in the world, and it's by Helena's side."

Jered lowers his sword and takes a step towards his son.

"No, it's not. It never was. You only think that way because you've been trapped down here for so long."

Silas begins to chortle. His laughter is deep and menacing.

"You should have stayed in the world of the living, Father. Coming down here was a foolish mistake on your part. It may even end up costing you your soul."

"I would trade places with you in a heartbeat, Silas," Jered declares. "I tried for years to make a deal with Lucifer to release you, but he never would. Maybe Helena will allow me to trade in my soul and release yours."

"Even if she does accept your sacrifice, what makes you think I will?" Silas challenges. "I've found a home with her here, and I like the person she's helped me become."

"You can't mean that," Jered says firmly. "You don't know what you're saying."

"Who are you to presume to know what's best for me?" Silas argues as he takes a step forward. He towers over the rest of us at seven-feet tall. The backward legs and hairless white skin covering his lanky form brings back unpleasant memories of Sebastian transforming into his werewolf alter ego.

"Being down here for so long has warped your mind, Silas," he says, in what sounds like a futile attempt to reach his son. "Let me try to save you."

"Don't bother," Silas replies. "Helena has already promised to send me back to the land of the living."

Everyone remains silent after hearing this revelation. I'm certain we're all thinking the same thing. Whatever Helena's reason for sending Silas back to Earth, it can't be good.

"Why would she do that?" Jered finally asks, needing to know more about Helena's plans for his son. "What does she want you to do for her there?"

Silas laughs again. "Do you think me so fickle that I would betray her to help you? She has earned my trust and loyalty over the years. The only emotion I feel when I look at you is contempt. This loving father act you're putting on is wasted on me. I no longer care what you want or what you think. I don't even consider myself your son anymore. You mean less than nothing to me now, and the sooner you accept that fact the better off we'll both be."

Silas vanishes back into the fog, leaving us alone in silence.

"That's what your children used to transform into?" Roan asks out of curiosity. "Those are the things that are howling out there?"

"Yes," I tell him as I look back at the other War Angels. "They were cursed because of our disobedience to God, and forced to transform into werewolves every night."

"Do you think Helena plans to send them all back to Earth?" Gideon asks. "The Watcher children who are down here," he clarifies.

"I have no idea," I reply, slowly shaking my head.

"Why would she send him back?" Jered says, but I know it's not a question he expects any of us to answer. He's simply thinking out loud. "She has to be planning to use him against us in some way."

"I don't think that's something we need to worry about right now," Mason says to him. "Let's all stay focused on what we came here to do, and that's finding Anna and Lucas. We're going to have to play Helena's game in order to do that, and I suggest we move as quickly as possible. The less time you all spend in here the better."

"Mason's right," I say. "We have to keep moving."

"But which way?" Zane questions, looking dubiously at the fog surrounding us. "We can't see the castle through this fog. We could end up moving further away from it instead of towards it."

"We're going to have to take a leap of faith," I tell them.

"Helena said you might be able to feel Anna," Alex says. "How is that possible?"

"When God opens the link between soul mates, you can feel their pain," Jess explains.

"But it has to be a deep pain," I remind her. "One that practically tears your heart or body apart."

"What do you think Helena is going to do to Anna to make her feel that way?" Cade asks worriedly.

Of all the War Angels, he has the closest personal relationship with Anna. He was, after all, the War Angel she created as Seraphina to protect her during the war in Heaven. I'm sure that's why she chose him to be our son's guardian angel. Their connection to one another was extremely strong during the war because it was designed to be that way. Of any class of angel, the Guardians of the Guf were the most important. They were charged with creating the War Angels to ensure that the rebels didn't win.

"I have no idea what her plans are," I reply. "The first time I felt the connection with Anna was right after she received the first seal."

"So the pain can either be physical or emotional?" Atticus asks.

"Yes," I answer.

"Either way," Roan says, "Helena plans to torture Anna."

The immense guilt I feel for wanting her to cause Anna enough pain to set off the connection between our souls weighs heavily on my heart. I need to find her and Lucas, and the only way I can sense her in Hell under our current circumstances is for that to happen. My only solace is the fact that I know Helena won't kill my wife. In her twisted mind, she truly believes Anna is her sister. Perhaps they are connected to one another in some odd way. I have no way of knowing the ins and outs of being made the way they were. Each of them had been brought to life from parts of Lucifer's soul. I can't deny that the circumstance in which they were created is unique, and it isn't like there's a handbook explaining the consequences of being conceived in such a fashion.

All I do know is that I need to find my family before it's too late. I need them back. My sanity depends on it.

CHAPTER FIVE

(Anna's Point of View)

While Helena is away, doing God only knows what to Malcolm and the others, I walk over to the bed to check on Lucas and make sure he's all right. As I sit on the edge of the bed, I lay a hand on his side in order to prove to myself that he's still breathing. The gentle rise and fall of his ribcage reassures me that he's simply in a deep sleep. In a way, I envy his slumbering state. I don't know if she realizes it, but Helena did Lucas a kindness by providing him an escape from Hell for a time. I feel on the verge of hysteria from being trapped here, but I know I can't give in to my fear.

The deal I've made with Helena may have been coerced out of me, but it was the best I could do, given the circumstances. What I've agreed to sets my heart on fire with worry. It's not that I doubt Malcolm will do everything he can to win this game of hers. I have complete faith in him, but I also trust Helena as much as I would a viper slithering up my leg making promises that it won't bite me. I know her too well to believe that she's doing this just for the entertainment factor. She believes she can come out on top in this wager. I feel as if I'm missing a piece of a larger picture, and that's preventing me from seeing how she plans to manipulate things into her favor.

"Stop it, Anna," I berate myself.

Worrying over something I can't change won't do me or anyone else any good. I need to figure out a way to help Malcolm and the others, even if I can't physically be with them. How can I make sure they succeed in their game against Helena? She'll definitely try to outwit them. She might even try to wear them down physically, but torturing them in that way just seems beneath even her. She finds her happiness by messing with people's minds. She only uses physical abuse as a means to an end.

"Well," I hear her say from the same spot she was standing in before she left, "the game is afoot, as it were. Let's see just how strong lover boy is."

I stand from the bed and walk over to her while asking, "What have you done to them?"

"Would you like to see?" she asks with an excited smile. "Look out that window," she instructs, pointing to a paned window with black curtains draped around it. When I first entered this room, it was a windowless space. The sudden appearance of this new addition to the room tells me that Helena can change almost anything she wants to here just by willing it into being. I walk over to it and peer outside. It's apparent from the angle of my view that the room we're in is very high off the ground. It might even be in the tower of a building. Far in the distance, I can see Malcolm and the others fighting. I have to squint to make out who it is they're battling against. When I do, I quickly turn to look at her.

"You're making them fight mirror images of themselves?" I ask, horrified by the notion. "Why would you do that?"

"What better way for them to work through their own issues? If you think about it, this could actually be beneficial to them in the long run."

I turn to face Helena fully, crossing my arms over my chest.

"And how, in your uniquely twisted sense of logic, do you believe you are helping them?"

"It's the perfect way for them to express the self-loathing they feel for themselves," she answers, as if her reasoning is sound. "Each of them hates something that they did in the past. What better way to work through those issues than punish themselves for their transgressions?"

"Are you planning to use their guilt against them to win?"

"I'll use whatever works best," she says, shrugging nonchalantly.

"How long are you going to make them fight themselves?" I ask, turning back to the window to watch the love of my life and my friends fight their doppelgangers. Among the group, I notice two people with Malcolm who shouldn't be in Hell. "Is that Jess and Mason?"

Helena lets out an exasperated sigh. "Yes. Those were the two souls I couldn't identify earlier. I don't know what good they think they can do here."

I let out a derisive laugh. "Even you aren't that dense," I say, turning back to look at her. "They're here to protect Malcolm and my friends from you."

"Well, I can assure you that they'll wish they never came after I'm finished with them."

"Can you even do anything to them?" I ask.

"Maybe not to their souls," Helena admits. "Those seem to be protected from me, but I can still see their memories. They've each been keeping secrets from each other. It seems a shame for them not to share with the group. Since I plan to make most of your friends work through their worst memories, I don't see why those two shouldn't participate in the fun."

"Is that what torturing is to you? Fun?" I ask in disgust.

"The best kind," she smiles.

"Are you going to make Cade relive his worst memory, too?"

Helena's expression becomes impassive with the mention of her soul mate's name, and I know I've hit a nerve.

"What I do with or to him is none of your business, Sister. If I were you, I would worry more about what Malcolm is hiding from you."

I feel my heart begin to beat a little faster, because her statement sounds more like a threat.

"I don't think you can show me anything about him that would surprise me," I tell her confidently.

Helena giggles. "Oh my, you are too much sometimes, Sister! Malcolm is a treasure trove of guilt. He's done more wrong than good in his life. Don't you know that about your own husband?"

"He's already shared his past with me. He hasn't tried to hide who he was from me."

"I can assure you there's one thing that you don't know about him," she says haughtily. "He didn't even share this little gem of a secret with his dearest Lilly. I'll bet you anything that when you see it, you and your children will think twice about going back to him."

"There is nothing you can show me that would make me second-guess Malcolm's love for us."

Helena grins. "We'll see."

She vanishes from my sight, and I'm left to watch Malcolm and the others fight against themselves over and over again. It seems like hours pass by, but I can't be sure since there's no way for me to keep track of time in the room. Eventually, I have to pull a chair over by the window because standing for so long begins to hurt my back. After a while, the fighting finally comes to an end, and Helena reappears before the others. The scenery around them changes to one with a lush meadow full of flowers and a small picturesque pond. I instantly recognize my mother and Alex lying underneath a weeping willow near the water's edge. This has to be a replication of his worst memory, but how can such a seemingly-tranquil scene be something he doesn't want to remember? When he leans over and kisses my mother, I let out an involuntary gasp in surprise.

My mother told me about her relationship with Alex in Heaven, and I know for a fact that she felt a motherly love towards him, not a romantic one. Apparently, his feelings for her weren't as platonic. My heart goes out to him when my mother pushes him away and quickly sits up. I can't hear the exchange between them, and I can barely make out Alex's expression, but I do see him phase away. Had he felt embarrassed about mistaking my mother's love for him as a romantic interest? I'm sure his heart was probably broken, and I have to wonder if they resolved this issue before he left Heaven. Maybe that was another reason my mother seemed so concerned about his welfare. I had to assume that the scene took place before Lucifer returned to Heaven. There wasn't any way Alex would have made such a move on my mother if he had seen her with Lucifer before this moment. After being parted from one another for so long, I sincerely doubt my parents will leave each other's sides for any length of time.

It brought a great deal of joy to my heart to know that I helped them find one another again. Who wouldn't want their parents to be reunited after such a long separation? Knowing that I helped my father finally find peace within himself was a gift any daughter would be proud to receive.

I continue to observe the others as the scene changes yet again. This time I see the living room in New Orleans appear with a girl sitting in front of the fireplace, crying. I don't recognize her, but with her long brown hair, and considering the fact that she's wearing a wedding dress, I assume she's probably one of the descendants who preceded me. As I watch the scene, I see Malcolm enter the room and speak to the girl. Finally, he sits down beside her and pulls her into his arms as she continues to sob. I have no idea why this would be Malcolm's worst memory or why Helena thinks it would surprise me. Was the girl extra special to Malcolm in some way?

When I see Helena address Jered first and not Malcolm after the scene ends, it appears that this might have something to do with him instead of my husband. I can't quite piece together what's going on, though. Suddenly, my view of what's happening with the others is obscured by a dense fog that covers them like a blanket. I'm unable to see anything else.

Helena reappears in the room a few minutes later.

I turn in my chair to face her. "What's the fog meant to hide? Is there something happening out there that you don't want me to see?"

"Not everything is about you, Anna," she snaps. "I thought I would add a little suspense to Jered's family reunion."

"Family reunion?" I ask in confusion. It takes me a few seconds to catch on, but when I finally do, I feel flabbergasted by Helena's audacity. "Is Jered's son here?"

"Oh, he's been here for quite some time now," she tells me with a pleased smile on her face. "Silas has become one of my star pupils. It took a few hundred years to break his spirit, but now he's one of my most loyal generals. I know I can rely on him to do anything I tell him to."

"And what is it that you want him to do for you?"

"Right now, I want him to make his father feel pain. Jered has only himself to blame for what his son has become. If he hadn't led Silas down the path of mayhem and murder, he wouldn't even be here. And poor Mason, he feels the guilt of an executioner since he's the one who delivered the death blow that sent Silas to me."

"He didn't have any choice," I protest in my ancestor's defense. Malcolm had told me the story about the Watchers who came to Jess' mother's house to attack them. Jered had been among the group. He was the only Watcher who accepted Mason's offer to earn God's forgiveness.

"It's a moot point now," Helena says with a dismissive wave of her hand. "I have Jered's son under my command, and that's all that matters. I imagine this will tear him up inside for years to come." She sighs in complete satisfaction about the matter. "I really couldn't ask for more to punish him with."

"Don't you get tired of hurting people?" I ask, wondering how she can find so much joy in other people's misery. I understand that she's Hell incarnate, but how can any sentient being enjoy the misfortune of others with such zeal? It's a concept I have a hard time comprehending.

"Their pain only makes me stronger," Helena explains. "I was made to drink in the misery of others and become more than I am through the power of their pain. If you have a problem with the way I am, you should blame our father. I'm only doing what he taught me to do, so stop looking at me like I'm some creature who just slithered out from underneath a rock. I'm doing what I was made to do in this world. What is it that the humans always say? Oh yes, you can't have good without evil. Just consider me a necessary component to the universe, Anna. I am a constant that can never be changed. If I did, the universe would be thrown into chaos, and I can assure you that it would be a worse place to live in."

"But you can change," I tell her. "I've seen the way you are with Cade. You can't ignore the connection the two of you have."

"I don't deny it, but if you think it will change who I am, you're a romantic fool."

"And if Cade thinks he can change you, are you going to call him a fool, too?"

"The worst type," Helena snaps. "Lucifer brought you into the world to only do good, but he created me to destroy good by any means necessary."

"You can't be that one-dimensional, Helena," I argue. "No one can only be one thing. You can't be pure evil, just like I can't be pure good. Those are just concepts perceived by others. They don't exist in reality."

"You can think that if you want, but I know the truth. I've accepted who I am, and I relish in the power it gives me. So should you."

I pity Helena for her beliefs. And I pity Cade even more because his soul has been tethered to someone who will never be able to love him the way he deserves.

"Stop looking at me like that," Helena says, scowling at me.

"I can't help it," I tell her. "I feel sorry for you and the life you have."

"Well, I don't!" She professes a little too fervently. It makes me wonder if her words are just a front to protect herself from the possibility of finding happiness in something other than the pain of her victims. "You're such a self-righteous bitch, Anna. It's hard for me to believe Lucifer enjoyed being around you so much. I guess it took you betraying him to understand the mistake he made when he created you."

Involuntarily, my back stiffens after hearing Helena's rude remark.

"I wasn't a mistake," I inform her.

She laughs. "You were the biggest mistake of our father's life! If he hadn't created you, his fall from Grace would have never happened. You may have been one of his greatest achievements, but you proved yourself to be his greatest failure in the end. If you want someone to blame for what our father went through during his life, look no further than a mirror, Anna. Of course, I don't lay the blame for his disgrace all at your feet. I'm thankful to you. If it wasn't for what you did, I never would have been born. But, I suppose I'm jumping ahead of myself. We should probably start at the beginning."

Helena stares at me for a moment, and I can feel her rummaging around in my mind, searching for something.

"Hmm," she says a little disappointedly, "I see God showed you things in Heaven in a way your teeny tiny human brain could comprehend them. How boring; but I suppose if you're going to feel the full effect of what I'm about to show you, it'll have to do."

The room we're in is instantly replaced by the moment of my birth in Heaven. I quickly stand from my chair and look over to where the bed with Lucas lying on it should have been.

"Where's Lucas?" I demand.

"Oh, don't worry about him. He's fine. He doesn't need to be here while you and I take a trip down memory lane. Though, they aren't your memories since you have none from being Seraphina. As I promised you earlier, I'm going to show you things from Lucifer's perspective. He may have left, but his memories will stay with me forever."

We're standing in a grand building made of what looks like crystal. The light of Heaven shines through its walls, giving it a happy, warm luminescence. I know exactly where we are. It's the Guf, the repository where all souls are created.

In the scene, I see Lucifer and God standing together inside it. Lucifer smiles as he places one of his hands over his heart. He pulls his hand away from his chest, and I see a white glowing orb resting on his palm. He throws the orb into the air, and it explodes like a firework. Suddenly, I'm standing in front of him. Although, it isn't really me. It's simply a representation of me as Seraphina.

Lucifer walks up and holds his hand out to her.

"Welcome to the world," he says, smiling triumphantly.

Seraphina stares at Lucifer's hand for a moment before cautiously placing one of hers into it.

"Who am I?" she asks. "Where am I?"

"You're in my Father's home," Lucifer tells her. "We call it Heaven. And your name is…" he pauses and I can tell he didn't think up a name beforehand. Finally, he says, "We will call you Seraphina. Do you like that name?"

"I don't know," she answers truthfully, like a child. "I'm not sure what I like."

Lucifer tightens his grip on her hand and says, "Then let's figure that out. I will be your guide, and we'll discover who you are meant to be together."

She looks uncertain about his offer at first, but then she smiles at him and nods.

"I would like that," she tells him. "I want to see everything."

Helena freezes the moment and snickers. "Can you believe our father used to be so…*soft*? He's fawning all over you for no good reason."

"No good reason?" I question, wondering if we watched the same memory. "He just made me. How else would you expect him to react?"

She snaps her fingers with an irate look on her face, and the scene changes to one she's shown me once before.

Lucifer is lying on the ground, holding a pulsating black orb in his hand.

"I've already seen your birth," I remind her, knowing this is the moment right after Michael brought my father to Earth to begin his exile.

"Yes, but you didn't see everything," Helena tells me just as Lucifer phases away.

The first time she showed this to me, she ended the scene here. This time we phase with him.

He's standing in a space that is entirely devoid of light, except for the dim radiance emanating from the glowing black orb. It's just enough to illuminate his facial features.

"We'll show my Father just how depraved humanity can become," Lucifer snarls as he stares at the orb. The expression on his face is that of a madman. It makes me realize just how far he had to come to ultimately find redemption.

He hurls the orb out into the darkness. It explodes in the air in a purple spray of light. An arched entryway appears, revealing a space that isn't as dark as the one we're standing in, but it's not a great improvement. I watch as my father walks through the portal with determined strides. Helena and I follow him, and I find that we're standing in a darker version of the Guf. Where the Guf in Heaven is filled with warmth and light, its counterpart in Hell is filled with coldness and shadows.

"I've made you to prove to my Father how wrong He is about humanity," Lucifer says as he looks around his new realm, with a mixture of pride in his creation and utter hate for God. "In the end, He'll have to admit that they never should have been created. Every soul we capture will be yours to devour. I will fill you with all of their hate and fear, and one day, you and I will have enough power to finally snuff out the human race. Together, we'll destroy anything that tries to stand in our way."

Helena stops the scene and looks at me.

"Now you tell me, does that sound like I had much of a choice in what I became?"

I have to admit, "No."

"You always make it sound like I chose to be the way I am, but what you don't seem to be able to grasp is the fact that I don't know how to be any other way."

"But you could learn, Helena," I counter. "Lucifer is gone. He finally realized how wrong he's been all these years. Fundamentally, the reason you were made no longer exists."

"As long as humans roam this universe, I serve a purpose," she tells me. "Only with their annihilation can I finally find peace."

"That's an unrealistic goal. Humanity will always find a way to survive. We always have and we always will."

"None of you can survive if you have nowhere to live."

"So your plan is to destroy the whole universe?" I scoff. "Lucifer has already tried to do that, and he failed. What makes you think you can do any better? How do you plan to destroy something that is infinite?"

Helena just stares at me.

"He wasn't strong enough to harness the power of the seals like I have."

"But you're still not strong enough to destroy the universe, or you would have already done it."

"No, I'm not strong enough yet, but I can be in time."

"How?" I ask, pressing for an answer. "And how do my children factor into your plans? I know you're not protecting them for my sake. So, what is it that you want them to do for you? The seals are their souls now. It's not like you can steal them from Liam and Liana."

"Why don't you let me worry about what I have planned?" Helena replies snidely. "And stop getting me off topic. We're here to learn more about your life with Lucifer while you were Seraphina. I have more to show you, if you think you can handle it."

"I can handle it," I say, lifting my chin a little higher in defiance of her challenge.

Maybe if I keep her preoccupied it will help Malcolm and the others in some way. I have no way of knowing if it will aid them in their quest to find Lucas and me, but surely it can't hurt to keep her away from them.

That's my reasoning at least. I just hope I'm right.

CHAPTER SIX

Helena changes our surroundings back to the Guf in Heaven. Lucifer and Seraphina are standing next to a stream of light that shimmers like a translucent pillar of gold, located in the center of the room. Since the shaft of light seems to reach well beyond both the ceiling and the floor, it's impossible to tell where it begins or ends. Floating within the light's warm glow are a multitude of small white orbs. Some are brighter than others and seem to be begging for attention as they twinkle like stars.

It's odd to see me physically represented in the recreation of Lucifer's memory. Since the bodies of angels are composed of energy and not flesh and blood, Helena is using the same tactic as God did to show me scenes that took place in Heaven. Giving Seraphina my human form also adds a level of connection between us that wouldn't be there otherwise. Even though I have no recollections of being her, I know everything Helena is about to show me happened to my angelic counterpart.

"Go ahead, Seraphina," Lucifer encourages, his eyes alight with expectation. "Try to pull out one of the orbs that's ready to be made into a soul."

"What if I can't do it?" she asks him, her voice quivering slightly, with a great deal of trepidation.

"You can," Lucifer says reassuringly. "You are the first Guardian of the Guf. It's time for you to fulfill your potential and make more angels to fill the halls of Heaven. Wouldn't you like to have others to talk to besides just me and God?"

"I'm perfectly happy with it just being us," she admits. "What if we get so caught up with the new angels that we end up not having time for each other anymore?"

Seraphina looks worried about the prospect of losing time with Lucifer and about the drastic changes that are going to take place in her life. I can't say I blame her. If all you knew was about to be altered forever, I think anyone would be frightened by what might happen. Considering the facts as I know them now, she had every right to be apprehensive.

"I would never let anything or anyone come between us," Lucifer promises as he takes hold of one of her hands. "You are the light of my life, Seraphina. Until I made you, I didn't truly understand the love my Father feels for me. Now, being a father myself, I grasp what it means to love someone else with your entire being. I promise that no one will ever separate us from one another. Do you trust me enough to believe that?"

"Of course I do," she says in earnest. "You would never lie to me."

"Then trust me now when I say you can do this." Lucifer lets go of her hand. "But you can only do it if you try."

I watch Seraphina take a deep breath to steady her nerves. Cautiously, she slides her hand into the pillar of light, palm up.

"Now, remember what I told you. You can only coax an orb of energy out of the Well of Souls. You should never try to force one out before it's ready to be born."

"What would happen if I ever tried to force one to come out?" she asks as I watch one of the brightest orbs in the well float down and rest on her outstretched hand.

"The energy would dissipate and that soul would never have a chance to come into being."

Seraphina cups her hand around the orb and gently pulls it out of the well.

"What's your next step?" Lucifer asks as he attempts to lead his daughter in the right direction, instead of blatantly telling her what to do.

"I think about all the attributes I want the soul to have," she answers.

"And remember, it's important that you make each soul different. No two souls should ever be the same. Otherwise, what's the point of existing? No one wants to be exactly like someone else. Being an individual is a very important part of being alive."

She nods. "Yes, I understand, but shouldn't we make a few souls a little more special than the rest?"

"What do you mean by 'special'?" Lucifer asks, looking intrigued by her suggestion.

"Well, I was thinking that we should make some angels who can lead the others. Like one could be the bravest, and one could bring comfort to those who need it. Perhaps we could even make one who can see into the future and let us know if we're doing everything right."

"Hmm…" He ponders her suggestion for a while before saying, "You know… you might be on to something. It's possible we will need more leaders one day to help us. Since the orb of energy you're holding is so bright, I think it would be a good candidate for one of these special souls. What do you think?"

"Yes," Seraphina says as she looks down at the orb and smiles. "I think it would make an excellent archangel."

“So you plan to make them just like me?” Lucifer looks amused by her pluck.

“Similar. No one could ever be exactly like you, but they will need your strength if they’re meant to lead the other angels.”

He smiles at her with a great deal of pride. “Have you thought of a name for your archangel?”

“Yes. I’m going to call him Michael.”

“Michael,” Lucifer considers the name and nods his head. “I like that. It’s a strong name. Bring him into the world, Seraphina, and let’s start building our family.”

With a snap of her fingers, Helena changes the scene to a different day in the Guf. It must be sometime in the future because the Guf is full of guardians busily shaping new souls. Lucifer is walking among them. He’s talking and laughing with the other guardians as if they’re all old friends.

“He looks so happy,” I comment to Helena, smiling for the first time since I entered Hell. My reaction is impossible to contain. Lucifer’s joy is so blatantly obvious it’s infectious, even if what I’m seeing is only a memory. “I’ve never seen him so carefree and open with others.”

“The poor, deluded fool thought he could never feel happier than he did in this moment,” Helena says with a great deal of disdain in her voice over the matter. “He was everyone’s hero back then. At least until you decided to ruin his life by making the first human soul.”

I hear Seraphina squeal with joy in Lucifer’s memory. He rushes over to her and asks, “Are you all right, Seraphina?” He looks down at the soul she’s created. It glows golden like the energy in the Well of Souls. “What is it? Why isn’t it transforming into an angel?”

“It’s not an angel,” she tells him excitedly. “It’s something different, Father.”

God phases in beside them in the Guf.

“Seraphina,” God says as He gazes at the soul she created, “you’ve conceived something new for Me.”

She nods with pride in the memory. “Yes, I have. Isn’t it the most beautiful soul you’ve ever seen? I gave it everything it needs, and added in the ability to imagine wondrous new possibilities for itself.”

“It’s perfect,” God praises. “It will be the first in a long line of souls who will safeguard the Earthly realm. I’m very proud of you, Seraphina. You did what I wanted without even knowing that I required a soul like this to be made.”

“But, what is it, Father?” Lucifer asks, still looking dubious about the soul his daughter just crafted.

“A human,” God replies. “One day, they will be the overseers of both Heaven and Earth. I will need you to serve them as you do Me, Lucifer, and help guide them in their new existence.”

In that instant, I see the joy of Heaven fade from Lucifer’s eyes. As he stares at the first human soul, his entire face turns stone-cold. I realize I’m witnessing the first moment Lucifer begins to hate humanity. My heart begins to ache with the knowledge that I was directly responsible for his despair.

The scene fades and turns into one of Seraphina sitting on a small grassy knoll, facing a setting sun that has turned the bottom half the sky a fiery orange while leaving the top half a sapphire blue. I hear singing unlike anything I've ever heard before. The voices lift the gloom shadowing my soul, and bring hope into my heart that everything will be fine.

"Who is singing?" I ask Helena.

"That caterwauling is from the Heavenly Host," she replies with a slight shiver of revulsion. "I've always hated this memory, but it's one you need to witness for yourself."

"How many times have you watched it?" I ask, knowing Lucifer used to recreate his memories quite often in Hell. She wouldn't have any choice but to view whatever memory he wanted to relive.

"More times than I care to think about," she replies curtly. "Just watch the stupid thing, and bear witness to the moment Lucifer decided he had to stop loving Seraphina in order to do what had to be done."

Helena's words make my heart tighten with impending dread. When she started this journey through Lucifer's memories, I knew she would eventually try to hurt me with one of them. That is her talent: causing pain through grief. I do my best to steel my heart against what I'm about to see. I remind myself that my father and I have built a connection to one another now, but I have to wonder if it's as strong as his was with Seraphina. Did I lose a portion of his love back then that I will never be able to earn back? Is there still a part of him that blames me for the way his life turned out? Will he ever truly be able to forgive me and understand that I didn't make the first human soul to spite him? I'm not sure. I'm not even sure I can ask him those questions face to face without losing my nerve. I may not like the answers my father has to give me.

Lucifer phases in beside Seraphina on the hillside, and sits down next to her so they can watch the sunset together.

“I’ve always enjoyed listening to their singing,” he tells her, a look of contentment on his face. “It brings a sense of peace to my soul that nothing else does.”

She looks over at him and asks, “Can I help you in any way?”

Lucifer meets her gaze with a melancholy smile. “You’ve done enough, Seraphina,” he tells her without elaborating further. I know the true meaning behind his words, and apparently she did, too.

“I didn’t know creating a human soul would upset you so much. I thought you would be proud of what I was able to accomplish on my own.”

“I was proud of you before you created that *abomination*.” Lucifer spits the last word out in disgust. “I will not serve those things like my Father wants me to. I refuse to follow through with His order.”

“But God has plans for the humans,” she reminds him. “He wants them to take care of the Earthly realm.”

“We could have done that just as easily and probably a lot better than they ever will,” Lucifer replies tersely. “Those things are prone to self-destruction, Seraphina. Mark my words. They’ll end up destroying what God has created, and everything we love will be lost to us forever.”

“I don’t believe that,” she says with conviction, “and deep down, I don’t think you believe it either.”

He presses his lips together, and I prepare myself to hear his angry words. Instead, he sighs heavily and turns his gaze back towards the sunset. They sit in mutual silence for a long time before Lucifer finally stands up. He holds out a hand to Seraphina.

“Dance with me,” he invites softly. “I think this might be the last time I ever hear the Heavenly Host sing.”

She takes hold of his hand and stands up in front of him.

"Why would you say that?" she asks, looking confused; frightful of his words. "What are you planning to do?"

"Let's not quarrel right now," Lucifer practically begs. "I only want to dance with you… one last time."

"Why will this be the last time?" Seraphina asks tearfully.

He doesn't make a reply as he takes her into his arms.

"Do you want to know what he was feeling in this moment?" Helena asks me as she holds her hand out to me.

I feel like I owe it to my father not to shirk away from this moment or his feelings. Helena is offering me a window into his soul, and I can't ignore the opportunity. I place my hand on hers, and she gently twines our fingers together. Almost instantly, I experience a sorrow so intense all I can feel is a raw, gaping hole where my heart should be. Lucifer's sense of loss is so strong I immediately begin to cry. He is grieving not only the loss of his once-happy life in Heaven, but also the loss of his only child. He never expected to find joy in having a daughter of his own, but once experienced it was a hard thing to abandon. He didn't want to leave Seraphina behind, but he knew she would never condone, much less join, the war he was about to start. He was determined to prove to God that humanity needed to be destroyed before they corrupted the beautiful world He'd created on Earth. Lucifer viewed humans as the worst kind of plague, and he was certain they would ravage the universe and cause destruction wherever they went. He wanted to protect God from Himself and earn back His love and trust. Obviously, Lucifer had already fought over humanity with his father before this moment, and God refused to listen to his advice.

There was a time when his Father would have come to him and asked his opinion on matters before making an important decision. Now, God placed humanity on a higher pedestal than his own angels, and that was a fact Lucifer couldn't accept. He hated humans, and he was beginning to hate his Father for choosing to love them more than him.

As I watch Lucifer take his first step in his last dance with Seraphina, I can feel his heart shatter into pieces that will never fit back together the same way again. He knew she might never be able to forgive him for what he was about to do. He was preparing to plunge Heaven into civil war in order to save it from the destructive clutches of humanity. This dance with Seraphina was his way of saying goodbye to her, at least for a little while. It was possible she might never be able to understand his actions, but he felt like his sacrifice would be well worth it in the end. He hoped the war would open the eyes of others to the threat humanity presented and that at some point she would join him and stand by his side.

Of course, that never happened, and Lucifer's heart would never find true peace again for a long, long time.

"Look at him," Helena says scathingly. "What a pathetic fool he was to think he could win against God. It takes a lot of arrogance to believe you can make the Almighty bend to your will and follow your lead."

"Lucifer was wrong in what he did, but he was following his heart," I argue.

Helena looks over at me. "Are you actually defending his actions? Do you believe he was right in starting the war?"

"No," I say with a firm shake of my head. "He was wrong, and he finally understood that in the end. Humanity isn't a plague on this universe like he thought. We're its only hope of survival, and that's what God was trying to tell him."

"Trust me, the universe would survive just fine without humanity running around in it like little worker ants," Helena assures me.

"It would survive, but it would remain stagnant, unchanging. Humans provide something vital to the universe."

"Oh really? And what is this miraculous contribution you believe your kind adds to the grand scheme of things?" she challenges.

"Imagination," I tell her. "We think of ways to use what God provided and make it into something else. The world itself hasn't changed since its creation. We still only have what God put here in the beginning, but we've learned how to use what He gave us and improve our lives. We can travel through space to colonize other planets, and that was only possible because we imagined we could do it."

"You also found ways to destroy what was given to you," Helena points out. "Or have you forgotten about the Great War and all the wars that came before it?"

"No, I haven't forgotten, but have you failed to realize that humanity always finds a way to survive? We're still trying to fix what was broken by the last war, but eventually we'll become stronger than we were before it happened."

She snorts derisively. "I think that's wishful thinking on your part, Sister."

"No. It's a fact. History often repeats itself. I suppose if there is one thing that humans have a hard time with, it's learning from their mistakes. We tend to make the same ones over and over again because, at the time, we believe we're fighting for the right cause. It's one of our greatest weaknesses, but we weren't made to be perfect. All we can hope is that we do better the next time we're faced with the same adversity."

Helena returns her gaze to the scene of Lucifer dancing with Seraphina. A far-off look comes into her eyes and I have to ask, "What are you thinking?"

"Nothing you would care about," she whispers, keeping her eyes fixed on Lucifer as he holds his daughter so lovingly.

I know there's no way I can help her unless she willingly begins to open up to me. This feels like an opportunity for her to share something important about herself. All I need to do is tread carefully and try to earn at least a little bit of her trust.

"I do care, Helena." I squeeze her hand lightly to stress my words to her. "Tell me what you're thinking about."

She doesn't pull her hand away from mine like I feared she would. Instead, she closes her eyes, and the scene of Lucifer and Seraphina fades away. Like pieces of a jigsaw puzzle being put together, another scene replaces it. My father is standing alone in the middle of Hell's dark version of the Guf. He looks sad and lonely.

"This is the day of your eighth birthday," Helena tells me in a detached voice as she opens her eyes to look at Lucifer's image. "Lucifer had just come back from visiting you, and I knew how sad he was over having to leave you again. I don't know why he kept torturing himself with those yearly visits for so long. Every time he came back from Cirrus, he would come here and reminisce about his time with you as Seraphina. Sometimes he would spend weeks reliving the old days. On this day, I did something…" Helena's voice trails off and I'm not sure she's going to finish her tale. After a few seconds, she clears her throat and begins again. "I did something I thought would make him finally stop visiting you."

A flash of red captures the corner of my eye, and draws my attention back to the scene. Standing in front of Lucifer is a young version of me, wearing a frilly red dress with a puffy skirt. Since Helena mentioned it was my eighth birthday, that age seems about right for the vison of me.

"Have I visited Hell before and just don't remember it?" I ask her, confused as to why I would be here at this age.

"That's not you," she tells me in a detached voice. "It's me pretending to be you. It was the first time I ever attempted to use my power to manifest a physical form for myself."

I don't say anything because I'm not sure where this is leading. Helena is showing me this moment from her past for a reason, and I don't want her to stop. I fear if I start asking too many questions, she'll close herself off to me again, and that's not what I want.

"I thought…" Helena begins, but stops yet again as she considers the scene before us with a critical eye. Her head tilts slightly as she stares at the memory of herself standing in front of Lucifer. Her brow creases, as if she's having a hard time putting into words what it was she was thinking on this day. "I guess I thought if I could give Lucifer what he wanted the most, he wouldn't feel the need to go to you every year. I wanted him to stop caring about you so much."

I can't prevent myself from asking, "Why?"

Helena glances in my direction. “Because I knew if he didn’t stop, I might lose him to you one day, and that’s exactly what ended up happening.”

I remain silent. She knew I would be Lucifer’s weakness even before he admitted it to himself.

She releases her hold on the scene before us and I hear her version of me say, “Don’t be sad, Father. You will always have me.”

Lucifer’s expression tells me that he’s shocked to see Hell take on a physical form for the first time, and that he’s also confused by why it would choose to present itself to him as me.

“What are you doing?” he asks in dismay. “How is this even possible?”

“You created me like you did her, Father,” Helena tells him in her childlike voice. “I thought you would be able to understand that better if I took on her form, but I can look like whoever you want me to be. I just thought if I looked like Anna, you would stop feeling the need to go see her every year. I can be her for you.”

With a roar of anger, Lucifer rushes Helena and grabs her by the forearms. He yanks her up into the air until they’re eye to eye, and begins to shake her so vigorously the curly brown ringlets on her head bounce uncontrollably.

“You will never take her place, do you understand?” he yells. When she doesn’t make a reply, he shakes her even harder. “*Do* you understand me?”

“Yes,” I hear Helena sob. “Yes, I understand!”

Lucifer releases his hold on her arms, and her little body drops to the ground with a distinct thud.

She begins to weep, hanging her head low, unwilling to look back up at him.

"Why can't you love me like you do her?" she asks pitifully. "What's wrong with me, Father?"

"I am not your father," Lucifer says viciously. "You are nothing more to me than a means to an end. Stop deluding yourself by thinking that you're my daughter. I only have one daughter, and her name is Anna."

He phases, leaving a weeping, child-like Helena on the floor.

I turn to look at my Helena. A single tear rolls down her cheek as she continues to watch the memory. Unexpectedly, my heart goes out to her in a moment of compassion. Maybe she wasn't as heartless as she wanted others to believe. Perhaps a kernel of good wormed its way into all the hate Lucifer used to create her. If Helena can feel emotional pain, it's quite possible she can change and evolve into something more than she was originally designed to be.

"I need to go," she tells me, quickly pulling her hand out of mine.

"Wait," I say, acting on instinct rather than common sense.

I put my arms around Helena in an attempt to comfort her. I hear her sniff once, which prompts me to pat her reassuringly on the back. I have no idea what to say to her about what Lucifer did. I mean, I can't exactly blame him for his reaction. It was harsh, but also natural. She never should have appeared to him for the first time looking like me. If she had chosen a different body, he probably wouldn't have reacted so poorly. From what I just saw, it appeared that Helena simply wanted love and acceptance from him. Who would have imagined that from her?

Helena allows me to comfort her for a little while longer, which is surprising. When she does finally pull away, her eyes shimmer with tears but she seems determined not to let them fall. The space around us reverts to the bedroom where Lucas is still sleeping.

"I'll go get you some food," she tells me, thinking of an excuse to leave for a while. "I'm sure you could both use something to eat."

"Thank you," I tell her.

"You're welcome," Helena replies before hastily vanishing from my sight. I know she isn't phasing down here because I never see her leave behind a phase trail. If she did, it's possible I could follow it and escape, which is probably the reason she *isn't* phasing. Though, I'm not sure if her ability to stop people from phasing in Hell also restricts her from doing it. This is her domain, after all. I would imagine she can do almost anything she wants to in it.

Seeing Helena become so emotional has thrown me for a loop. I had no idea she sought Lucifer's acceptance. It was obvious she was jealous of me at one time, even though she had no reason to be. My father did visit me on each of my birthdays until I turned ten, but I didn't know that until recently. Millie was the one who told me about his yearly visits. She didn't even tell my papa about them during the time they were happening.

I've peeled back yet another layer to Helena's personality, and I'm not quite sure what to think about it. All I do know is that I feel pity for her, and selfishly hope I'm slowly breaking down the barriers she's erected to protect herself from being hurt by others. If I can do that, there's hope I can convince her to let us go.

CHAPTER SEVEN

(Helena's Point of View)

What an idiot! All I had to do was shed a tear, and now I have Anna eating out of the palm of my hand. She feels pity for me. *Me* of all people! It took every ounce of self-control I had not to start laughing triumphantly when she brought me into her arms for a loving embrace. What a sentimental fool my sister is to believe anything Lucifer ever did actually hurt me. Manipulating her emotions is child's play, and I intend to keep her on a short leash until I don't need her anymore.

I may have slightly embellished the scene I just showed her with half-truths to gain her sympathy, but believing anything that I show her in Hell is real is her own fault. She should know me better than that, but her innocent, gullible nature when it comes to family matters seems to prevent her from using her basic reasoning skills. I am Hell. I use people and bend them to my will. It's simply what I do.

As I walk through the fissure that is still open between Hell and Cirrus, I can't help but feel an overwhelming sense of accomplishment. I have no doubt Anna will do everything within her power to make me feel like I matter in the world, even if our father tried to make me believe otherwise. I didn't have to over-exaggerate the scene of me appearing to Lucifer as a young Anna by too much. The only thing I added in was the waterworks. I didn't know how to cry back then. It wasn't in my repertoire of emotional responses until recently. In reality, when Lucifer shook me I lost my ability to keep my physical form, and so I vanished. But, for dramatic effect, I showed her something I knew would tug at her heartstrings and make her more pliable to my will. I've learned over the years that very few humans can resist the effect of a crying child. It seems to excite some sort of primordial emotion within their psyche.

I phase to Anna's palace in Cirrus to snoop around a bit. I do intend to take her some food, but I don't think she expects me to return right away. After all, I'm supposed to be attempting to sort through my emotional baggage and find a way to ease my sorrow over being rejected by Lucifer all those years ago.

I can't prevent myself from laughing out loud at the absurdity of such a notion. The sound of my laughter echoes in the empty halls of Anna's home. I have to admit that I like her palace a lot better when it's devoid of humans. It doesn't feel so…*happy*.

I decide it will be beneficial to look through Anna and Malcolm's private chambers to see if I can discover something I can use against them while they're trapped in my domain. Plus, I'm just curious to know what my sister treasures in her life. Most humans like to keep mementos of what's important to them. I want to know what my sister cherishes most.

As soon as I walk into her chambers, I feel cradled by an aura of peace and tranquility. Even though Anna isn't here, I can still feel her presence. The room itself is filled with the warmth of natural lighting from the outside. The rays of the sun stream into the space through the windows and large opening that leads out onto the verandah. A gentle breeze lifts the sheer white curtains hanging in the space between the living room and the terrace, stirring the scent of freshly cut flowers. The chamber is decorated with comfortable-looking furnishings in light-colored fabrics and woods. I notice at least a half-dozen crystal vases holding skillfully-designed bouquets scattered all around, providing the source of the floral aroma permeating the air.

The glint of something shiny on the fireplace mantel catches my attention. I walk over for a closer inspection and find an old-fashioned framed photo of Lucifer and Amalie. I remember this picture and wonder how it came to be in Anna's possession. Lucifer thought he had found true happiness with Amalie, and that's what they'd shared for a time. Then she got knocked up with Anna and died during childbirth. Her death caused Lucifer to lose his mind to grief. I didn't realize it at the time, but Amalie's death was actually a blessing in disguise for me. It was the catalyst that sent him spiraling down into a pit of despair so deep that I thought he would never find his way out of it. If his natural instinct to protect Anna hadn't been so strong, he would still be with me.

I don't blame him for the way he felt, and in the end everything worked out as it was supposed to. I managed to recover most of the seals despite the odds that were playing against me. I finally gathered enough power to emerge from the pits of Hell to venture into the Earthly realm. Lucifer may have lost sight of our goal, but I haven't. Humanity still needs to be destroyed, and my sister has given me the means by which to do it.

The photo of Lucifer and Amalie isn't the only picture sitting on the mantel. There is also a framed holographic image of Anna, Malcolm, and Lucas. It's from their wedding day, and they're all smiling as if they have a bright and wondrous future ahead of them. It's often amused me how people think their lives can sustain such happiness. No one can stay that cheerful forever. I don't care how much you might love one another. Something always happens to make you face reality.

"You really shouldn't be here," I hear a rancorous, yet familiar voice say behind me.

I turn around and come face to face with Hale, the self-proclaimed leader of the rebellion angels that Lucifer left behind after his exodus to Heaven. The fact that the person responsible for their fall from grace has been welcomed back into Heaven has sent them all into a feeding frenzy. Having no better target for their rage, they all decided Anna and her offspring should be the ones made to suffer for Lucifer's betrayal. I've done my best to protect her and the babies, but Hale and his group obviously became restless and decided to attack her against my wishes. It's just as well. I won't make them suffer for ignoring my orders. Their actions caused the babies to seek me out for succor. I got what I wanted, even if it wasn't the way I had planned to get it.

"And why shouldn't I be here, Hale?" I ask.

"We've placed charges on the propulsion system keeping this city in the air," he tells me, looking especially pleased with himself. "On my command they'll be blown, and Cirrus will fall out of the sky and into the ocean."

"And what exactly does doing such a thing gain you?" I ask out of curiosity.

"Revenge," Hale replies heatedly. "Anna may have gone to you for protection, but she's left her city vulnerable. When she finally does poke her head out of Hell, she'll discover that her home is lying at the bottom of the sea."

"Seems a bit childish of you," I comment, finding the whole situation amusing.

“It will cause her pain, and that’s all I care about.”

“What do you think Lucifer would say about your plan?”

“I don’t care what he would think!” Hale rails angrily. His otherwise-handsome features are contorted into an ugly mask of rage. “His opinion means less than nothing to me now.”

“I think you’re just jealous,” I taunt. I do think that, but I’m also tweaking his anger up a notch. It’s always so much fun to poke at the hearts of the rebellion angels. Not all of them completely lost their sense of right and wrong during their fall from grace. A lot of them considered what they did in Heaven with Lucifer as the ultimate sacrifice for the greater good. They sincerely believed they were on the right side of the war, but isn’t that the way it is in every war? Each side always thinks it’s right. That’s why wars are fought. And who’s to say one side is more right than the other? It all comes down to a difference of opinion, nothing more. “I believe you wish you had been given a chance at redemption so you could finally go home. Does that sound about right, Hale? You can’t reach Lucifer anymore, so you’ll punish Anna as his proxy.”

“There’s no way a *thing* like you can understand how I feel,” Hale says, looking at me like I repulse him.

“I assure you that I can understand a great deal more than you give me credit for,” I say. “And don’t forget that I can end your life with just a thought, Hale. So watch your tongue when you address me, or I’ll cut it off and shove it down your throat, literally.”

“Then why don’t you just go ahead and do it, Helena?” he challenges. “If you’re so worried about Anna and the babies, why haven’t you killed us all, and gotten us out of the way?”

"I need you to do something for me."

"Like father like daughter, I suppose," Hale replies snidely. "And what exactly is it that you want us to do for you?"

"All in good time," I tell him. "I'll be sending someone to you when the moment is right. He'll lead you in the direction I want you to go."

"And who exactly is this someone?" he asks suspiciously.

"His name is Silas, and he'll be able to tell you exactly what you need to do."

"Silas…" Hale considers that name for a moment before asking, "Isn't that Jered's son?"

"Yes."

"And what makes you think I'll take orders from the child of a Watcher?"

"You'll either do what he tells you to or spend an eternity being my plaything in Hell. Which would you prefer?"

"Neither."

"Well, unfortunately for you that's not an option you will be given. Do what he tells you to do, or I promise you'll regret it. That also goes for all the other rotten little rebellion angels under your command. Please make sure you let them know what to expect."

The pinched expression on Hale's face tells me he's enraged by what I've just said, but he's not stupid enough to make a snide reply.

"And when can we expect him to come?" he asks instead.

"I'm waiting for the right time, but I suspect it won't be too much longer. Now, why don't you go scamper off and enact your petty little revenge plan? Do you want me to tell Anna that you've sunk her city, or do you want it to be a surprise for when she comes back?"

"You can tell her. I want her to suffer for as long as possible."

"Very well. I'll let her know when I get the chance."

"Good," Hale says sounding self-satisfied. "And make sure she knows I'm the one who did it."

"I'll be sure to mention it, but does she even know who you are?"

"Maybe not yet, but she will."

He phases and I hear the first bombs go off in the city. On impulse, I grab the picture of Lucifer and Amalie from the mantel before phasing to my Earthly home in Nimbo.

I go directly down to the kitchen in the palace and tell the cooks to prepare something worthy enough for a queen. The people of Nimbo love me, so they immediately set to work on the task that I've given them. I instruct the cooks to pack it up and have someone bring it to my rooms once it's ready.

Since I have a few minutes to wait, I go up to check on Levi. I don't like leaving him alone for very long. When he gets bored it usually leads to trouble, and I'm trying my best to maintain a certain standing for us in Nimbo.

When I had Levi take over the body of Zuri Solarin, I knew the Emperor of Nimbo had a certain reputation with the ladies. Our marriage was supposed to be one that finally calmed the emperor's ravenous appetite for the fairer sex by introducing true love into his life. If he started bringing strange women into his bed, the illusion we were cultivating, that of a happy marriage, would be ruined, and that was something I wouldn't let happen.

I find him in his office with Nimbo's Minister of Finance, Joseph Shea.

"And you're sure we can handle the financial burden of bringing them here to live?" Levi asks as he sits behind his sleek, burnt orange desk, which has a design that seems to defy gravity. Its wave-inspired shape sweeps up and out in front of him in an impressive curve.

Joseph sits in front of Levi's desk in a chair that only appears when someone wants to sit down to speak with the emperor. It's made from miniature polymer balls that rise up from the surface of the floor when they sense someone is about to sit down. The balls conform to the person's body to provide a comfortable seating experience.

"Yes, Your Majesty," Joseph says. "I believe we can incorporate at least ten thousand Cirruns here in Nimbo comfortably. It shouldn't put a strain on our housing situation or economy. However, I would caution against bringing in more than that number. I realize you want to help them in their time of need, but allowing too many to take up residence here would place our economy in peril."

"That's exactly what I wanted to know," Levi says, smiling Zuri Solarin's legendary, charismatic smile. "Since the empress is here," he says, lifting his gaze to look at me standing behind Joseph, "we can discuss what needs to be done later."

Joseph quickly stands from his chair and turns around to face me. He bows at the waist.

"Empress Helena, I didn't realize you were there. My sincerest apology for not acknowledging you sooner."

“Oh, Joseph,” I say good-naturedly, “you were perfectly fine. I quietly slipped in here to see if I could steal a kiss from my husband.”

Levi chuckles, and practically jumps out of his seat to walk over to me. I have to admit, he plays the role of the besotted emperor quite convincingly. He sweeps me up into his arms and kisses me soundly on the lips in front of our audience of one. The fact that Levi has his mouth over mine appalls me more than I like to think about, and when he tries to slide his wet tongue between my lips, I pull away, laughing to hide my revulsion.

“I think we’re embarrassing Joseph, my love,” I say, looking at the Minister of Finance sheepishly while I place a placating hand on Levi’s chest.

Joseph clears his throat nervously before saying, “I should really be going so the two of you can have some time alone. As soon as you hear back from Cirrus, please let me know, Your Majesty.”

Joseph scurries toward the office door and makes a hasty exit.

I push away from Levi and quickly wipe my mouth with the back of my hand.

“What was that all about?” I ask him, wishing I had some soap and water to take away the taste of him on my lips. “What is that devious little mind of yours up to?”

“I thought we would help Catherine secure some votes,” Levi states with a satisfied grin. “I’m sure Anna and Malcolm will have a hard time finding homes for all the Cirrun refugees. If Catherine goes to her people and tells them that she made a bargain with us for some of them to have a temporary home here, I’m confident the people chosen to live in our city will give her their support when the time comes.”

"It's a good enough plan, I suppose, but I wouldn't count on the election taking place anytime soon."

"And why is that?" Levi asks. "What do you know that I don't?"

"Hale and the others just blew up the Cirrun propulsion systems to send it to the bottom of the ocean."

Levi stares at me unblinkingly for a moment, like he didn't hear what I just said. I'm about to ask him if he did when he busts out in laughter.

"Are you serious?" he asks between chuckles as he attempts to control his mirth. "That's classic! I should have thought about doing that myself. Poor Anna; she's losing everything at once."

"That's not all," I say. I go on to tell Levi about everything that has transpired in Hell. After I'm finished, there is a smile so large on his face I almost worry his head will literally split in half.

"Can this day get any better?" he asks, and I know it's a rhetorical question. "Why do the babies seem to trust you so much, and how are they so self-aware about what's going on around them?"

"I'm not sure," I admit. "They seem to know I am the only one who can protect them from the rebellion angels. I don't know how they understand that, but I couldn't have asked for more from them."

"You still haven't told me what your plans are for Anna's children," Levi points out yet again.

"And like I told you the last hundred times you tried to find out, it's none of your business."

"Oh, come on, Helena, at least tell me if you're planning to tear their little souls out of their bodies for yourself somehow."

"No, I don't intend to do that. Is your curiosity satisfied?"

"Not really," he grumbles. "But I guess it's the best I can hope for from you. I really don't understand why you refuse to tell me. It's not like I'll shout it from the rooftops. If you haven't noticed, I don't have a lot of confidantes. I actually can't think of one besides you."

"The less anyone knows about my plans the better," I tell him, becoming irritated with his incessant prodding. "I just came up to check on you. I need to get back to Anna and the others. I would hate for them to get bored because I wasn't being a good hostess."

"What's that in your hand?" Levi asks, looking pointedly at the picture frame I'm holding.

"Just something to make Anna cry when I tell her that her city is now underwater. The gesture might even make her think that I care about her," I reply, showing him the photo of Lucifer and his insufferable wife.

"Well, if you need some back-up, you know where I am. I wouldn't mind playing with Malcolm in Hell if you plan on a good old-fashioned torture scenario."

"I'll keep that in mind," I say, wondering why Levi would think I needed his help to do anything in my own home.

I phase out of his office and return to my rooms. I have one of the servants bring up the doctor who has attended to the needs of the Solarin family for years. When I ask her for what I want, she looks at me in confusion.

"Are you pregnant, Your Grace?" the doctor inquires, glancing at my flat stomach.

"Oh, heavens no," I reassure her with a small laugh. "It's not for me. It's for a friend."

"Is she having complications with her pregnancy? I would only give a patient such medication if they were having problems."

"She's an extremely private person," I explain. "I'm not sure she'll seek out medical help when the time is right, so I wanted to be as prepared as possible for every eventuality. Can you get me what I need?"

"Yes," the doctor answers hesitantly, "but this is a very unusual request. If you weren't the empress, I would probably refuse to help."

"I completely understand and would respect your judgment if you decide not to lend me your aid. It's only that I fear for the life of my friend and her babies. I simply want to help them as much as possible in case something unforeseen occurs."

"Well, like I said, if you weren't the empress I would decline this request, but you are my empress, and I trust your judgment in this matter. When do you need the medicine?"

"As soon as possible, if it's not too much trouble."

"I can have it ready in about ten minutes, if you don't mind waiting."

"That's fine. I have to wait on a delivery of some supplies I'm taking to them anyway. And can you tell me how to administer the medication when it's needed?"

"It's in liquid form, so all she'll need to do is drink it."

"Wonderful. Thank you so much for your assistance in this matter. If there's ever anything I can do for you, just let me know."

"Thank you, Your Grace. I'll go get what you need and be back shortly."

The doctor phases and I sigh in contentment.

My plans are going along so smoothly it's almost as if destiny itself is smiling down on me. I'll have everything I need soon.

The thought makes me smile.

CHAPTER EIGHT
(Anna's Point of View)

As soon as Helena leaves, I hear a big yawn come from the direction of the bed. I turn around to find Lucas slowly sitting up and rubbing the sleep from his eyes with fisted hands.

"Mommy?" he says drowsily, dropping his hands onto his lap and opening his eyes to search for me.

I quickly walk over to the bed and sit on its edge. Lucas throws himself into my welcoming embrace, tightly wrapping his arms around my neck. I greedily accept his hug. I feel sure we both need the comfort of each other's love now more than ever. I'm still not sure why the babies decided to bring Lucas to Hell with us. Perhaps they didn't realize that by phasing me, they would inadvertently phase him here, too, since I was holding him at the time. Hopefully, my son won't become too curious about the reason behind why he was even allowed to enter Hell. I'm sure if he had been wholly human, he wouldn't have been permitted into Helena's realm of existence, but since he carries the soul of an archangel the rule of exclusion didn't apply to him.

"Can we go home now?" he asks, innocent of the reality of our situation. I'm not sure how honest I should be with him, but I know lying isn't the way to go.

"Not yet," I say, kissing his forehead, "but we'll be able to go home real soon, sweetie."

Lucas pulls away to look me in the eyes. "You can't take us home, can you?"

It may have been a question, but I can see he already knows the answer.

"No," I reply, shaking my head with a deep sense of regret, "but your daddy is trying his best to reach us. I'm sure he'll find where we are soon, and we'll all be able to go back home together."

"Daddy's here?" Lucas' demeanor instantly perks up and his eyes glow with a new sense of hope. "He'll rescue us for sure. He won't let anything stop him."

"I want you to understand that we're not in any danger here," I say. "Helena won't hurt us."

"Just being here is hurting us," Lucas tells me with more wisdom than a six-year-old should have about such things.

"What do you mean by that?" I ask, wondering what clarity he has received about our situation that I haven't.

"Do you remember my friend, Gabriel? The one who stayed with me in the Garden of Eden?"

"Yes," I say hesitantly. "What about him?"

"He showed up in my dreams and said we needed to get out of here quick."

"Did he explain why?"

"He said the longer we stayed here, the more power Helena would gain over us. It was something about her draining energy from our souls."

Well, this certainly put a new spin on things. I remembered Lucifer telling me something similar once, but I can't say I feel any different. Surely, if Helena is gaining a foothold into our souls just by us being here, I would have noticed a change.

"We won't have to stay here much longer," I say confidently. "Your daddy will make sure of that."

Lucas doesn't say anything. He just puts his arms back around me again, seeking comfort only a parent can give.

Almost an hour passes by before Helena returns with a basket full of food to share with us. She makes a small black dining table with three matching chairs appear in the room so we can eat together. While Helena is serving us our meal, she tells me about Levi's plans to invite some of my citizens to live in Nimbo.

"And why would he do that?" I ask, suspicious of Levi's uncharacteristic offer of goodwill.

"To help Catherine, of course," Helena replies, handing me a white container with my food and a bottle full of water. "Drink up. You haven't had any water for hours. I've heard the human body needs lots of fluids to stay hydrated."

While she hands Lucas his meal, I open the bottle and practically drink all of the water in one gulp. I hadn't realized how thirsty I was until I had something to drink in my hands.

"Here you go, my little angel," Helena tells Lucas. "I also had the cooks in Nimbo make you a chocolate cake for dessert. You like chocolate, right?"

"Why are you being so nice?" he asks, eyeing her suspiciously. "You're not a good person. Why are you acting like you are?"

She looks taken aback by his blunt questions. "You're my guests. I may be evil, but I do have manners."

"I think you want something from us," Lucas says wisely. "That's what I was told."

"Oh really?" Helena asks intrigued by his statement. "And who told you that?"

"Gabriel."

I wince slightly because I'm not sure what will come out of Helena's mouth next. She knows I don't want Lucas to know that he's actually Gabe reincarnated. I want my son to be able to live his life without thinking about the sad, albeit noble, way his first life ended. It would do no one any good for him to know the truth.

"How exactly did you come by this information from Gabriel?" she replies, sounding even more interested.

"He told me in my dreams."

"I see." Helena stares at Lucas for a moment, as if she's trying to decide something about him. Instead of shying away from her gaze, my son stares back at her just as intensely.

"You should eat," she tells him, being the first to break their eye contact. She sits down in her chair at the round table and opens her container of food. "A growing boy needs his food."

The meal Helena has brought to us consists of roasted lamb with asparagus tips, herbed potato slices, and a buttered roll. As I begin to eat the food, I quickly discover that I'm starving. Every mouthful of food taste like the best thing I've ever eaten for some reason. It doesn't take long before I've devoured everything that she brought me. Helena notices when I've completed my meal, because she pulls out another container with the same food in it and sets it down in front of me.

"Since you're eating for three, I thought you might end up needing a little extra food," she explains.

"Thank you," I say, considering her thoughtfulness very uncharacteristic. I don't say it out loud, but my expression must voice my thoughts for me.

"I *am* capable of thinking about the needs of others," she informs me, almost sounding offended by my surprise, "especially when it's my pregnant sister."

"Does that make you my aunt?" Lucas asks, looking perplexed by such a possibility.

"No," I'm quick to respond. "Helena is not your aunt. We're not real sisters."

I glance in Helena's direction, and notice she's using her fork to toy with the food in her container as she considers my continued refusal to acknowledge our connection. For a moment, I'm sorry for protesting so vigorously that she and I aren't related. After seeing her remembrance of Lucifer's rejection, I feel an overwhelming sense of guilt for rejecting her, too.

"At least," I begin, "not in the way you think of sisters."

Helena lifts her gaze from her food to watch me, waiting for me to say more.

"Lucifer made our souls from his," I tell Lucas. "Because of that, we *are* kind of like sisters."

In my peripheral vision, I can see a small, pleased smile appear on Helena's face, relieving a little bit of my guilt. Even though we're the complete opposite of one another, I feel bad for making her feel as though she means nothing to me. I'm not sure if it's just my hormones causing me to pity her, or if it's the way she seems to be reaching out to me that's doing it. I know I have to watch my back where she's concerned, but Helena seems broken in many ways. Considering how Lucifer treated her, it's no wonder she's so screwed up.

After we finish our entrees, she places a container on the table. Through the clear material, I can immediately see a chocolate cake. When she lifts the lid, the intoxicating aroma of the sweet confection seems to fill the room, making me ravenous to satisfy my sweet-tooth. Playing the part of the perfect hostess, Helena cuts three slices of cake and places them on small white porcelain plates for each of us. She even brought extra utensils for us to use. I pierce the cake with my fork as Helena hands a fresh one to Lucas for him to use. When I bring the first bite of cake up to my mouth, I notice that both of them seem to be frozen into place staring at one another. As Helena was handing Lucas his fork, the tips of their fingers apparently touched. I've seen this far-off look on my son's face before, and I know he's having a vision of the future. But I'm not sure why she seems to be frozen into place, too.

A few seconds pass before both of them are able to move again. Lucas gasps in shock as he comes out of his trance-like state, and I see Helena's face transform into a mask of unmitigated rage. I watch in horror as she swings her free arm back as far as she can and aims her open palm towards my son's face. For me, the action is almost like it's happening in slow motion, even though it isn't.

A well of protectiveness quickly rises from the pit of my stomach, and I react on emotional instinct without having to involve my brain in what happens next. Before Helena's hand can reach Lucas, I use my telekinetic powers to lift her off the floor and toss her body hard up against the nearest wall. I immediately stand from my chair, causing it to fall back onto the floor.

"Don't you ever," I say heatedly, barely able to control my fury as I look at her, "raise your hand to my son again! If you lay one finger on him in anger, I swear to you I will move both Heaven and Earth to find a way to end your existence. Is that understood?"

Helena gasps for air as she lies on her side on the floor, attempting to recover from being slammed against the wall with so much force. Slowly, she pushes herself up into a sitting position. The stunned look on her face doesn't remain there for long. It's soon replaced by the anger I witnessed earlier as she stands to her feet.

Helena's heated gaze remains on Lucas. He swiftly gets out of his chair and comes to stand beside me. I place a protective arm around his shoulders and bring him in as close as I can to my side.

"What you saw will never happen!" Helena tells him viciously. "I am not that weak!"

"I can't help what I see," Lucas says in a small voice.

"It will never happen!" She yells again, even more hysterically. "Do you hear me?"

I have no idea what they're talking about, but I do know Helena is about to lose control of her anger, and that isn't a good thing for anyone.

"You need to calm down, Helena," I say, tempering my own emotions to get a handle on the situation before things dissolve into madness. "Lucas' visions don't always come true. They're just possible futures. Whatever he saw may or may not happen."

"It won't!"

"Since it was something that concerned you, then you're the only one who can stop it from taking place. Don't blame my son because of his gift. He can't control what he sees, and he certainly can't control what you decide to do in your life."

"Don't *ever* touch me again," Helena snarls at Lucas. Her dead-eyed stare tells me she's close to making sure he never sees anything, much less the future, ever again.

"Trust me, I won't," he says, shivering slightly as he makes his promise to the mad- woman standing in front of us.

"Maybe you should leave for a little while," I suggest to Helena, not wanting to take a chance on her losing what common sense she has left and harming Lucas. If she does, I know it won't end well for any of us, and I have three children counting on me to diffuse the situation before things get out of hand. I can't afford to lose my own temper and place their lives in jeopardy by trying to protect them. The smart move is to get Helena away from us for a while, at least until she has her emotions under control. The steady, murderous gaze she is directing towards my son worries me. It's almost as if she blames him for whatever it was that she saw while touching him.

Thankfully, she vanishes from the room, and I breathe a sigh of relief. The tension has been neutralized for now, but I have no way of knowing what kind of mood Helena will be in when she returns. The more I know about what happened, the better I can prepare for the worst.

I pick my chair up off the floor and sit back down in it. I take Lucas' little hands into my own and ask, "What did you see? What made her so mad?"

Lucas takes a deep breath, as if to steady his nerves before he speaks.

"I saw her running down a dark hallway," he tells me, a far-off look in his eyes as he remembers his vision.

"Ok," I say, feeling confused as to why this would anger Helena so much. "Was anyone else with her?"

He becomes thoughtful for a moment before saying, "No. She was alone, but she was crying really hard and looked scared."

Well, that definitely wasn't what I expected to hear. "Do you know why she was so upset?"

Lucas shakes his head. "I don't know. It was almost like she was running away from something."

"And you couldn't tell what it was?"

Lucas shakes his head again.

I bring him into my arms. "It's okay. Like I told Helena, you can't help what you see."

"I've never done that before," he whispers, sounding frightened.

I pull back to look into his eyes.

"Done what exactly?" I ask.

"Shared a vision with someone else," he answers. "I didn't even know I could do that."

"Maybe your powers are growing stronger as you get older," I suggest.

"I wish I could control them better."

"That might come in time, too, sweetie. You're growing up, even though I would rather you stayed my little man instead."

"I'll always be your little man," Lucas promises, placing his arms back around my neck. "I won't ever leave you, Mommy."

I hug my son back and don't make a reply. It's a child's pledge. I know at some point Lucas will need to become the man he's meant to be. His future lies outside the safety of my arms, but, like most parents, all I want for my son is for him to have a happy and fulfilling life. I know I won't be able to protect Lucas forever, and in order for him to grow I will eventually have to let go so he can find his place in the world. No parent should hold on to their children so tightly they're unable to discover who they're meant to be. At some point, you have to trust that you raised them well, and that you've prepared them to face life's many adversities on their own.

"Where do you think she went?" Lucas asks, breaking my train of thought.

"Somewhere far away, I hope." Even as I say the words, I have a bad feeling Helena won't waste her anger. She'll find a target for it, and I fear her focus will lead her straight back to Malcolm and the others.

CHAPTER NINE
(Malcolm's Point of View)

After Helena leaves, we decide the best course of action is inaction, at least for now. If we move in the wrong direction, it might pull us even further away from Anna and Lucas and cause us to lose what ground we've already gained to reach them. There is a slim chance we could choose the right path, but, in this fog, and considering the fact that we are playing by Helena's rules, it isn't likely we would be that lucky. The howls of the Watcher children continue to fill the air all around us. I can see the toll their continued presence is taking on Jered. I look over at Slade and see pity on his face for what our fellow Watcher is enduring.

Slade's own son, Romulus, didn't find out about his father's hellhound bite and subsequent decision to sell his soul to Lucifer until after Slade's death. Rom was as clueless as the rest of us about his father's treachery until it was too late to help him.

Slade and Rom had begun their journey towards redemption together by choosing to help Lilly and protect her from Lucifer's followers back in the day. After Jess and the other vessels sealed the Tear, they both went before God and asked for His forgiveness for their past transgressions. But after Slade died, and we all learned of his deceit, Rom ended up feeling like an outsider to our group and avoided the rest of us as much as possible. He seemed to feel guilt by association. None of us blamed him for Slade's actions, but Rom blamed himself for not seeing what happened to his father. He felt as though he should have known something was wrong. Rom was able to live out his life as a human, just as my own son was fortunate enough to do. At least Slade didn't have the added burden of knowing Rom was among the Watcher children here in Hell. His son was in Heaven now, a privilege Slade himself seemed to want to earn again.

When Helena reappears before us, the look of anger on her face warns that this visit won't be as benign as her previous ones.

"How can you stand to have someone like Lucas around all the time?" she asks me in a grave tone.

I involuntarily grip my sword tighter. "What have you done to him?" I demand.

"Nothing…yet. And go ahead and use that sword on me, Malcolm. I dare you to. Anna couldn't hurt me with her powers. What makes you think your puny sword can do anything to me?"

Cade steps up with a murderous look on his face. "Tell me you haven't hurt Lucas, Helena. He's an innocent in all of this."

Helena looks at Cade like she hates him more than any of the rest of us.

"He's fine!" she snaps irately. "I haven't harmed the miracle child."

"That's good to hear," Jess says, her voice low and threatening. If you could will someone dead, Helena would be vaporized by the look Jess is giving her right now.

She stares at Jess for a moment before saying, "Of anyone here, I suppose it's only right that you feel the most guilt over his current predicament. After all, you're the one who killed him in his first life."

Jess' face falls in shock, like Helena just slapped her.

"Oh," Helena says, as if she realizes something important. She looks around at the War Angels and says, "Do we need a little tutorial about what happened on alternate Earth? I would hate for the rest of you to be clueless about what I'm talking about. Although, it really does have more of a punch if you see it for yourself."

She snaps her fingers, and the fog rolls away from us like waves moving in reverse.

I swallow hard when I see the scene she's conjured for us to watch. It's an exact replica of the moment Gabe sacrificed himself to save us on alternate Earth. I quickly look over at Jess, and see tears fill her eyes from a well-spring of unforgotten grief as she looks at the illusion of Gabe standing behind the Gabriel of that alternate reality. His arm is outstretched and his hand is just about to touch his counterpart on the shoulder. The scene is frozen, giving us all time to soak in the details.

I've tried my best to forget this instance from my past, and that fact has often made me feel a deep sense of guilt. The truth is that it hurts too much to think about losing Gabe here. He was the bravest of us all, and sacrificed everything he was or ever would be in this moment. He did it not only to ensure that we all made it back home, but to also to end the Apocalypse on alternate Earth. He proved to everyone who witnessed his sacrifice that it wasn't necessary to have superpowers to be a hero. All that was required was a sense of right and wrong that led your heart to do whatever needed to be done, no matter the personal cost.

We're standing in a replica of the crater on Mt. Rainer. Jess, Mason, Jered, and I were the only ones visible to the Gabriel in this reality, but the other vessels were standing invisible behind us to bear witness to Gabe's sacrifice and to make sure he was surrounded by loved ones when he left us. Since this is Jess' memory, we can see everyone, including JoJo. The grief on my dear friend's face tears at my heart. I spent a great deal of time with her after we returned home. I promised Gabe I would look out for her and their son, Gabriel. I kept true to that pledge and have looked after their descendants ever since. With Lucas being the last of their line, it seems appropriate that Gabe would come back to Earth as him.

I look up into the dark sky and see what's left of the moon as it approaches this Earth. As this moment transpires, I know that the remnants of the moon will be torn apart by the Earth's gravity field to form a ring around the planet that bears Gabe's name, the Kinlan Ring. I thought it a fitting monument to my friend's life and what he gave up to save us all.

"Remember this moment, Jess?" Helena says as she walks around the back of Gabe's figure, taking in the scene. "Sorry, that really was an unnecessary question, wasn't it? Of course you remember. This is your memory, after all. Hmm, what do you think Gabe felt when he touched his counterpart in this world? Excruciating pain, or nothing?" She walks over to Jess to stand directly in front of her. "Unfortunately, I have no idea, but I do know you felt so much guilt it practically ate your heart away."

Mason places his body in between Helena and Jess as a protective barrier.

"At least Jess has a heart," he tells her scathingly. "To be so powerful, you seem awfully petty when it comes to revenge, Helena. Did Jess' relationship with Lucifer make you so jealous that you're willing to use anything you can to hurt her?"

Helena begins to laugh. "Oh, that's rich coming from you, Mason." Her eyes narrow on him. "You're a fine one to talk so condescendingly to me about jealousy. Does Jess even know what you used to do to satiate your own?"

I notice Mason's back stiffen after Helena's accusatory question.

"I thought not," she says triumphantly. "Otherwise, there wouldn't be so much guilt associated with those memories of yours."

"What is she talking about, Mason?" Jess asks, sniffing and wiping the tears from her eyes with the tips of her fingers.

"Why don't I just show you what I'm talking about?" Helena says snidely to Jess as she peers at her over Mason's shoulder. "I'm sure we would all love to see what haunts Mason the most."

The scene changes and I see Jess and Lucifer sitting at a cozy candle-lit table in the Eiffel Tower restaurant. They're the only ones in the restaurant because he had a yearly standing reservation for this day. He would rent the space from the owner to make sure they received the best service and had privacy. While we were on alternate Earth, Lucifer bargained for alone time with Jess in exchange for his help with certain things there. His first request was for an hour on her birthdays. When we needed his help a second time, he upped the ante to one whole day at any time of his choosing once a year. I knew this had to be one of her birthdays, because he always took her there for supper to celebrate. I have a sinking feeling I know why Helena is showing Jess this particular scene. Jess may not, but I'm sure Helena will happily clear up her confusion.

"What does my memory of this birthday have to do with Mason?" Jess asks, still clueless even after all these years. I thought for sure Mason would have told her about this by now. He'd had years in Heaven to come clean with this particular secret.

“The two of you really should talk more,” Helena says with a disparaging laugh. “After all this time, she still doesn’t know how you stalked her and Lucifer on their dates, Mason?”

“I wasn’t stalking her,” he says defensively. “I was trying to protect her.”

“Hmm, no,” Helena says, drawing out the negative, indicating that Mason is lying. “You may want to believe you were being noble in your actions, but that’s not entirely true, is it? It may have started out that way, but after so many years of Lucifer doing nothing but being a perfect gentleman with Jess, I think your behavior could definitely be categorized as stalking. Did you know he was aware that you were watching him with your little wifey? At the time, it just added joy to these little excursions of theirs, especially this one.” Helena looks at Jess and smiles wickedly. “I think you know why I chose this particular birthday, don’t you, Jess?”

“Yes,” she answers in a hollow voice. “I know why.”

Jess looks shell-shocked about discovering Mason’s secret in this way. I’m sure it isn’t how she wants to appear to Helena, but it’s a natural reaction she’s unable to conceal.

Helena’s smile turns triumphant. “Well, I don’t want everyone else to feel left out of this conversation. Let’s watch this scene together and discover what happens.”

The scene is set into motion and we all watch what should have remained a private moment between Jess and Lucifer.

“What is this,” Lucifer begins as he pours some Dom Pérignon Champagne into Jess’ long-stemmed glass, “your forty-fifth birthday?”

"Please, don't remind me," Jess groans as she reaches for her refilled glass.

As she takes a sip, Lucifer says, "You're not that old, and you still look good for your age."

"Did you just compliment or insult me?" she asks, setting her glass back down near her plate. "It's hard to tell with you most of the time."

"After all these years, I thought you would be able to distinguish the difference by now."

"You're still an enigma to me," Jess admits, eyeing him curiously. "I can't always tell what's going on inside that devious little mind of yours. In fact, I thought you would have gotten bored with these yearly visits of ours by now and stopped making me honor my debt to you."

Lucifer sits back in his chair, eyeing Jess across the table. He shrugs his shoulders a bit and says, "It's the only time we get to talk without your overbearing husband listening to every word we say to each other."

"Mason isn't overbearing, and he doesn't spy on us," Jess professes.

He remains silent as he considers her words.

"Anyway," he says, deciding to move on to another subject, "how is Luke doing?"

Jess narrows her eyes on Lucifer. "Every time you see me, you ask about Luke. Why is that? And why won't you tell me why you were so mad when you discovered I conceived him while we were on alternate Earth?"

"Can't I be concerned about your youngest spawn with Mason?"

"No," she says succinctly. "You've never asked me how my other children are, yet you never miss an opportunity to ask about Luke."

"Well, if you don't want to tell me, you don't have to, Jessica," Lucifer says. "I'm just trying to make small talk to pass the time."

A waiter rolls a silver cart with a three-tier birthday cake on it to their table, interrupting the conversation. The cake is covered with white fondant and expertly decorated with purple and white edible flowers. Sitting on the top layer of the cake is a candle in the shape of a large, glittery, purple '45'.

"Thank God it's almost one o'clock in the morning on this side of the world." Jess shakes her head at the blatant advertisement of her age.

"You're not nearly as old as I am," Lucifer tells her, as if it should bring her a small bit of comfort.

"But you don't age physically."

"I admit it's a perk of being what I am, but I don't think you would want to live forever even if you were given the chance, Jess. There's only so much you can do in this world to pass the time. After a thousand years, you would get bored of your existence and wish you could die."

"I never said I wanted to live forever," Jess replies. "But if I could grow older in years without my body suffering for it, I wouldn't mind that arrangement."

"Complain to my Father about that particular human frailty. I've never understood why He makes your bodies fall apart at the end of your lives, either. I mean, I can see the advantages to doing it to ensure you all die one day, but it seems rather cruel of Him to allow you to gain so much knowledge during your lives then limit your ability to use it at the end."

"Since we know what's coming, maybe He thinks it will urge us to do all we can while we're still physically able."

"Perhaps," Lucifer concedes.

While the waiter is cutting slices from the cake, Lucifer leans further back in his chair and raises his left arm to gain the attention of the small string quartet sitting on the other side of the restaurant. He nods his head to them and they being to play some music.

Lucifer looks back at Jess and holds his hand out to her.

"Care to dance?" he asks.

Jess allows herself to smile a little bit before she places her hand in Lucifer's. The ease with which he brings Jess into his arms as she casually places her hands on his shoulders tells everyone watching that they've danced like this many times over the years.

As they sway to the slow music in perfect unison, Lucifer says, "Can I ask you something?"

"I don't know," Jess responds cautiously. "Can I reserve the right not to answer your question?"

"Yes. If you don't want to answer it, you don't have to."

"Okay, then you can ask me."

"Do you find me attractive?"

Jess looks at Lucifer as if he's lost his mind.

"Well, you picked a great body to inhabit, if that's what you're asking," she replies, looking puzzled by his need to ask such a question.

"Are you really that superficial? Does attractiveness to you only equate to physical beauty? I thought you were more evolved than that, Jessica."

"Why do you care if I find you attractive?"

"I don't necessarily care. I just want to know if you do or not."

Jess sighs heavily as she considers what she should say next.

"You're intelligent," she finally answers, "and on occasion you can be funny. You're loyal, even though your loyalty is rarely on the right side of an argument. But you have your opinions about things and you normally stick to them. At least you're consistent."

"Hmm, consistent," Lucifer muses, looking confused by Jess' use of the term, "not exactly a characteristic most people attribute to a romantic hero."

She lets out a small laugh. "I'm not sure I would ever tag you with that description, Lucifer."

"I'll have you know I can be extremely romantic with the right partner. Women tend to find me extremely attractive for many reasons other than my body."

"Oh, really?" She asks, sounding doubtful of Lucifer's boast. "And what exactly do you do to romance these women?"

Lucifer immediately stops dancing and leaves Jess' side to walk over to the string quartet. As he whispers something to the musicians, he takes off the jacket of his tuxedo and tosses it carelessly onto a nearby chair. As he continues to give them instructions, Lucifer pulls off his black bow tie and throws it onto the coat. The musicians are smiling at whatever Lucifer is saying while he unbuttons the top of his shirt and then proceeds to rolls up his shirtsleeves.

When Lucifer turns around to face Jess again, the quartet strikes up the first notes of a tango. With a determined look on his face, he walks towards her like a tiger hunting its prey. Jess' eyebrows lift slightly in surprise, and she begins to slowly walk backwards to stay out of Lucifer's reach. Her actions simply play into the movements of the dance. When

Lucifer reaches her, he wraps one arm around her waist, pressing hard against the small of her back until she's flush against him.

"Lucifer!" Jess says in alarm. "What are you doing?"

He smiles devilishly and quickly spins Jess around into a dip as he lunges forward on one leg, easily supporting her back with both of his hands.

Jess lets out a small yelp in surprise but ends up laughing at Lucifer's unexpected antics. He pulls her back into a standing position and drops his arms away from her as the music continues to play. Jess shakes her head in exasperation at Lucifer and turns to walk away, but Lucifer goes to her and wraps an arm around the front of her waist, pulling her back up against him again. Jess smiles, looking amused by his actions as he dances her backwards to where they started. Lucifer spins her until she's facing him again. He places a guiding hand on her back while holding her hand and stretching her arm into the air in a customary dancing stance.

The tango has always been a vibrant, playful dance between two partners. There's no other dance that encompasses such a give and take between people while allowing them to display a passion that's both alluring and dynamic. As we watch Lucifer lead Jess in this conversation through dance, I chance a glance in her and Mason's direction. Both of them are watching the scene with somewhat blank expressions. I can't tell exactly what either of them is thinking.

At the end of Jess' tango with Lucifer, he dips her one last time as the last notes of the song are played. Jess laughs, obviously having enjoyed the dance. As she smiles up at him, he leans his head down so close to hers their noses are almost touching. Jess stops laughing as she looks at Lucifer with a mixture of confusion and anticipation.

He doesn't say anything for a long time. He simply gazes into her eyes as if he's looking for the answer to an unasked question. Jess seems to know what that question is and says, "Stand me back up, Lucifer."

He doesn't comply.

"Are you sure that's what you want, Jessica?" he asks in an intimate whisper.

Jess swallows hard before replying, "Yes. I want to go back home now."

Lucifer hesitates, but finally stands them both upright again.

"Don't you want a piece of your birthday cake before you leave?"

"No. Mason and the kids made me one today. I don't need any more cake. I just need to go home. Please don't make me tell you a third time."

"Very well," Lucifer says, looking slightly perturbed. "I suppose our hour together is over."

"Yes. It is."

Lucifer turns to retrieve his jacket and tie, and Helena stops the scene as he's in mid-stride.

"Well…well…well…" Helena says, sounding impressed by what we all just witnessed, "that was *quite* a heated moment between you and my father, Jess. Who knew the devil could tempt you into betraying your vows with just a dance?"

"I didn't betray Mason," Jess informs her.

"Maybe not with your lips," Helena concedes, "but a small part of your heart wanted that kiss. What is it that people say? Oh yes, that men and women can't be friends without sex coming into play at some point during the relationship. I know for a fact Lucifer would have satisfied any carnal desires you had for him on that night. Though, he did feel a little torn about the whole situation. He wanted you to give in, yet he also wanted you to deny him. Secretly, he hoped you would stand firm in your love and commitment to Mason. Otherwise, you would have just been another little monkey who couldn't decide what she wanted out of life. He was proud of you here because not many women could have resisted him in full-out seduction mode, but you did. I guess I should congratulate you for passing his test. Now, why don't we look at this from another perspective?"

The scene reverses to the point where Lucifer is taking off his jacket in front of the quartet.

"I think it's time you saw it the way Mason did," Helena tells Jess as the room zooms out and we're suddenly standing outside in the middle of the Eiffel Tower on the section directly across from the restaurant. The Mason from that time is standing by the railing in a dark wool coat, looking through the window and watching Jess and Lucifer's date. We're standing just behind him as the scene begins to play again.

"Poor Mason," Helena says with false sympathy. "What did it feel like to watch Lucifer try to seduce your wife? Did you doubt her loyalty to you?"

"I never doubted her," Mason replies tersely. "But I certainly didn't trust him." He turns to look at Jess while the scene replays in the background. "I couldn't stand these little dates you had with him, Jess. I'm not perfect, and I should have told you that I followed you every time he took you somewhere."

"Every time?" Jess asks, looking stunned by this new piece of information. "I never saw you."

"Oh, but Lucifer did!" Helena is quick to add in. "And Mason knew Lucifer caught him spying on the two of you."

"Is that the real reason he tried to seduce me here?" Jess asks Helena. "Did he want to hurt Mason by tempting me to be unfaithful to him?"

"I guess that's something you should probably ask my father the next time you see him."

The joy on Helena's face falters. She closes her eyes as if she's experiencing pain. She begins to repeat the word 'no' to herself over and over again. It's as if she believes saying the word enough times will make something untrue.

Finally, she opens her eyes and stares at Jess with even more hatred than before.

"It figures," she says, snapping her fingers and making Jess disappear in a puff of smoke.

Mason turns on Helena with murderous intent.

"What did you do to Jess?" he demands.

"Stop being so overly-dramatic. She's fine," Helena tells him with a roll of her eyes. "It's not like I can kill the two of you anyway. Believe me, if I could I would, just for the sake of my own amusement, but seeing as how you're already dead what's the point? I simply put her in a different section of Hell. I think it might be time to split up this happy little group of adventurers for a while anyway."

Helena snaps her fingers again and the War Angels disappear, leaving only me, Jered, Slade, and Mason.

"How are we all supposed to reach the castle if we're not together?" I ask her, remembering that it was one of her rules in this sadistic game of hers.

"Well, that's the beauty of this game of ours, Malcolm," Helena says. "All of you will need to survive the next tests on your own, and I never said you all had to reach the castle at the same exact moment. If I were you, I would just worry about reaching your family before time runs out."

"But why are you making Jess face things alone?" Masons asks angrily.

"She isn't alone," Helena replies with a sadistic smile as the fog begins to roll back in, obscuring our view of things once again. "But you'll have to find her to discover who she's with. Now, if you gentlemen will excuse me, I have a group of War Angels to go play with, and I believe the children you all helped curse want their own playtime with the lot of you. Far be it for me to hinder the revenge they seek."

Helena vanishes, leaving us worse off now than we were before she came.

The howls of the Watcher children linger in the fog and sound even louder now, indicating that they've moved closer to where we are.

"I can't do this, Malcolm," Jered says, shaking his head vehemently. "I refuse to fight my own son."

"I don't think they're going to give us much of a choice," I tell him as the fog begins to swirl around us like a living creature. I can hear the rhythmic clatter of claws striking the ground like a war drum. "Get ready," I tell the others as I hold my sword in front of me and assume a fighting stance. "They're coming."

Just as the last word leaves my mouth, the black-clawed paw of one of the werewolves penetrates the fog right in front of my eyes. As it makes a vicious downward slash that would have torn half my face off, I twist my body to the right and strike with my sword before it has a chance to retract its arm. My blade slices straight through its elbow, causing it to howl out in pain as it disappears back into the fog with a pitiful whine.

The four of us quickly gather in a circle with our backs to each other. It's impossible to tell in which direction the Watcher children will attack next. The fog is definitely giving them an advantage over us.

"Silas!" Jered calls out. "Stop this! I will not fight you."

We hear a deep, throaty sound that falls somewhere between a chuckle and a growl in response to his words.

"What's happened to you, Father?" Silas mocks. His words sound as if they're coming from everywhere at once, and I instantly know he's part of the pack that's running around us. "You used to be so savage and cunning. It appears your time on Earth has made you soft and slow-witted."

"I'm stronger now than I ever was before," Jered replies. "It took your death to show me how wrong I was about everything. I only wish I had realized it earlier. I could have saved you if I had."

"You should worry about saving yourself," Silas replies spitefully.

One of the wolves launches himself at Mason, but my friend is able to hold his ground and pierce the Watcher child through the gut with his sword. I see a flash of gold surround Mason but it vanishes at quickly as it appeared, making me wonder if I saw it at all. Mason lifts a foot and kicks the wounded werewolf off his blade, propelling him back into the fog.

"Why don't they attack us all at once?" Slade asks. "That would be a more effective tactic than trying to take us out one by one."

"I think this is meant to slow us down more than anything else," I reply. "It's not like they can kill us."

"But we can tear your heads off," Silas taunts from his well-hidden spot in the fog. "Even you can't regenerate from something like that quickly enough to save your wife and children."

"Silas," Jered begs his son, "can't you see that Helena is just using you?"

"Like you used me while I was still alive?" Silas questions scathingly. "At least I know where I stand with her. She's never lied to me, and she appreciates what I have to offer."

"What are you offering her?" Jered asks. "Your allegiance? To what end?"

"I will not be bated by your questions, Father, so stop trying. I will not betray Helena!"

Jered's words seem to make Silas lose his patience. The sound of the werewolves circling us comes to an abrupt stop, and the fog ceases to spin anymore. The air around us grows quiet with anticipation and all I can hear is the breathing of my fellow Watchers. I grip the hilt of my sword with both hands and hold it out in front of me as we wait for their attack.

I don't have to wait long.

Five Watcher children appear out of the fog in front of me, at a full-out run. I'm able to stab one of them in the chest, but the other four do exactly what they were sent in to do: split up our defensive circle.

As I'm about to pull my sword from the wounded werewolf lying on the ground in front of me, I feel another wolf leap onto my back, clutching my shoulders with its sharp claws. With a roar that is a mixture of both frustration and pain, I reach behind me, grab the wolf's head, and yank as hard as I can, detaching the creature's head from its shoulders. A warm blanket of blood covers my back as it slumps forward, almost knocking me off my feet. I quickly throw the wolf head into the fog and step forward to remove the dead weight of its body from my back.

Just as I free my sword from the Watcher child still on the ground, another one comes at me with its head bowed, and rams me hard in the stomach. The momentum of the strike easily tosses me into the air a few feet. I end up landing flat on my back and losing the grip on my sword from the force of the impact. Another Watcher child immediately pounces, hovering over me on all fours. I barely have time to grab the sides of its head before it tries to bite my face. With its teeth bared, it snaps its jaws at me, drooling like a rabid dog. Suddenly, the wolf yelps in pain as it's propelled off me by a swift kick to its side from Jered.

I grab my sword and quickly get back onto my feet. When I look around, I notice a couple of the werewolves running back into the safety of the fog, dragging their fallen comrades behind them. Both Jered and Slade have random scratch marks all over their torsos. Only Mason appears to be unscathed from the fight.

The howling resumes, letting us know that the wolves may have retreated but they haven't gone very far. More than likely they're taking a moment to heal from their wounds before attacking us again.

"I don't think they're going to leave us alone," Slade says, mirroring my own thoughts. He hefts the shaft of his mining pick over his right shoulder as he peers into the fog, listening to the howls of the damned children of the Watchers.

"Helena is probably using them to keep us here, or, at the very least, lead us in the wrong direction," Jered replies.

"I think we should try to push forward while Helena is preoccupied with the War Angels," Mason advises me, since I'm the one who will ultimately have to make the decision about our next move. "It's possible we could end up going in the wrong direction, but we won't know unless we try."

"I agree," I say. "I can't stand here and do nothing. Thankfully, whatever Helena tried to do to Anna didn't work. I didn't feel her pain, so I can't use that as a way to find her; at least not yet."

There is always a chance that Helena will attempt to cause my wife pain in another way. A part of me wants that to happen just so I can find my family. The guilt of that admission weighs heavily on my soul, making me wonder if Hell is influencing my thoughts in ways even I can't understand. Right now, all I can do is pray that we choose the right direction to travel in, and find Anna and Lucas before it's too late.

"Which way do you want to go?" Jered asks me.

It doesn't really matter which direction we take since none of us can see through the fog, but everyone is looking to me to make the decision.

"This way," I tell them as I turn around and start walking.

It's as good a direction as any other. I just hope I'm walking closer to my family instead of further away.

CHAPTER TEN

(Jess' Point of View)

I find myself standing on a replica of my front porch in Cypress Hollow, looking out towards the quaint neighborhood I used to live in. Of all the homes Mason and I owned around the world, I have always loved this one the most. The familiar sound of a creaking rocking chair makes me spin around to seek out the source of the noise.

"Why did you come here without me?" Lucifer asks, looking disappointed in my exclusion of him in this mission. As he brings his chair to a standstill, I notice Anna's hellhound, Luna, sitting beside him. She's so different from the hounds I've fought in the past. Her clear blue eyes remind me so much of Anna's new eye color.

"Are you real, or something Helena has conjured up to torture me with?" I ask, not trusting anything I might see or hear while I'm in Hell.

Lucifer absently begins to stroke the fur of Luna's back. "If you want to prove to yourself that I'm the real deal, ask me a question that she wouldn't know the answer to."

"Ok," I say, quickly thinking of something that only my Lucifer would know. "What were the first two words I said to you when you returned to Heaven?"

Lucifer grins.

"Welcome home," he answers.

I breathe out a sigh of relief.

"You shouldn't have come back here, Lucifer. Even you aren't boneheaded enough to think returning to Hell is a good move for you. I have things handled, so just go back home," I tell my friend as I sit in the matching white rocking chair next to his.

"Considering the look on your face, I would say that statement is far from the truth. My daughter and my grandchildren are in danger, Jessica. You should have told me what was going on so I could come here with you to help."

"Honestly, I wasn't sure if you would be a help or a hindrance. It's too soon for you to be back here. This used to be your realm, remember? You're still trying to come to terms with the things you did when you were acting out against your Father. Helena will just play with your new-found guilt and use it to her advantage."

"It wasn't your decision to make," he says, growing angry. "No matter how noble your intentions, you should have told me what was happening to my own child."

"Lucifer, don't lose your temper," I plead. "Helena will use it to manipulate your actions here. This is her domain now, not yours."

"It was always her domain," he tells me. "She just didn't realize that until after I lost Amalie and began to wallow in my own self-pity. Once I stopped ordering her around, she understood who the real master of this place was."

"Helena is a real piece of work. You out-did yourself making her."

"She served my purposes well for a long time, and even if she hasn't accepted it, she's still providing mankind with what it needs. There will continually be those in the world who deserve an eternity of torment, and that has always been and will always remain Helena's whole reason for existing. I foolishly thought punishing human souls was solely for my own enjoyment, but it turns out I was doing what my Father always wanted me to do: serve mankind."

"You served humanity by torturing their souls?" I begin to wonder if being back in Hell has twisted Lucifer's sense of logic.

"Yes. Unless they're insane, everyone in the world thinks about me at least once before they commit a sin depraved enough to bring them here after death. The thought of Hell and what happens here has prevented more crimes against humanity than I fostered in my time. No one in their right mind would want to come here and endure what this place was made for."

"I still think you should go back to Amalie," I beg him. "She's practically done nothing but mourn your separation since her death. Don't make her suffer anymore."

"She's the one who told me to come," Lucifer says, striking down my one good argument to make him leave. "I'm not about to go back to my wife without being able to tell her our baby and grandchildren are safely back home."

"Do you know everything that's happened while we've been here?"

"I know what my Father told me before I left, but what just happened, Jessica? I get the distinct impression Helena made you experience something that upset you a great deal."

"I'd really rather not talk about it," I grumble, sitting back and slouching in my chair with my arms crossed in front of me.

"I need to know," Lucifer prods gently. "I can't help you unless I have all the information at my disposal. What did she show you?"

I think about his request for a moment and decide I need to understand the motive behind what he did on my forty-fifth birthday. He's been working through his guilt lately. I would like to know if he feels any guilt for what he tried to do that night.

"Do you remember when I turned forty-five?" I ask him, sitting up straighter in my chair as I watch his expression closely.

"Ahh," Lucifer says as his face flushes with understanding, "I suppose she told you about Mason following us around all those years. I have to admit, I'm surprised he didn't tell you about that himself before now."

"I guess even dead, he felt guilty or embarrassed about it. Probably a little bit of both if I know my husband, which I do," I say. "I don't blame him for doing what he did. I do wish he had been the one to tell me, but all of that is in the past. There's nothing to be done about it now, and it doesn't make me love him any less."

"I never suspected that it would, which is why I never told you about his shadowing of us on those occasions."

"His motives, I understand. He was just jealous and trying to protect me. It's yours on that night that I'm a little fuzzy about. What would you have done if I had turned stupid and given in to you that night?"

"I would have taken you to my bed and given you a birthday gift you would have never forgotten," Lucifer says cheekily. "I've been told I'm quite an unselfish lover, by more than one woman, I might add."

"And after we had this wild night of passion," I say with a roll of my eyes at such a concept with him, "what would have happened to us?"

"I never would have come to you again."

I think about this for a few seconds before asking, "Were you trying to push me away, or ruin my marriage?"

Lucifer continues to pet Luna as he contemplates his answer before giving it.

"I was trying to push you away before it was too late."

"What do you mean by too late?"

"I thought that if I coerced you into being unfaithful to Mason, it would shatter the respect I had for you. And if I could coax you into my bed while he watched, that would just be the icing on the proverbial cake."

"Why would you want to lose your respect for me?"

Lucifer sighs. "I was becoming too dependent on our friendship, and I didn't like feeling as if I needed you in my life. You were the only person I cared about back then and that made you my weakness. Also…you were getting older, and I knew I would lose you to death eventually. I decided I would try to break my connection to you before you went to live with my Father. It was the one place I couldn't follow you to."

"Lucifer," I say, reaching out to touch the arm he has resting on the chair, "I wish you had the clarity of mind back then that you do now, and I'm so glad you found Amalie. All I ever wanted was for you to find a way back to your Father because I knew you would never truly be happy until you did."

I then proceed to pinch Lucifer hard on the arm.

"What was that for?" he asks, taking his hand off the hellhound to rub away the pain from the spot on his arm. "I thought we were having a tender moment of truthfulness, Jessica. How did I earn physical violence from you?"

"That's for trying to seduce me *and* for trying to push me away. You're damn right you needed me. I was the first one who finally got through that thick skull of yours and made you start thinking about what you were doing."

"Well, I know that *now*," Lucifer says defensively, still rubbing his sore spot. The hellhound whines and lays her head in Lucifer's lap, looking up at him with pity in her eyes for his superficial wound.

"What's up with the hellhound, anyway?" I ask. "Why did you bring Luna here?"

"She should be able to help us find Anna and Lucas," Lucifer says, finally ceasing to rub his arm as he places a hand back on the soft white fur on Luna's head.

"Why are her eyes blue? Every hellhound I've ever fought had black eyes."

"It's because she's been raised to be kind," he answers. "All hellhounds are born with a pure heart. It's only the way they're corrupted here in Hell that makes them vicious. From what I understand, Luna has proclaimed herself as Lucas' protector. She has a special connection to the boy that will help make it easier to locate him. If we find Lucas, we find Anna and the babies."

"Do you know where in Hell we are?" I ask. "Or have you lost your mojo for navigating around this joint?"

"Well, Helena has disabled everyone's ability to phase down here, and I can't teleport myself around Hell anymore since I lost my connection to it. From what my Father told me before I left Heaven, Helena has set up finding Anna and Lucas as a game. All we have to do is play by her rules and win."

"How are we going to find the others?" I ask.

"We don't need to. We just need to get to the castle. As long as you all make it there and find Anna, you win. Is that correct?"

"Yes."

"Then all we have to worry about is getting you to the castle. Malcolm is capable of getting everyone else there."

I have to smile. "There was a time you wouldn't trust him to walk a dog. Now you have faith that he'll be able to save your daughter. I find that ironic."

"I can't say my opinion of Malcolm as a person has changed very much," Lucifer says, to set the record straight. "Old habits of loathing die hard where he's concerned, but I can't dispute the fact that he loves my daughter and his children more than anything else in his life. He'll win this game Helena is making him play, or die trying. Of that, I have no doubt."

I stand up from my rocking chair. "Okay, so where should we start?" I ask, looking down at Luna. "Do we just follow the dog?"

"Hellhound," Lucifer corrects, also standing from his chair. "Basically, yes. We follow her." Lucifer looks out at the neighborhood I grew up in and raised my children in. "All of this is just one big deception. Nothing you see is real, even though it might feel like it is and react as if it were. Luna will be able to walk us through Helena's illusions and keep us on a straight path to Anna and Lucas."

"So, she's going to act like a bloodhound?"

"Yes, basically."

"All righty then. Let's get going. The sooner we meet up with the others, the better I'll feel."

As we walk off the porch and follow Luna, a sense of impending doom enters my heart. With Lucifer's unexpected arrival in Hell, I have a bad feeling Helena is going to do something stupid to exact revenge on him for leaving her. A woman scorned is never a good thing, and it's even worse when she's the embodiment of Hell.

CHAPTER ELEVEN
(Helena's Point of View)

War Angels. They're like juicy little morsels filled with ooey, gooey, guilty goodness. Luckily for me, the ones who came with Malcolm are the best of the bunch. These particular War Angels are practically bursting with remorse for what they did during the war in Heaven. It's almost as if they thought they had a choice, which is a downright ludicrous notion. God didn't give them an alternative. He designed them to be war machines, and that's exactly what they turned out to be.

I remember the one and only War Angel who came down to Earth with the Watchers. His name was Aiden, and he ended up marrying Lilly's daughter, Caylin. Their first-born was a girl they named Kate. She was the first in a long line of descendants who preceded my sister's birth. Jess' son, Luke, ended up marrying Kate. Their union joined the two bloodlines together for all eternity. I knew that would lead to trouble, and I suppose it did in a way. I wasn't sure I would like Anna when I first met her, but I did. I can see a lot of similarities between us, even if she refuses to acknowledge them herself.

As I travel to the section of Hell where I placed the War Angels, I feel giddy with anticipation. One of them has a doozy of a secret to share with the others. It's been like a boil on his soul, growing larger with the passage of time. I can't wait to slice it open and let it ooze all over their brotherly love for one another. I want to see just how strong their bond actually is.

When I reach their location, I find them all standing together in a group, weapons at the ready, prepared to fight whatever I send their way.

My attention is drawn to Cade first as he moves to stand between his brothers and me. He's the only one of them who isn't afraid of what I might say or do next. It's not because he's my soul mate and assumes I won't single him out for his sins. It's because he has nothing to hide or to be ashamed of, unlike some of his brothers behind him.

"Why have you separated us from the others, Helena?" Cade asks me in a voice that commands an answer.

"We may have a connection to one another," I tell him tersely, "but that doesn't give you the right to demand anything from me. While you're in my home, you'll mind your manners and abide by my rules. Is that understood?"

"Hmph," the angel named Xander says. "You're going to stand there and give us a lecture about having good manners? That's a bit hypocritical of you, isn't it? You're the one keeping Anna and Lucas down here against their will. No one has said it out loud yet, but I'm betting you blackmailed Anna into going along with this little game of yours. I know she wouldn't agree to it unless she had no other option."

"I wouldn't call it blackmail," I reply. "I simply gave her a choice. I could either kill all of you instantly, or allow you to have a chance to earn her and Lucas' freedom."

"Would you have really done that?" Cade asks me, giving me those puppy-dog eyes of his. "Would you have killed us all just to prove a point to her?"

"In a heartbeat," I tell him without hesitation.

He tilts his head as if he just noticed something about me. "You're lying."

“No, I’m not,” I protest, feeling sure I meant exactly what I said.

Cade stares at me hard before saying, “Yes, you are, but you don’t seem to know it because you’re even lying to yourself.”

“He’s right,” Ethan, the leader of the War Angels says, coming to stand by his brother-in-arms. “I don’t think you would have killed us, or at least not all of us.”

“It doesn’t matter!” I reply, losing my temper as they play a semantics game. “The point still remains that I can kill all of you if I want to, but I won’t because Anna and I made a deal.”

“Then why did you split us up?” Cade asks again. “Was this a part of the deal you made with Anna?”

“Not specifically,” I admit. “But I didn’t allow for a negotiation on the details. The goal still remains the same. All of you must reach the castle and enter it to find Anna within the 24-hour period I gave you. Like I said before, it doesn’t necessarily mean that you all have to come at the exact same time. I’m sure some of you will make it there before the others do.”

“What are your plans for us?” Gideon asks as he walks up to stand on the other side of Cade. “You must have separated us from the others for a reason.”

“I’m so glad you asked me that, Gideon. I think I have a way to help all of you get over this mental block you have about the war. Seriously, boys, why do you burden your souls with so much guilt? You did what you were told to do, nothing more. You really need to let go of all the baggage you keep carrying around with you. I mean, honestly, there are literally only two of you who have a real reason to feel any remorse about what you did back then.”

"Two of us?" Cade asks, perplexed. "What do you mean by that?"

I smile and look over his shoulder to find my first victim.

"Oh, Xander," I call, drawing his name out as I address him. "We should work out your issues first, since they seem to cause you so much internal strife. Although I'm confused as to why you feel guilt over someone else's treachery. It makes absolutely no sense."

All of the War Angels turn their attention away from me and direct it towards Xander.

He looks around at his brothers uneasily.

"I don't…" Xander begins to say, but I hold up a hand to stop him before he can refute what I've said.

"As they say," I tell him, "a picture is worth a thousand words, and I can do one better than that."

I change our surroundings to a human's way of thinking about Heaven. I'm sure Anna is watching us, and I want to make sure she understands what she witnesses from her window. The ground is covered in a layer of puffy white clouds, and the sky is a baby blue color. As I look at the way the War Angels are dressed, I decide to add in an accessory that humans have associated with angels almost since the beginning of time. With a snap of my fingers, all of them instantly have large black and white feathered wings springing forth from their backs.

They all act surprised by their new appendages, but Cade is the only one who uses them to fly over to me.

"Why are you doing this, Helena?" he asks, searching my eyes for something he desperately wants to see: mercy.

"Because it's who I am," I tell him, feeling no shame in admitting it to him. "This is what I do. It's all I know."

"But it's not all that you can be," he argues. "You're one of the most powerful beings in all of creation. What more could you possibly want?"

"I need for the universe to feel my pain," I blurt out, without even considering my words first.

"There's more to life than pain," he whispers. "If you would let go of this need you have to hurt others, I could show you another way to live."

Cade looks at me, the promise of a better life naked in his eyes. If I reject who I am and follow him into the light of the future, we could build a life together that would rival the happiness Anna has built with Malcolm. The thought of outdoing my sister in such a way intrigues me, but only for a moment. If I give into Cade's request, I would end up losing who I am, and I'm not about to do that for anyone.

I hold out my hand and use my powers to propel Cade through the air, forcing him to go back to his brothers.

I return my attention to Xander.

With a twitch of my index finger in his direction, I pull him across the ground until he's standing in front of me.

"Now," I say, looking him up and down appraisingly, "why is it that you feel so much guilt, Xander?"

"I should have seen who he really was before it was too late," he finally admits. I have a feeling it's the first time he's put his guilt into so many words. "If I had, I could have saved him."

I let out a derisive laugh. "You angels and your incessant need to save people from themselves. Is that an angelic requirement or just an annoying trait?"

"We care about what happens to others," Xander says as he looks at me with repugnance. "But I don't think that's something a creature like you would know much about."

"*Au contraire*. I do know a little something about that, but I don't let it control who I am or let it influence my life enough to make me self-destruct. Considering the fact that you've let yourself devolve into a sinner during the short time you've been on Earth, it's amazing you can retain this self-righteous attitude of yours in front of me. Why don't we show your brothers what's really going on in that little brain of yours? I'm sure they would all like to know why you keep trying to find ways to forget who you are."

I materialize the memory Xander has been trying to forget with his boozing and whoring on Earth. Since Heaven didn't allow for such things, I suppose he thought the sins of Earth could help him forget this moment from his past. It was an act that forged him into someone who would do anything in order to forget the first time he had to kill.

"You'll have to excuse my need to embellish this scene. You see, I'm almost positive that Anna is watching this from her room, and I want to make sure she understands what she's viewing. So, I've taken a few liberties here and chosen a human form for Xander's Vanguard mentor, Puriel."

"Puriel?" I hear Zane, Xander's true brother, ask as he looks at the memory I've reconstructed behind me. "What does he have to do with this?"

I can already tell by the guarded look on his face that he suspects what it is his brother has been hiding from them all these years.

Xander stares at my interpretation of the angel he looked up to at one time.

"That's a very good question, Zane," I praise sarcastically. "Why don't we watch and see just why it is your brother keeps trying to forget this moment?"

I unfreeze the scene and stand back to watch.

"You can't believe what you just said," the Xander within the memory says to Puriel in disbelief.

"Yes," Puriel nods with certainty, "I do. I believe Lucifer has been right all along. We're fighting on the wrong side of this war, and we should join Lucifer's rebellion before it's too late."

"You know I can't do that. It goes against everything I was made to believe in and fight for."

Puriel places his hands on Xander's shoulders, looking him straight in the eyes with the intensity only the mad have. "You are your own person. We were all created to believe that God is all-knowing, but we were also given free will. You can make up your own mind about what you should believe in."

"I'm sorry, Puriel, but I have made up my mind," Xander says. "I believe we should protect humanity from Lucifer and the others. Why do you believe we shouldn't? I just don't understand how you can be a member of the Vanguard and think this way. You were chosen by God Himself to defend humanity."

"I'm tired of being brainwashed by Him," Puriel says with pure venom. "Lucifer's right: We rarely think for ourselves anymore. We just follow whatever He says without questioning His orders. It's time we started thinking for ourselves instead of just blindly following Him."

"You're speaking blasphemy," Xander argues. "All He wants is peace. It's Lucifer who has caused this war. You have to know he will never win. Why do you think God created my class of angel? We will win this war for Him. Don't turn your back on us, Puriel. You'll regret it."

"Are you threatening me?" Puriel asks, his black wings flaring out on his back.

"I'm asking you to change your mind and see reason. If you join Lucifer's side, you become my enemy, and I don't want to lose you, my friend."

Puriel calls his sword to his hand. "You've already lost me."

With those words, he swiftly raises his sword against Xander. War Angels are known for their quick reflexes, and Xander proves he's no exception to that rule. He calls his heavy flail to his own hand and knocks Puriel's blade away from him.

"Stop this!" Xander pleads. "I don't want to fight you!"

"I'm not giving you a choice," Puriel counters. "Either you fight or you die. You're right; War Angels were made to win this war for God. If we can't persuade you to rebel against Him, then you're a danger to the rest of us. I may be the only one who can kill you because your feelings for me make you weak."

"I am not weak," Xander growls, swinging his flail as he and Puriel begin to circle one another, each trying to find an opening to strike the other. "Please, don't make me kill you."

“I’m not that easy to kill,” Puriel declares as he charges sword-first towards Xander.

They continue to fight for what seems to be a long time. I finally get tired of watching it.

“Why don’t we just skip to the end?” I tell the others as I speed the memory up. Finally, I see Xander about to make the killing blow to Puriel’s soul. I freeze the moment Xander’s spikey flail pierces the other angel’s soul. To emphasize the importance of what’s happening, I drop the illusion of Puriel’s human body and let Xander see his victim in his angelic form for added effect. Since an angel’s true form is made from pure energy, it’s easier to see the glow of Puriel’s soul this way. In slow motion, I let Xander relive this moment in excruciating detail. We all watch as Puriel’s soul extinguishes, marking the true death of an angel.

The expression on Xander’s face in the memory matches the one on his face now, total devastation.

“I don’t see why you still feel guilt over this,” I say. “Unless you actually thought Puriel was right.”

“No,” Xander replies, his voice gravelly with pent-up emotions. “I knew he was wrong.”

“Then is it the fact that you never told anyone you were the one who killed him that’s haunted you all this time?” I ask, wanting to discover the source of Xander’s self-hatred.

When Xander continues to stare at the scene and doesn’t make a reply, I know I’ve found the root of his problem.

Zane walks over to his brother and places a hand on Xander’s shoulder.

"It wasn't your fault," he tells him. "He didn't give you any choice. You had to kill him or he would have killed you."

Xander turns his head to look at his brother. "If it was the right thing to do, why did I feel like I had to hide it from all of you?"

"Oh, oh!" I say, holding up my hand and wiggling my fingers because I'm sure I know the answer to this question. "I would have to say you felt embarrassed that you couldn't change Puriel's mind, and that he thought so little of his relationship with you that he tried to kill you. I have to admit his actions were a little underhanded. Since you wouldn't join him, he was going to use your feelings for him against you so he could slay you. Honestly, I don't see why you still feel guilt over executing such a nasty piece of work like Puriel."

"I hate to agree with Helena," Gideon says to Xander, "but she's right. You shouldn't feel shame over Puriel's death."

"He was my first friend and the first angel I ever killed," Xander confesses. "I'm not sure I'm meant to forget what I did."

"No, you're not supposed to forget it," Ethan tells him, sympathetic to his fellow War Angel's plight. "But you need to let go of your guilt. Puriel made you fight him. He would have murdered you if you hadn't defended yourself, and that's all it was, Xander: self-defense. I just wish you had confided to one of us what happened. I guess I should have been a better leader so you would have felt like you could come to me with this."

"Oh, good grief," I say in exasperation, shaking of my head. "You angels and your guilt complexes. Sometimes things just happen, and it's no one's fault. Have you ever tried to think about it that way?"

None of them makes a reply, giving me an answer with their silence.

“Anyway,” I say, making the scene of Xander and Puriel disappear, “only one of you has the right to feel true guilt over something.” I look over at Atticus and smile beguilingly. “Would you like to share with the class, Atticus, or should I tutor your friends about your treachery?”

All eyes turn to Atticus, who is looking delectably guilt-ridden.

“What is she talking about, Atticus?” Ethan asks.

Atticus’ face mirrors the shame he’s been hiding in his heart for thousands of years.

“I…” He stops as his gaze drifts to the ground at his feet, unwilling to look his brothers in the eye.

When it appears he isn’t going to continue with his confession, I do it for him.

“He worked with Lucifer for a time,” I say, filling in the blank to move this along a little bit faster. “Atticus, here, gave away a few secrets to the enemy, if I remember correctly.”

I have to giggle at the shock on Ethan’s face after learning about Atticus’ disloyalty.

“Come on,” I have to say in disbelief, “not at least one of you knew this already? No one suspected that you had a traitor in your midst? Surely you guessed something was going on when Lucifer started picking the exact right moments to attack the veil where all those precious human souls were residing.”

“Why would we suspect one of our own?” Cade asks me. “We’re a family.”

"Families are overrated; trust me," I tell him. "They can turn on you faster than strangers most of the time." I look back at Atticus. "But you, what's your excuse? Why did you take Lucifer's side?"

"I let his words bore their way inside my soul," Atticus finally answers. "I didn't understand why God seemed to love humans more than He did us." He looks over at Ethan for understanding. "He made us to win the war, but it was almost like we were just a means to an end for Him. He didn't seem to care that most of us would end up dying in battle. Our souls weren't as important as the humans were to Him."

"Atticus," Ethan says reproachfully, "you know that isn't true."

"I know it now," Atticus says, "but when we were first born, all I saw were my brothers dying to protect a race that God treasured more than his angels. We were expected to lay down our lives for them. It didn't seem fair to me at the time, and I rebelled against the idea that my life meant less than a human one."

"But you understand that wasn't true, right?" Ethan asks.

Atticus nods. "Yes. It took me a while, but I finally understood that God made us to protect those who couldn't protect themselves against Lucifer."

"The information you gave Lucifer still led to a lot of deaths in the war," I remind Atticus. "Let's not forget that little detail."

"I never will," he says. "It will haunt me for all eternity."

"How nice for you," I quip.

Atticus looks around at his brothers. "All I can say is that I'm sorry for what I did. I came to realize how wrong I was, but by then the damage had been done. I was too ashamed to admit it to any of you. When I told our Father what I did, He forgave me, even though I didn't deserve it."

"I wish you had trusted us with your secret, Atticus. At least this explains why you're always so hard on yourself," Ethan says. I can see by the look in Ethan's eyes that Atticus' actions in the war have added to his own guilt. Brilliant!

I feel a group hug coming on, so I do something before they can make me want to regurgitate my supper.

I change the scenery to the one in which I made our intrepid group of heroes fight themselves over and over again during the first few hours of their stay here.

The parched earth landscape and the dark, lightning-filled sky bring just the right amount of gloom to their next trial.

I place a shimmering purple barrier right in front of their goal: the castle.

"Who's ready for a little fun?" I ask them. With a snap of my fingers, a legion of angels forms a protective line in front of the castle on our side of the veil. "As you can see, the castle Anna is in is right behind the purple veil. All you have to do is defeat the angelic army protecting it. You have to kill every single one in a timely manner, or the barrier won't drop."

"What's the catch?" Roan asks. "This seems a little too easy."

"Thank you for asking," I say to him. As the ground beneath their feet begins to tremble, a loud crack can be heard directly behind them. When they turn to follow the noise, all of them see the crevasse that's forming, slowly crumbling the earth to form a deep chasm of nothingness. "I'm afraid you'll need to use those nifty new wings I just gave you to fight my army in the air. Now, be careful of the veil. It has a nasty sting to it. I'm sure you've all been told how painful my hellhounds' bites can be. Trust me… this will be a hundred times worse for you. You'll be in so much torment you'll beg for death. And there's a time limit, of sorts. You only have so much time to kill them all before they begin to respawn; so be quick about it, or you'll never win."

"Is that all?" Gideon asks sarcastically. "Would you like to tie our hands behind our backs, too?"

I smile and not nicely. "Don't tempt me."

I walk over to Cade, grab one of his arms, and snap my fingers, signaling to my minions in front of the veil that they should begin their charge towards the War Angels.

"Have fun, boys!" I say, teleporting Cade with me to a more secluded area: my bedroom.

I'll admit. The room could be more colorful. It's very similar to the one I have Anna resting in. I can't help it if I like black and silver.

Cade takes a quick look around the space before saying, "You need to take me back, Helena. They need my help."

As I take a couple of steps to stand in front of Cade, I slide my hand up his arm and across his chest. I love how silky smooth his skin feels against the tips of my fingers, yet the muscle underneath makes it taut to the touch.

"They'll survive without you," I tell him, thinking him handsome with the wings I've placed on his back. They give him a regal look.

"Why have you brought me here?" he asks, yet his words don't match his tone. He knows exactly why I've brought him to my bedroom. "I can't do this with you right now."

I lift a questioning eyebrow. "If not now, then when, Cade? You know as well as I do that we'll end up in a bed together at some point. It's inevitable. What's wrong with giving in to what we both want now? We belong to one another, right? Isn't that how the whole soul mate thing is supposed to work?"

"My friends are fighting to win this sadistic game you're making us play. Do you honestly think I'm the kind of person who would rather take you to bed than help them? If you do, then you don't know me at all."

"No, I don't know you, and you don't really know me."

"I'm beginning to wonder if I want to."

I feel a tightening in my chest after hearing Cade's words.

"I don't think either one of us has a choice in the matter," I say, ignoring the pain. "You may not like what I am or how I do things, but this is me, Cade. I'm heartless, and I do what I have to in order to survive."

"You don't need Anna or Lucas, Helena. You would survive just fine without them. Why can't you let them go without making us play this stupid game of yours?"

"I *will* let them go, you fool. I just need some more time."

"Time for what?"

"For my real plan to unfold."

"And what is your real plan?"

"Why would I tell you that?"

"Why are you telling me anything?" Cade questions, eyeing me curiously. "You didn't have to tell me what you just did. I think you want to tell someone what you're planning. You may even want someone to stop you from doing it."

"I'm not sure it's going to work, and if it does I certainly don't need you telling my sister about it."

"I won't let you hurt her children," he says stubbornly.

"Good grief!" I yell. "How many times do I have to say that I'm not going to hurt them? I have no intention of killing any of them! None whatsoever! In fact, if it wasn't for me they would probably already be dead. I've been protecting them since Lucifer left to live the good life with Amalie. Why can't any of you see that?"

"Because nothing you do is for unselfish reasons. Yes, you're protecting them, but why? What's your end game here, Helena? Are you planning to steal their souls? Can you even do that?"

"I can't steal souls. They can only be given to me."

"Then, what is this? A long con? Are you planning to twist them in some way so their souls end up here in Hell when they die? Will that give you enough power to do whatever it is you want to do?"

"If they want to give me their souls, then I will gladly take them. Don't bother trying to get me to tell you more, because I won't."

"Then take me back to my brothers so I can help them. You can't force me to make love to you."

"Make love?" I scoff. "I just wanted to have sex. Who said anything about love? Would you rather I let Levi satisfy my needs in his bed? He's been begging to have the privilege of pleasuring my body for quite some time now."

"You wouldn't let a mangy mongrel like him inside you," Cade says with certainty. "I know you at least that well."

"True enough," I admit, unable to make myself pretend otherwise. "I'm not that desperate yet, but if you keep denying me I might find someone else willing to satisfy my needs."

"You can do what you want. I'm not your keeper."

"No, you most certainly are not." This conversation is not going in the direction that I wanted it to. "Very well, go back to your brothers. Just remember to stay away from the barrier."

I send Cade back to the fight. I feel more frustrated now than I did before. Despite myself, I begin to miss the self-righteous fool.

I teleport back to where the War Angel fight is taking place. As I watch them battle against my minions, even I have to admit that they're the best warriors I've ever seen. It's no wonder Lucifer's followers didn't have a chance against them. Even without being able to phase in and out of the fight, they move with incredible speed and precision. Of course, my attention centers on Cade. Watching the way his muscles move as he wields his silver great sword, makes me imagine how it would feel to have his body wrapped around mine. I guess I shouldn't be surprised that he rejected my offer of sex. His memories are so pure it should have been plain to me that he would think of it as 'making love'. His thinking is so quaint it borders on disgusting to me. I'm still puzzled as to why the two of us were paired together. It doesn't make a lot of sense. I could understand God wanting to punish me, but why punish Cade? What did he do to deserve such a doomed fate?

I vow that the next time I invite him into my bed, I won't take no for an answer. I'll find a way to make it happen.

Cade notices me watching him fight, and for a second his focus is split. It's just enough time to give his opponent an opening to kick him in the stomach and propel him towards the purple veil. Without even thinking, I stop Cade from spinning through the air, inches away from a lifetime of pain. He looks down at me in shock, but quickly recovers and smiles as he flies back into the fray.

"Damn him," I mutter to myself, feeling weak because I let my feelings for him interfere with the natural course of events. If it had been anyone else about to fall into the veil, I would have just laughed. But it was Cade. I couldn't let him get hurt.

I ponder this for a moment, but decide not to dwell on the matter. It might give me a headache or make me realize something I'm not ready to face yet.

Anyway, I have someone I need to go see. I'm sure Lucifer is wondering where I am right about now. His return here shows how much he truly loves Anna. She's always been his favorite, but we'll see how long that lasts.

CHAPTER TWELVE

One of the loveliest things about my home is that I can transform it into whatever I want. The laws of physics bend to my will here, and I know exactly what's going on in every section of it at all times. It's almost like being omnipotent, except my power only reaches as far as my domain.

As I stand at the center of an old-world dirt crossroads, awaiting Lucifer and Jess' arrival, I feel my heart begin to pound with anticipation. I can't wait to see my father again and tell him exactly what I think of him. He may try to deny that I'm his child, but it's time he acknowledged that he created me. Hale and the other rebellion angels weren't the only ones Lucifer abandoned on this stupid rock hurtling through space. He left me behind, too, and I'll never forgive him for that.

The scene I've created for our reunion is one Lucifer has used many times before on unsuspecting travelers. During a time when humans still walked most places, they would almost always end up at a crossroads at some point in their lives, literally and figuratively. Lucifer may have never directly made humans sin, but he definitely liked to push them in that direction. A whispered word of encouragement can go a long way in the human psyche. Their minds are so pliable when they're confused about whether they should go left, right, or straight ahead. The crossroads is a symbolic representation of human choice. You can go left and give into your desires, go right and rise above your basic instincts, or go straight with blinders on and never choose a side. Generally, after Lucifer talked to someone, he or she typically chose to go left in their lives, recklessly throwing caution to the wind and giving in to their deepest and darkest desires. Lucifer was a master manipulator, and he used that skill effectively every chance he got.

The first sign of their imminent approach is the glow from the hellhound's blazing coat in the semi-darkness of night I've recreated. I remember Lucifer selecting her out of a newly born litter of hellhounds to take up to Anna. Levi had just ripped off the head of her robotic dog, and it was questionable whether her down-world friend would be able to restore Vala to working condition. Fortunately for my sister, Vala was repairable, but not before Lucifer gave her one of my puppies. He didn't even ask if he could take her! He just grabbed the pup and left. Typical Lucifer; always doing whatever he wants without thinking about the repercussions to others.

"Well, well, well," I say as the trio approaches me, "what do we have here? Jess and Lucifer's Excellent Adventure? I'm sure people would pay good money to see the two of you fighting your way through Hell. I have to say that I'm surprised to see you here again, Father. I thought for sure you would stay hidden where it's safe. Tell me, what brings you back so soon? Did you miss me?"

"You know why I'm here. Give us Anna and Lucas, Helena," Lucifer says in his most intimidating voice. It used to bring me in line to do his bidding, but all I want to do now is laugh in his face. I know I'm more powerful than he ever was during his reign here, and he knows it, too.

"Sorry, but you lost the right to order me around the moment you gave up on who you were truly meant to be. You are still dead, aren't you? Or did God resurrect you just to annoy the hell out of me?" I can't help but laugh at my own joke, but the two standing in front of me aren't as amused. "You people really need to get a sense of humor."

"This body is only temporary," Lucifer says, ignoring my attempt at a joke. "Once Anna is safely back home, I won't be returning here. Well, unless you do something this idiotic again."

"Anna, Anna, Anna," I say in aggravation. "Everyone worries *so* much about Anna! Why is that? It's not even like she's all that special."

"She's my daughter."

"So am I!"

I notice Jess stare at me, an annoyingly quizzical look on her face.

"What?" I snarl at her. "Why are you looking at me like that?"

"I think," she begins, studying me even more closely, "this is the first time I've truly understood what's wrong with you, Helena."

"Oh, really?" I ask, doubtful Jess could have any deep insight into my character. "What sort of divine enlightenment do you think you've just received about me?"

"It's obvious you're nothing but a spoiled brat who never thought her father loved her enough while he was alive. Everything you've done up to this point is just your version of a temper tantrum."

I feel rage infuse every cell of my new body, and immediately lash out at Jess. I lift my left hand to throw a flaming ball of energy at her, but it ends up glancing off a transparent gold shield that surrounds her like a bubble. It was invisible to the naked eye until it was needed. I should have known God wouldn't send His holier-than-though champion back without some sort of protection from me. I throw one at Lucifer just for kicks to see if he's protected, too, and, of course, he is.

"Well, the two of you are no fun to play with," I complain, growing even more aggravated.

"We're not here to play games with you, Helena. We're here to get my daughter back. Now, where is she?" Lucifer demands hotly.

"That's for me to know and for you to find out, big guy." I wink at Lucifer to test whether or not I can still enrage him, or if being in Heaven has completely neutered his personality.

Apparently, Heaven hasn't changed him that much.

With a growl of frustration, Lucifer rushes me. He grips my throat tightly with his left hand and throws me down on the ground, causing a puff of dust to rise from the dirt road.

"Take me to her now!" he demands.

Even though he's cut off the air to my lungs, I'm still able to smile up at him.

He's back. That do or die hellfire look in his eyes hasn't been extinguished yet. The old Lucifer has come out to play with me even though he said he wouldn't. Maybe if I push him just the right way, he'll decide to return to me and we can pick up where we left off. What is it the humans used to say? You can't teach an old dog new tricks? It looks like that might be the case for my father. What would he be willing to exchange for Anna's release? I'm sure if I asked him for his soul, he would gladly hand it over in order to save her. After all, he gave his life to protect her from me. I doubt there's anything he wouldn't sacrifice for his sweet, precious Anna.

"Lucifer!" Jess rushes over to him and begins to wrench at his arm. The sight of her distress tickles something inside my soul, and I begin to laugh.

Poor Jess. She's slowly seeing all her hard work crumble to the reemergence of Lucifer's true self. She spent so many years endeavoring to change her friend, even though he wasn't ready to be transformed. Her friendship and love weren't enough to make him want to be a better man. Only when he saw himself through Amalie's eyes did that unexpected miracle take place. She was the only one who could make Lucifer face up to who he had become. She held up a mirror to his soul and forced him to stare into the abyss. He ended up detesting what he saw in the reflection. He tried to be a better man for Amalie, but all he did was fail her miserably before she died.

"Lucifer, stop!" Jess begs, yanking on his arm with even more force. "You're doing exactly what she wants you to do! Don't let her win."

Damn it.

If there's one thing Lucifer hates most in the world, it's losing. Why did Jess have to put it in those terms when I was just gaining the upper hand?

He instantly lets go of my neck and stands back up.

"She's not worth it, Lucifer," Jess tells him. "Think about Amalie and Anna. They both need you. Don't let them down by giving into Helena's jabs. She's trying to goad you into losing your soul again. Can't you see that? She wants you back here with her."

"Why would she want that?" Lucifer asks in bewilderment, staring down at me as I try to gasp for breath to refill my lungs.

"I think she's lonely."

"You know," I croak as I sit up, rubbing the soreness out of my neck, "I *am* right here. I can hear what you're saying."

"Good," Jess says in that sanctimonious tone of hers. "You need to hear the truth. You're behaving like a child who's mad because her favorite toy got taken away."

I stand to my feet. As I look at her, I don't even attempt to hide my hatred.

"You know less than nothing about my relationship with Lucifer!"

"I know enough to tell when someone is acting out their jealousy, Helena, and right now you're practically green with envy."

"Envious of whom exactly?" I question. "Amalie? God? You?"

"Anna," Jess answers calmly, so sure of her answer. "You're jealous of how much Lucifer loves her and how much he despises you."

After listening to her words, my blood begins to boil and all I want to do is smash her smug face into the ground. When I look over at Lucifer, I see a look of dawning pass across his features. He meets my gaze as if he's seeing me for the first time in his life.

"Anna's my child. You're just a construct I created to serve my will, Helena," Lucifer tells me, as if I should be able to discern the difference between Anna and myself. "I never meant for you to become self-aware, and I certainly didn't intend for you to become flesh and bone."

"That's all I've ever been to you! A means to an end!" I scream, unable to hold in my rage and frustration. "You've never been able to see me as real."

I reach out and grab Lucifer roughly by the arm. "How does that feel, Father? Don't I feel real enough to you yet?"

"I am not your father, Helena," he states in frustration, wrenching his arm out of my grasp. "How many times do I have to say that before the truth of it finally sinks in? I don't care how many bodies you make for yourself. You will never be a real person! This isn't some fairytale. I'm not Geppetto, and Jess isn't the Blue Fairy. You will never be a *real* girl."

As Lucifer's words settle into my heart, I slowly take a step back from him.

"You don't see me at all, do you?" I ask in a whisper. "You'll never see me no matter what I do or what I become. I'll never be someone you can care about."

"You are not a *someone*," Lucifer says. "You are a *something*."

I stare at him as my own sense of realization sinks in.

"Fine," I say. "If that's the way you see me, then there's nothing I can do to change your mind, but I know who and what I am even if you don't." I turn my back to him. "Good luck finding Anna with that hellhound of yours. By the time you reach her, I'll already have what I want from your precious daughter."

"What do you want from her?" I hear Lucifer yell at me as I walk away. "Helena! What are you planning to do?"

I don't turn around. I just keep on walking until I fade from his sight and teleport myself back into Anna's room. When I see her lying on the bed, sweating profusely, I know what I just said to Lucifer is true. He may find Anna, but he's already too late to help her.

"Helena," Anna says when she sees me in the room, "I think something's wrong with the babies. I need a doctor."

"You need to get my dad," Lucas tells me from his position next to Anna on the bed. He's sitting there cross-legged, holding her hand.

"Oh, I think we can handle things just fine by ourselves," I assure them both.

"I thought you wanted to protect my children," Anna argues. "Please, Helena, I know something's wrong. I need your help."

"I've already given you my help," I tell her, walking over to her side of the bed. I have to admit she does look pale. "Oh dear, I hope I didn't put too much of that medicine in your drink. Honestly, I forgot to ask what else it might do to you besides start your labor."

"You drugged me?" Anna asks in disbelief, her eyes frantic with worry now.

"With everyone trying to reach you, I couldn't very well wait around for it to happen naturally. The babies are almost full-term anyway. If you think about it, I'm doing you an enormous favor. You can finally get rid of that gigantic baby bump you've been toting around for the last few months. Although, I seriously doubt your figure will ever be the same again."

Anna places a protective hand on her stomach and looks at me like I've lost my mind.

"I think you're the craziest person I know," she tells me without a shred of doubt.

"Thank you," I reply. At least she called me a person and not a thing like our father just did.

That pompous ass deserves to have Hell rain down on him. If he and Jess weren't being protected by some Heavenly shield, that's exactly what I would do.

I observe Anna for a little while to judge how swiftly her labor is progressing. Other than a fine sheen of sweat across her forehead, I see no other signs that things are moving along fast enough. I don't dare give her any more of the medication. I don't want to harm the children. What to do…what to do…

"Oh!" I say as brilliance strikes. I may not be able to give her any more medication, but I can play with her emotions to help speed things along. "I almost forgot all about Malcolm and what he's been hiding from you. If you're going to bring his children into the world, you really should know what he's capable of doing."

"My dad is a good man," Lucas defends, looking fiercely loyal to a man he barely knows anything about. His counterpart, Gabe, knows a great deal about Malcolm's past, but this reincarnation of him is innocent of Malcolm's rather shady history.

"You're right, Lucas. Your dad is a good man," Anna says.

"If I were you," I say, "I wouldn't let your little angel witness what I'm about to show you. I'm sure what his father did would only feed his nightmares."

I know Malcolm has shared some of his past with Anna. She knows what he used to be and the way he used humans to satisfy his own needs, carnal and otherwise.

"He might not want you to see his worst memory, Lucas," Anna says. "Helena isn't going to give him a choice about reliving it, but I think we should give him the choice of sharing it with you when he's ready."

I let out a derisive laugh. "Oh, trust me. He won't be sharing this moment from his past with our littlest angel."

"Why do you keep calling me an angel?" Lucas demands. "I don't like it."

"And why is that?" I ask, finding this curious.

"Because coming from you it sounds like a bad thing."

Anna sits up in the bed and brings Lucas into her arms.

"Stay here for me and your dad," she tells him before slowly moving her legs over the side of the bed and placing her feet on the floor. Instinctively, I go to help her stand up.

She walks over to the chair by the window and sits down. Her expression is defiant in the face of my threat. I can't help but admire the faith she has in her husband. I mean, it's a bit on the foolhardy side, but if there is one thing I can say about Anna it's that she always believes in the ones she loves.

"Can I make a request?" she asks.

"You can make it," I tell her, "but it doesn't mean I'll grant it."

"Let Malcolm see me," she pleads. "Let me be with him while you do this."

"Hmm." I mull this idea over and see an opportunity open up. "Request granted."

I turn to the window and zoom in on the image Anna is able to see from her room in the tower. From her vantage point, she can see Malcolm, Mason, Jered, and Slade walking in the thick fog, blindly trying to navigate their way to the castle.

The men look our way and see Anna. From their point of view, all they see is a window with Anna sitting in front of it. Malcolm's eyes widen in surprise when he sees the love of his life. He rushes over to the window to start banging on it, but when his fists go through the illusion, he realizes she isn't actually there.

"Lucas, come here for a moment," Anna hurriedly requests. "Let your dad see that you haven't been harmed."

Lucas scrambles off the bed and runs over to the window. He presses his hands against the clear pane of glass as he looks at his father.

Malcolm kneels on the ground in front of the window so he's eye level with his son. He raises his right hand, folds it into a fist, and places it over his heart. He thumps his chest twice while holding Lucas' gaze.

Lucas mimics his father's gesture with his own little hand and says, "I love you, too, Dad."

"Go back to the bed, sweetie," Anna says.

Lucas thumps his heart twice more for his father with his little fist before doing as his mother instructs.

Anna and Malcolm lock gazes. She holds out a hand and presses it against the glass. He mirrors her movement, even though his hand simply passes through the illusion of the window on his side. They stare at each other, and the love between them seems to manifest into a physical presence inside the room.

When Anna drops her hand away, she looks up at me and says, "Do it. Prove to yourself that Malcolm is strong enough to survive whatever horror you're about to make him relive. I already know he is."

"It must be nice to have so much faith in another person," I comment, finding her even more beautiful as she sticks up for her man while suffering through the first stages of the birthing process. I admire her ability to handle everything that's been thrown at her. She's strong, but is her love for Malcolm strong enough to forgive what I'm about to show her? The answer to that question is about to be answered.

CHAPTER THIRTEEN

(Malcolm's Point of View)

Being able to see Lucas and Anna again has healed my soul and fueled an already- burning desire to have them both back in my arms again. When I first saw the window appear, all I could think about was tearing it down to reach them. The sensible part of me knew that it was only an illusion, but I had to try anyway. I had to know for sure that they were out of my reach.

Anna doesn't look well. Her skin is deathly pale and glistening with sweat. If I didn't know any better I would say she's in labor, but the babies aren't due for another four weeks. Could stress be causing her to go into labor early? Dear Lord, please don't let that be the case. I refuse to have my children breathe their first breaths in Hell.

"I have to say I kind of like you on your knees, Malcolm," I hear Helena say behind me. "The position suits you well."

I withdraw my hand from the illusion of Anna and steel myself for what's about to come next. There's a reason Helena is allowing Anna to see me, and I know it's not out of the goodness of her heart. She's been systematically showing everyone the one memory that haunts them the most. I can only surmise that she's through playing with the War Angels. That only leaves Slade and me to harass.

"I guess you've come to show me my worst memory," Slade says, apparently having the same thought as me and deflecting Helena's attentions onto himself first for some reason. "Go on, then. Show it. I have nothing to hide."

Helena turns her gaze away from me to stare at him.

"Are you that eager to relive it?" she asks him. "I promised my sister she could watch Malcolm's memory, but if you want to go first who am I to deny you such sweet torture?"

The heavy mist surrounding us rolls away, and I instantly recognize where we are.

It's an exact replica of Brand's home in England. The scene Helena has conjured shows the Watchers engaged in battle with Lucifer's angels in front of the mansion. This is the day Lilly was able to stop Lucifer's plans to destroy the world, but not before he was able to make the Tear. I fought in this skirmish alongside Slade, but I don't understand why this would be his worst memory.

"You look puzzled, Malcolm," Helena says, sounding a little too happy about my confusion. "Didn't you know that this was the day Slade received his hellhound bite?"

She turns around and points to memory Slade lying on the ground, a hellhound standing over him. Its jaws are open and you can tell there's nothing that can stop what's about to happen next.

Helena unfreezes the memory so we can all watch the hellhound bite Slade on the shoulder. He cries out in pain, but no one hears him. We were all too busy with our own battles to notice what was happening to him.

I look at Slade. "Why didn't you tell one of us? We could have helped you."

"What good would that have done?" he asks me. "There was only one way to stop the pain, and I knew that."

"Still, you should have told somebody," Mason says, looking distraught over Slade's refusal to confide his secret to one of his fellow Watchers. "You shouldn't have gone through that alone. If you had told us, we would have stopped you from making a deal with Lucifer."

"In his defense," Helena tells us, "he did try to cope with the pain for a very long time. He suffered through it without anyone knowing, up until about a year after the Tear was sealed. Then he eventually succumbed to temptation, like most people do."

The scene changes again and we see Slade and Lucifer sitting at a small table outside a café in Venice, Italy. A gondola is passing by on the canal as Lucifer leans forward in his wooden fold-up chair.

"I have to say," Lucifer tells Slade, "I thought you would have come to me before now. Very few people make it this long without either going insane or giving up their souls. What took you so long, Slade?"

"I thought I could deal with the pain on my own," he admits. "I wanted to help the others find a way to close the Tear, and I've done that. I hoped one of you would have killed me by now."

Lucifer grins, confident he's about to add another Watcher soul to his collection.

"I told my brothers not to touch you," Lucifer informs him. "Why would I destroy someone who is so ripe for the picking?"

"I thought it might be something like that," Slade replies, looking like a man who is trapped in a situation that has only one way out. "That's why I'm here. I'm damned either way. You'll never lift the curse, and I can't go another day living like this. So take my soul, you bastard. Just stop this unending pain."

Lucifer studies him for a moment. It's almost like he's drinking in Slade's suffering one last time before it ends.

As Lucifer sits back in his seat, he declares, "Done."

The Slade in the memory takes in a large gulp of air. If you didn't know any better, you would have thought he'd been holding his breath for days and only now allowed himself to breathe. I know the truth of the matter. I know what it feels like to live with so much pain you wish you could die from it and even the simple act of breathing hurts. This is his first breath as a free man, yet he only traded in one pain for another that will never end. Slade is luckier than most. It's unheard of to escape Hell and be given a second chance to redeem your soul. I may never fully trust Slade again, but I don't begrudge him this opportunity to put all of his wrongs right.

I can see the toll reliving this memory is having on Slade, and against my better judgment I decide to deflect Helena's attention onto another target.

"Why don't you do what you really came here for, Helena?" I ask. "I'm feeling a little left out. It seems like I'm the only one you haven't tortured with a bad memory."

She smiles at me. "Oh, I saved the best for last. Didn't you know that's the way you're supposed to play the game, Malcolm? Your secret has been itching to be shown for centuries. I have to admit I didn't think even you could be so cruel to someone you love."

I know which memory she's talking about, and I've made my peace with it. I can only assume she hopes to drive a wedge of doubt between

Anna and me by showing it. That has to be one of the reasons she's allowing her to watch.

"Anna knows me," I tell Helena. "She knows what I went through, and she'll understand what I did."

"That sounds awfully naïve of you, Malcolm. What woman would want a man who could be so heartless?"

"You don't know what you're talking about," I tell her. "What I did, I did out of love."

"Love?" Helena scoffs. "Well, why don't we show the others what we're talking about and see if they agree with your view of the event?"

Helena changes the scene around us to the cave Sebastian and I lived in for most of his childhood. I'm sitting in an armless wooden chair before a small campfire. Sebastian is lying on a blanket across from me, in a deep sleep. His body looks about two years old, but he was much older than that by this point. Part of the curse heaped upon the children of the Watchers was a slow aging process.

There is a dead look in my eyes as I stare at my son. I remember the hopelessness I felt in this moment, and I know I'm about to make a decision that will haunt me for the rest of my life.

As the fire crackles, you can see a determined look take hold of my features the longer I gaze at Sebastian. I remember this night clearly. How could I not? I knew he was about to transform into a werewolf, and I also knew there was only one way to end his suffering. I had been sitting in that chair for a while, trying to decide if I loved my son enough to do what needed to be done.

I turn my gaze away from the scene and look at Anna as she sits on the other side of the window. She appears confused by what she's watching. I know why Helena has chosen to show this memory. She wants to place doubt in Anna's mind about how I will be with our own children.

I hear the chair in my memory creak as I stand from it. As I watch the events from my past unfold, I begin to worry that Anna won't understand my next actions. What if it's something she can't rationalize or forgive me for? She knows me better than anyone ever has in my life. I have to believe she'll figure out the motivation behind what she witnesses next.

Neither Mason, Jered, nor Slade knows what's about to happen. I've never shared this memory with anyone because I was too ashamed to admit my own weakness.

We all watch as memory-me walks over to the cot I used to sleep on while Sebastian and I called this cave our home. I guess it wasn't really a home. It was more like a prison for the both of us. The Watchers who tried to protect their children from their werewolf alter egos chose remote places like this one to live in. We couldn't risk taking our progeny into populated areas while they were so young. If we did we would be dooming their souls, because they wouldn't be able to control their bloodlust. They simply weren't old enough to understand the consequences of their actions. At this age, killing in their wolf form was a natural thing to do. Whether their prey was animal or human, it didn't matter. Meat was meat to them.

After living this way for so many years, I finally came to the conclusion that there was only one way to end Sebastian's torment.

I watch as memory-me pulls out a knife from underneath the pillow on the bed. I test its blade by pressing my thumb against its edge and drawing blood. It was sharp enough to do the deed in one, quick slice. In the memory, I turn my head to look at Sebastian.

"No," I hear Jered say beside me in disbelief. It's almost as if he believes saying it out loud will stop what's about to happen in my memory.

He turns his head away from the scene to look at me. He doesn't say anything, but I can see the incredulity in his eyes.

I dare to look over at Anna and see a mirror of Jered's expression on her face. Can she ever forgive the man I was back then for contemplating perpetrating such a horrific deed against his own son? Will she ever be able to erase the next few images from her mind?

I look back at the memory and watch as I walk over to Sebastian and kneel down beside him. With a gentle hand, I lift his head up by the chin to give me better access to his neck. I place the edge of the knife against the throbbing vein in his throat. The hand with the knife begins to shake uncontrollably. Tears begin to fall down my face as I realize I'm too weak to carry out my plan. I throw the knife into a corner of the room with a growl of rage. I'm mad at myself for being selfish. I thought the only way to free Sebastian of the curse my sin burdened him with was to end his life and release his soul. It was still unblemished, and I feared I wouldn't be able to keep it that way until he could die a natural death.

I force myself to look back over at Anna, hoping to see understanding in her eyes. Instead, I see utter loathing as she stares at me. I begin to walk over to the window but Anna shakes her head at me, telling me it's no use. I see her place both her hands on her protruding belly as if she's guarding our children from me. If the babies thought I couldn't protect them before, what do they think of me now, knowing that I almost murdered my first child?

"Please understand," I beg Anna, even though I'm sure she can't hear my plea. She isn't really there. I'm only seeing a projected image of her.

I watch as Anna stands from the chair. With disgust still in her eyes, she walks away from the window, taking my heart with her.

"Poor Anna," Helena croons. "She thought she found the man of her dreams, but now she knows the truth about you, Malcolm. You're willing to kill to clean up your mistakes, even if it's your own flesh and blood."

"She just needs some time to think," I say, coming up with a plausible excuse for Anna turning her back on me. "She'll forgive me. I didn't go through with killing Sebastian."

"True," Helena begrudgingly agrees, "but the fact that you even contemplated such a deed is probably weighing heavily on her heart. I mean, there's no guarantee that your little cherubs will come out normal. The odds are not in your favor on that one. In fact, since their souls are the seals I wager they'll be prone to the dark side of life."

"Why would you think that?" Mason inquires.

"The seals have absorbed an exorbitant amount of hate since they were created. That's what they were made for: to help maintain the balance between good and evil in the universe. I can assure you there has been more hate than goodwill perpetuated by humanity. It seems logical to assume that the babies will be more prone to hating than loving. Good luck keeping those two in line, Malcolm. Well, that is if Anna even lets you near them after witnessing your little memory."

"Don't listen to her," Slade tells me. "For all we know, that wasn't Anna in the window at all. It was probably just an illusion of her."

"Oh, I assure you, Anna was sitting behind that window," Helena looks at Mason. "Isn't that right, Mason? You can tell whether or not I'm speaking the truth, can't you?"

Mason hesitates before saying, "She's telling the truth."

"I still don't believe it was Anna," Jered adds. "She wouldn't turn her back on Malcolm no matter what she saw. Her love for him is stronger than that."

"Who would have thought you Watchers would be such hopeless romantics?" Helena laughs cruelly. "Well, I guess it really shouldn't come as that much of a surprise to me. After all, you did give up Heaven to bed the women you fell in love with on Earth. I guess it makes sense in a twisted sort of way."

"I won't believe anything you show me until I'm with Anna in person," I tell her, taking stock in the hope my friends are giving me. "I know she loves me. She wouldn't lose her faith in me so easily."

"You can believe whatever helps you cope with her abhorrence of you. I, for one, don't…"

Helena abruptly stops speaking. She closes her eyes and shakes her head.

"I should have tied that little angel to the bed," she growls angrily. When she opens her eyes, I see the insane expression of a murderer.

"Who are you talking about?" I ask.

"Lucas," she snarls. "It appears he took it upon himself to find Anna some help during her labor. I was enjoying your pain so much I became distracted and didn't realize he'd snuck out of the room."

"Labor?" Jered asks in surprise. "She's having the babies now?"

"I hope so. Otherwise, there's a certain doctor in Nimbo who will be feeling my unhappiness the next time I'm there."

"Jess is with her," Mason says with a smug smile. "I knew she would find Anna, no matter where you put her."

"Well, guess what? Lucifer is with her, too, and from what I understand my father and your wife had quite the heart-to-heart discussion about their relationship on Earth. Now, if you would all excuse me, I have to stop my father from taking away my prize."

Helena vanishes, but not before leaving us all with a parting gift.

The pain I experienced the first time I came to Hell fills my body once again, forcing me to my knees. I know I'm not the only one who feels the weight of guilt, as both Jered and Slade fall to their knees as well, holding their head in their hands. Only Mason remains unaffected by what's happening. He comes to me first.

"You have to fight her, Malcolm," he implores me. "You're a good person. You always have been. Everyone makes mistakes, and you have done more than enough to make up for yours. Our Father has forgiven you for the sins you committed. It's time you finally let go of your guilt and truly forgave yourself for what you did. You have to do this for yourself. Doing it for anyone else won't work."

"I can't…let…go…" I grimace, feeling suffocated by my own remorse. All I can see is Anna's face filled with contempt for me. Even if what Slade said is true, that it wasn't really Anna behind the window, the image of her hating who I was is permanently seared into my brain.

"You have to," Mason implores me.

I know Mason's right, but how am I supposed to learn how to forgive myself now, when I haven't been able to work that miracle for well over a thousand years? There is no way.

As hopelessness descends, the pain I feel grows worse. I'm trapped in a torment of my own making, and I fear there won't be any way for me to escape Hell this time.

CHAPTER FOURTEEN
(Anna's Point of View)

While I watch Malcolm's worst memory play out, my whole body begins to ache with misery. What dire circumstances led him to believe that killing Sebastian was the right thing to do? I know my husband as well as I know myself. He must have thought ending his son's life would release Sebastian from the mental anguish and physical pain of transforming into a werewolf every night. I know how guilty Malcolm felt for cursing his son to such a fate, and I know he would have done anything for Sebastian to end his suffering.

When Malcolm throws away the knife he's holding and begins to cry, I wonder if he's crying because he couldn't go through with it or because he almost did. Either way, all I want to do is take him into my arms and tell him everything will be all right. When the present- day Malcolm looks over at me, I reach out my arm and press my hand against the cool glass, yearning to tell him that what I just saw doesn't make me love him any less. He begins to walk over to me, but abruptly stops for some reason. I see his lips move as he says something to me, a pleading look in his eyes, but I can't make out his words. I watch as his gaze lifts, as if I've stood up, and then follows some phantom image to the left.

He turns his back to me as if he can't see me anymore. Confused by Malcolm's behavior, I try to figure out what he and the others are saying, but I'm not a lip-reader. I can't decipher what's being said between them.

"Anna," I hear a familiar and relieved voice say behind me, drawing my attention away from what's happening outside my window.

I gasp in surprise and feel my heart flood with hope when I see Jess and Lucifer enter the room. Lucas stands by the open doorway with a look of pride on his face. Luna is sitting contentedly beside him as he pets her on the head.

"I found you help, Mommy," he says as my saviors rush over to me.

"He sure did," Lucifer tells me with a smile. "Somehow he knew exactly where to find us."

"I saw you in a vision," Lucas tells us. "I'm not sure how, but I knew I could get to you if Helena stayed busy. Since she went to torture my dad, I figured it was a good time to go find you."

"I didn't even see you leave," I say guiltily.

"I was ninja-stealthy," Lucas says with pride, mimicking these ninjas by holding his arms out and walking in an odd sideways manner. I wasn't sure what a ninja was. I had to assume it was a down-world thing.

I feel one of the babies kick me hard, causing me to let out an involuntary gasp of pain.

"What's wrong?" Jess asks with worry, kneeling before me. "Is something wrong with the babies? If I didn't already know you're a month away from having them, I would say you're in labor from the way you look."

"I *am* in labor," I grimace. "Helena gave me some kind of medicine to start it early. She's determined to get her hands on my children."

"Why?" Jess asks, looking from me to Lucifer. "Can she steal their souls to absorb the last two seals?"

"No," he says absolutely. "Souls can only be given to her. Move, Jess. Let me pick Anna up and we can take her out a fissure."

After Jess moves out of the way, Lucifer easily lifts me out of the chair and into his arms, cradling me to him like I'm the most precious thing in the world. Lucas walks over to Jess, Luna following him, and takes one of Jess' hands.

"I can't leave Malcolm and the others," I protest.

"They would all agree with me that getting you out of here before these babies are born is the most important thing right now," my father assures me. "I refuse to have my grandchildren born in Hell."

"You used to like it down here," we all hear Helena say angrily. "I used to be your one and only sanctuary, Father."

"Stop calling me that," Lucifer orders curtly as he stares daggers at Helena, who is now standing by the open doorway, blocking our exit. "I don't know how many times I have to say that you are not my child, Helena. You're my creation gone wrong."

"Oh, so now I'm a mistake?" Helena practically screams. "Maybe you should have thought things through a little bit more before you created me from your own soul. You brought Seraphina and me into the world the exact same way. How are we any different from one another?"

"I loved her," Lucifer declares. "I never loved you."

Lucifer begins to walk towards the doorway with me safely in his arms.

"You have lost your mind, old man, if you think I'm going to let you leave with Anna!"

Helena roughly grabs one of Lucifer's arms, almost dislodging me from his hold as she tries to stop him. Jess grabs one of Helena's arms, trying to pull her away from us. The babies kick me simultaneously, causing me to squeeze my eyes shut as I scream out in agonizing pain.

"Oh, crap," I hear Jess say in dismay.

I open my eyes and notice that she's staring at something with a mixture of surprise and horror above my head. I follow her gaze to discover what has captured her attention and caused her to look so stunned.

Directly above my head, less than an arm's length away, is a vortex of lavender-hued clouds with what looks like tiny stars intermixed within them. In the center of it all, one of the stars shines brighter than the rest, beckoning me to touch it like a beacon of hope.

As I extend my arm and reach out my hand towards the star, I vaguely hear Jess scream, "Anna, no!"

The pull the star has on me to touch it is too strong for me to ignore, so I decide to disregard Jess' warning cry instead. When the tips of my fingers make contact with the star, I instantly wish I had listened to Jess.

My body feels like it's being broken down into finite atoms and then unceremoniously sucked through a straw by some unseen force. When I'm whole again, all I feel is excruciating pain. All I can do to maintain my sanity is remain lying where I am and squeezing my eyes shut to concentrate on my breathing.

"Anna!" Lucifer says in a panicked voice.

When he touches me, the pain I feel just seems to amplify, causing me to scream.

"Don't touch me!" I beg.

I lie there for a moment until my rapidly-beating heart slows to a steady pace. Once I can breathe normally, I force myself to open my eyes. I look up at the sky and see a million twinkling stars against the backdrop of a black sky, with no signs of Earth's celestial partner, the moon. Without that light source, the night is dimmer than it should be. Though, one prominent feature floating in the sky still reflects enough of the sun to provide some light to this world.

Malcolm told me a little bit about his adventures on alternate Earth. It wasn't a time in his life that he liked to talk about, but since Lucas was Gabe reincarnated, he felt it was important that I know what transpired here.

As I look up at the rocky debris that was once this Earth's moon, the name of the astronomical phenomenon encircling this planet comes to mind: the Kinlan Ring. It was named by the Watchers of this world in honor of Gabe's sacrifice to save it.

I hear Jess sigh heavily beside me. I look over at her and see her staring up at the ring, too.

"I never thought I would have to come back here," she says despondently.

As my physical pain begins to ebb away, I struggle to sit up so I can see where we are exactly. I feel a gentle hand push against my back to help me up.

"Thank you," I tell Lucifer.

I sit and take in our surroundings. We seem to be sitting in the middle of a forest of some kind. If it weren't for the tall glass and metal skyscrapers in the distance, I would have thought we were in the woods somewhere.

I look around at Jess and Lucifer, but notice one important detail.

"Where's Lucas?" I ask, feeling panic set it.

Both Lucifer and Jess quickly stand to their feet and begin looking around, calling out Lucas' name. I'm faintly aware that Helena isn't with us either, but she's the least of my concerns. Unless…

"Did Helena take him?" I ask, even more worried now about my son's absence.

"I don't think so," Jess tells me, still scanning the area for Lucas. "Lucifer and I would have seen her do something like that. She can't phase here yet. She doesn't have any points of reference to phase to. It's more probable that they were deposited at a different location. To be honest, I don't understand how we travelled here in the first place. The last time I came here it took the power of seven archangels to open the portal to this Earth. The vortex shouldn't have had enough power to open up again."

"Actually," Lucifer says, looking thoughtful about the situation, "I think we did have that much power." He holds up his right hand, and with his index finger out he begins to count. "Me, you, Anna, Helena, Lucas, Liam, and Liana."

By the time he's done, he has seven fingers raised in the air.

"I knew the babies would be powerful," I say, "but I didn't realize they would be as powerful as archangels."

If I wasn't worried about my children before, I definitely am now.

"When they kicked me," I tell them, "that's when the vortex of stars appeared. I think they caused it to open up."

"How would they even know about this place?" Jess asks.

"I told you it was a bad idea to become pregnant while you were here," Lucifer says to Jess in an 'I told you so' kind of voice.

"But you never said why!" she counters.

"This is why!" Lucifer replies in exasperation. "Your boy was always connected to this place. He was born of two Earths: This one because you were impregnated here, and ours because that's where you and Mason are from. Each Earth vibrates at a different frequency, and he was connected to both. Every generation after Luke ended up with the same connection. It's no wonder the babies teleported us here. It was the only way they could get out of Hell after Helena put Anna's life in danger by starting her labor early. Once Helena grabbed me and you grabbed her while holding Lucas' hand, it was a simple matter of willing the vortex to manifest. If we ever want to get Anna and the children back home, we have to find Lucas and Helena. Without their power, we can't reopen the vortex."

"Are you sure there isn't a way we can just leave Helena here?" Jess asks sarcastically, already knowing the answer to her question but hoping for a different one from Lucifer.

"We need her whether we want her to go back home with us or not," he replies.

"Right now, all I'm worried about is finding Lucas," I say, just as a contraction doubles me over in pain.

"I think we need to get you some medical help first," Lucifer replies, bending down and picking me up in his arms.

"It's been a thousand years," Jess says worriedly. "I don't even know if any of the Watchers are still around."

"I suggest we try Boldt Castle first," Lucifer says. "There may still be someone there who can help us."

"It's worth a shot." Jess takes hold of one of my hands, not only because she needs to be touching one of us before Lucifer phases, but I also think she knows I need the comfort of her touch.

Lucifer phases us to what looks like a small island with a large estate built on it. I have to admit that I had never heard of Boldt Castle before he mentioned it. It makes me wonder if it survived the Great War on my Earth or not.

The castle itself is majestic in size and truly does look like an old-world castle, with its many turrets and formidable stature. I could well imagine an empress or emperor living inside it.

A woman phases in a few feet away from us. She has straight dark hair and brown skin. From what I can see of her face in the dim light of night, her features are beautiful and evenly proportioned. She's wearing a white nightgown that catches the wind blowing off the water surrounding us, causing the material to billow around her legs.

She stares at us for a moment before saying uncertainly, "Jess?"

"Ava?" Jess replies, just as shocked.

The two women begin to laugh at themselves before they walk towards one another and hug.

"What in the world are you doing here? I thought you would be dead on your Earth by now," Ava says as she pulls away and looks at Jess. "You *were* human, right?"

"I *am* dead," Jess informs her. "God let me come back to Earth to help some friends."

Ava turns her attention to Lucifer and me.

“I’m surprise to see you back here, Lucifer,” she says, clearly leery of my father’s presence.

“Don’t worry,” Jess tells Ava. “My Lucifer finally saw the error of his ways and asked his Father for forgiveness in my reality.”

“Really?” Ava asks, unable to hide her surprise.

“Can we dispense with the catching up for now?” My father says in an agitated voice. “My daughter needs a doctor who can stop an induced labor. Do you have one here who can help or not?”

“Your daughter?” Ava quickly takes in my pregnant condition. “Take her inside to the living room. I know of someone who can help her.”

Lucifer wastes no time, phasing us to the living room inside the castle. Ava phases in with Jess but quickly phases away again, presumably to find me a doctor.

My father lays me on the leather couch in the room and props my head up with a throw pillow. He kneels down beside me, brushing away the hair matted to my sweaty forehead.

“How are you doing?” he asks worriedly. I know he wants me to reassure him that I’m all right, but the simple fact of the matter is that I’m not.

“I need you to find my son for me, Dad,” I say instead, reaching out and squeezing his arm to emphasize my words. “The best-case scenario is that he’s out there by himself. The worst one is that he’s roaming around a strange Earth with Helena. If you want to help me, find Lucas and bring him back to me.”

"I can go look," Lucifer says, sounding uncertain about his mission, "but you do realize that it's going to be like looking for a needle in a haystack. He could be anywhere."

"Odds are he's in New York City," Jess says. "The two times we've travelled here, we all ended up in the city somewhere, just like we ended up in Central Park. Still, the city is huge. Finding Lucas is going to be hard unless he brings attention to himself somehow."

"I'm not only worried about his safety," I tell them. "I'm worried being here might trigger memories from being Gabe. This is where he died. What if he begins to remember who he was?"

Lucifer leans in close and kisses my forehead.

"You try to get some rest," he instructs before standing up. "I'll do my best to locate Lucas. Maybe luck will be on my side." Lucifer turns to Jess. "Take care of her for me. I'll be back as soon as I can."

"Don't worry," Jess says, "I've got her."

He phases and I can see through his phase trail that he's returned to the wooded area we just came from to begin his search for my son.

"Jess?"

The sound of a familiar male voice causes my heart to pound with excitement, and I attempt to sit up.

"Oh no, you don't," Jess says as she walks over to me, pressing my shoulders back onto my pillow. "You stay right where you are."

The man walks around to the end of the couch so I can see him. He's dressed in a pair of tight-fitting black jeans and black T-shirt.

Malcolm told me about his doppelganger on this alternate version of our Earth, but it was hard for me to believe there could ever be two of him. I suppose there are multiple versions of my husband within the multiverse, at least physically, but as I look at this Earth's Malcolm, I quickly realize he isn't mine. He may look and sound just like my husband, but he's a far cry from the man I've given my heart to.

"It's good to see you again, Xavier," Jess holds her hand out to Malcolm's double. "How have you been?"

"As well as can be expected, I suppose," he says, shaking her hand and looking mystified by our unexpected presence. "No one has addressed me by that name since all of you left."

"Well, considering Anna, here, is Malcolm's wife back home, I think it would cause her less confusion if I called you Xavier instead."

He nods. "Of course. I've never minded the name."

Xavier looks at me with blatant curiosity before he smiles. "So, Malcolm finally fell in love?"

"He didn't have much of a choice," I tell him. "We're soul mates."

"And get this," Jess says, "Anna is also our Lucifer's daughter."

"Well, the plot thickens," Xavier says with raised eyebrows as he takes in this news. He looks at my belly and asks, "Wasn't it dangerous to travel here while you're pregnant? And where is Malcolm?"

"It's a long, twisted story," Jess sighs.

Just then, Ava phases into the room with a woman by her side. She's blonde and wearing a fitted white jacket with matching pants. In her hands, she's holding a small black case.

"Is something wrong with the babies?" Xavier asks worriedly, letting his arms fall back to his sides.

"My demented sister induced my labor with some medication," I tell him as the doctor walks over to me.

"Do you happen to know what the name of the medicine was that she gave you?" the doctor asks, setting her case on the coffee table.

"I'm sorry," I reply. "I have no idea what it was or how much she put in my drink."

"It's okay. It could only have been a couple of things. I have a drug that can counteract whatever it was as long as your water hasn't broken yet. Has it?"

I shake my head. "No. Not yet."

"Good." The doctor pats the hand I have resting on top of my belly. "Don't you worry about a thing. I can slow down what's happening."

"Slow?" Jess inquires. "You can't just stop it?"

"Once labor is induced," the doctor tells her, "it can't be completely stopped, but if …" the doctor looks down at me. "I'm sorry. What's your name?"

"Anna."

"I'm pleased to meet you, Anna. My name is Marie Chambers. As I was saying, we can't stop your labor, but we can place it on hold for a time and take away most of your discomfort."

"So how long can we prevent Anna from giving birth?" Jess asks.

"A few days at least," Marie replies. "Possibly even up to a week. But I would caution against preventing it for longer than that. Like all medication, what I'm about to give you might have side-effects."

"Will it hurt the babies?" I ask, determined not to take any if the answer is yes.

"No," she assures me. "Your babies will be fine. It's you who will have to suffer through them."

"What kind of side-effects are we talking about?" Jess asks worriedly.

"Mood swings, nausea, and fatigue, for the most part."

"I already have those just from being pregnant," I say, not seeing the problem.

"True," Marie says with a small smile, "but all of those symptoms will be magnified while you're taking the medicine. Honestly, I would suggest that you let the labor progress naturally, but Ava tells me that would not be a good option for you."

"No," I say. "I can't have the babies right now. Give me the drug you have to postpone my labor, and I promise you I'll have them after I get back home."

Marie doesn't look pleased, but she doesn't argue with me either. She reaches for her case on the table and opens it, pulling out a short, silver tube.

"This might sting a little bit," she warns me, placing one end of the tube against my arm.

I feel a small needle pierce my skin, but that isn't what causes me pain. As the fluid enters my body, I feel an intense stinging sensation that last a few seconds.

"There is enough medicine in this tube to get you by for at least a week. You'll need to take a dose every twelve hours. Like I said, it would be much better for you if you have your babies as soon as possible. How long will it take you to get back home?"

I shake my head. "I don't know."

Marie looks confused by my answer, but doesn't comment on it.

"Well, if you have any problems, don't hesitate to have Ava come and get me." She stands up and walks back over to Ava. "I need to get back to my other patients at the hospital."

Ava places a hand on Marie's shoulder and phases the doctor away, but instantly returns to the living room.

Xavier walks over to my side and lifts me off the couch, cradling me in his arms.

"What do you think you're doing?" I demand to know, offended by his actions considering the fact that he didn't ask me for permission first.

"I thought you would be more comfortable in a bed," he explains, looking bemused by my outburst. "Am I wrong?"

"Well, no," I concede, "but you should have asked me if I wanted to be moved by you. It's just common courtesy."

"I'm sorry," Xavier says sincerely. "I was only thinking about your comfort. You're absolutely right, though. I should have asked first. I'm just not used to asking for permission before managing something I know needs to be done."

"I'm not someone you can just man-handle," I inform him.

He smiles. "No, I can definitely see that. To be honest, you're the first woman who's ever complained that I picked her up to take her to my bed."

"Oh no, you're not," Jess says feistily with her hands on her hips. "You take her to one of the other rooms. There are a ton of them in this joint. She doesn't need to be in your bed."

"I didn't mean that the way it sounded," Xavier explains. "Not exactly, anyway. I just thought she would be more comfortable in my bed because my room is clean and the bed has fresh sheets on it. The other rooms, besides Ava's, haven't been used for a long time. They'll need to be prepared before anyone can use them."

"Well, you should have started off with that," Jess huffs. "Anna gets your room and you get the couch, buster."

Xavier chuckles. "That was the plan, Jess. I would never disrespect Malcolm's wife by making passes at her while she's my guest. Her honor is safe with me."

"That's something I never thought I would hear you say about a woman," Ava jokes. "Why don't you go put Anna in bed while Jess and I make her some hot tea?" She loops an arm around one of Jess' and begins walking her out of the room. "Now, tell me everything about Nina and Rafe's life. How many babies did they end up having?"

I don't get to hear the rest of their conversation after they leave the room.

"Would you prefer I phase you to my room or walk you up there?" Xavier asks.

"I would rather you walked me up," I say without explaining why, and he doesn't ask. He just follows through with my request.

As we walk out of the room, I find myself studying Xavier's profile. It's amazing how exact every detail about him is to my Malcolm. From his naturally arching black eyebrows to his chiseled chin, all of his features look identical in every way.

I was glad he didn't question why I wanted him to carry me to his room. He may not be my Malcolm, but he's the closest thing to my husband that I can get to right now. I close my eyes and rest my head against his shoulder, imagining that he is my Malcolm. My eyes begin to burn with tears because my heart misses the special connection he and I share. I hoped allowing Xavier to hold me would lessen the loneliness I feel, but it's done the exact opposite. I miss my husband even more now, and can't prevent myself from crying over the emptiness I feel inside my heart from his absence.

Even though I openly begin to sob, Xavier remains stalwart in his duty. He doesn't say a word as he carries me into his room and sits me on a bed that's already been turned down. He takes off my shoes and tucks my feet underneath the comforter before pulling it up to my waist. I watch him walk into the bathroom attached to this room and walk back out with a box of tissues in his hand. He sits on the side of the bed and angles the box towards me.

"Thank you," I tell him, plucking out the top tissue from the box and wiping my eyes with it.

"Why are you here, Anna?" Xavier asks in a soft, undemanding voice. "If you're too tired to tell me, I can go downstairs and ask Jess, but I get the feeling it might do you some good to talk about what's happening."

I realize he's right. Maybe if I discuss things with a complete stranger, I can start to make sense of it all.

"It's a long story," I warn him. "In order for you to understand everything, I'll have to start from the moment Malcolm and I first met."

"I would actually like to know about that," Xavier admits, looking slightly embarrassed for being curious about my relationship with his double. "It gives me hope that I'll meet someone one day, too. I've never heard of anyone having a soul mate here, though. Do you think that's something that only happens in the Origin?"

“I’m not quite sure,” I say, finding it strange that soul mates don’t exist in this reality. “My father or Jess might know the answer to that question.”

“It’s not important,” Xavier says, but I can tell from the expression on his face that it’s important to him, even if he protests that it isn’t. “Tell me how you and Malcolm met. How did he convince you to fall in love with him?”

I have to laugh at that. “It was totally the other way around,” I admit. “I had to do everything I could to make him realize he couldn’t live without me.”

“He refused you?” he asks incredulously. “And here I thought Malcolm was smarter than that.”

“He was just being stubborn, and trying to do the noble thing instead of the right one.”

“Then tell me your love story. I would like to know how it all started.”

As I tell Xavier how Malcolm and I found each other, I realize what an extraordinary life we’ve led so far. The love he and I share has transcended time and space. This detour in our lives is just a small part of our story, one that will be passed down from generation to generation. I have no doubt whatsoever that we’ll be reunited soon, and when we are I vow nothing will separate us from one another again.

CHAPTER FIFTEEN
(Helena's Point of View)

Well… that smarted.

I remember when Lucifer made the trip to alternate Earth. He complained about the discomfort he felt traveling back and forth between realities. Now that I have a body of my own, I understand what he was talking about.

I find myself standing in an alleyway between two glass-and-steel five-story buildings. I'm a little surprised by how clean such a space looks. As I recall, Lucifer and Jess were deposited in a similar location when they traveled here. Interesting. I wonder if it's the same exact spot.

As I look around the area, I notice a pair of pint-size brown shoes peeking out from behind an automated blue recycling bin. I have a feeling I know who they belong to. As I walk over to see if I'm right in my assumption, I discover an unconscious Lucas lying supine on the concrete. I guess I can see why Anna's motherly instincts kicked in when Lucas came into her life. He is cute for a miniature human, even though his ability to see the future is immensely annoying.

I turn away from Lucas and walk up the alleyway to the city street. I'm surprised to find a thriving New York City bustling with activity. The streets are filled with hover cars and the sidewalks with people. From Lucifer's memories, this world was on the cusp of collapse thanks to Lucian and the princes of Hell opening the seals here. They almost succeeded in bringing Hell to Earth. If Gabe hadn't sacrificed his life to stop them, this world probably wouldn't exist anymore.

I look back down the alleyway, wondering where the others are, when I notice Lucas' feet twitch.

I could leave him here to fend for himself. He's cute. I'm sure someone would help him find his mommy. Considering the change in my luck, he would probably end up running into a serial killer with a penchant for chubby-cheeked children.

With a groan of frustration, I spin on my high-heels and march back over to where he is. When I reach him, he's struggling to maintain his balance as he sits up and rubs his head.

"Wow," he says grimacing, "that sure did hurt."

"Is your body damaged in any particular spot?" I ask curtly.

"No. It's an all-over kind of hurt." Lucas tilts his head and looks up at me with only one eye open. He's still grimacing from the pain he feels when he asks, "Where's my mom?"

"I'm sorry to say she isn't here. I'm afraid you're stuck with me until we can find her and the others."

"What happened to us?" Lucas asks, slowly standing to his feet. "Where are we? Somewhere in the down-world?"

"Look around us. Does this *look* like the down-world to you?" I ask sarcastically.

He takes in the well-kept alleyway and modern buildings. "No," he says, "it's too clean. Are we in another cloud city?"

"Oh, good grief," I say in frustration. "We're on an alternate Earth. The one your father traveled to with Jess. Didn't he ever tell you about it?"

Lucas shakes his head, looking confused by the concept. "No. He never told me."

"Figures. He probably didn't want to scramble your brain with too much information."

"Why would telling me about this place do that?"

I could tell him the truth. There wasn't anyone here to prevent me from doing it. What would telling him about his first death do to his tiny human brain? I'm honestly not sure. No, I should probably keep the information to myself for now. I might need this kid to get back home. If he goes bonkers trying to cope with the knowledge of a past life, he won't do any of us any good.

"Listen, kid, right now you and I have one common goal: Find the others and get back home. Why don't we concentrate on working towards that goal together?"

"So you're not going to kill me?"

"Why would I kill you? I need you to help us get home. I think it's going to take all of us to work that small miracle."

"Then let's go find them," Lucas says determinedly. "The sooner I get away from you the better."

"You're a cheeky little thing," I say, reluctantly finding myself admiring his spunk.

"I don't like you," Lucas states with conviction. "I know I'm not supposed to hate people, but if I did you would be someone I hate."

"Did your self-righteous parents tell you not to hate people? I can assure you, my little angel, that they have hated plenty of people in their own lives. It seems a bit hypocritical to place such a restriction on your feelings. You can't help who you dislike any more than you can choose who you love."

“Do you love Cade?”

The question catches me off-guard. I was hoping to expound upon the merits of hating others, and he has to bring my feelings for Cade into the conversation.

“Why would you ask me that?”

“I’ve heard things,” Lucas says mysteriously.

“And what exactly have you heard?”

“Things,” he says even more vaguely.

“Things…” I muse, wondering if Anna has been negligent in her son’s education and has unconsciously restricted his vocabulary.

“Well, do you love him or not?” Lucas asks more incessantly.

“What business is that of yours?” I ask, wondering if he’s this impertinent with his parents, too.

“Cade’s one of my best friends,” he states as a fact. The fierce look of protectiveness on his face shows me just how loyal he is to him. “I don’t want you to hurt him. I overheard Cade and Ethan talking about how you’re supposed to be his soul mate. If you ask me, I think God made a mistake doing that, but my parents always say He works in mysterious ways. Cade being your soul mate is sure enough mysterious. I just hope God knows what He’s doing.”

“Are you always this opinionated?” I ask, wondering how so much can come out of someone so small.

“My dad told me I should always speak my mind.”

“Did he also tell you that children should be seen and not heard?”

“No…” Lucas looks offended by my question.

"It's something that's worked for centuries. I suggest you try it while you're with me."

"You said you weren't going to kill me," Lucas says suspiciously. "Have you already changed your mind?"

"Not yet," I say cryptically, "but give me time. Peace of mind might sound better than going home if you continue to be argumentative with me."

"I'm not doing that," he says defensively. "I'm just saying the truth."

"Truth is a very subjective thing, my little angel."

"Can you please stop calling me that?" he asks in aggravation.

"Don't get your feathers all ruffled, little angel. I'll stop calling you that if you stop talking about Cade. I don't want to think about him right now."

"How come?" he asks with a tilt of his head.

"He's a distraction I don't need at the moment," I say, finally realizing something. "Maybe that's why God put us together. Maybe He thought Cade would distract me from my mission."

"What's your mission?"

The innocent way Lucas makes his inquiry tells me he doesn't understand the consequences of asking such a question. If anyone else had shown me such impertinence, I probably wouldn't have hesitated in ripping out their throat.

"*That* is none of your business," I inform him. "Now come along. We need to figure out a way to find everyone else. I'm sure they're looking for you."

"My mom will be worried about me," Lucas says with certainty as he walks up to my side.

“I’m sure she is,” I agree.

I begin to walk down the street with my little angel following along beside me. If anyone had told me I would become Lucas’ babysitter, I would have laughed in his or her face. Lucas was right about one thing, though. Anna is most certainly beside herself with worry about his safety. I have to say the thought brings me a degree of pleasurable satisfaction. It’s nice to have at least one thing to be happy about, given the circumstances.

The city is buzzing with activity, even though it’s nighttime. It must not be that late or most of these people would be in bed by now. I get strange looks from passersby. I look down at my clothing, wondering if there’s something wrong with it, but I don’t see any visible damage to the red dress I’m wearing.

As I study the people on the street, I notice they’re all wearing either muted or monochrome colors. In fact, the brightness of my dress makes me stick out like a sore thumb.

“These people must have lost their sense of style after the Apocalypse,” I mumble, more to myself than for Lucas’ benefit, but he hears me anyway.

“Maybe they just don’t like red,” he suggests.

“Why would anyone have an aversion to the color red?”

“How should I know? I’m just a kid.”

“Touché,” I reply, wondering if Lucas could be on to something with his observation. In a weird way, it would make sense if red is banned from use on this world. It could be that the color was outlawed because of Ravan Drake. She did wear it every chance she got, and I’m sure, even after so many generations, they might still associate the color red with her.

“I may need to find some different clothes to wear while we’re here.” I look down and notice for the first time what Lucas is wearing. His white shirt and brown pants don’t seem too out of place here, but my red dress is definitely sending out bad vibes to the crowd of people walking by us.

“Come on. I need to find a clothing store.” I begin to walk across the street when I feel Lucas place his little hand into mine. I look down at him questioningly. “What do you think you’re doing? I thought I told you never to touch me again.”

“I can’t walk across streets without holding an adult’s hand,” he tells me, as if I should have known this bit of information already.

“Just how many rules do your parents make you follow?”

“Lots.”

“Eh, very well,” I say, tightening my grip on him since no visions of the future are unexpectedly popping up inside my mind. “Let’s go. I see some shops on the other side of the street. They should have something I can wear to blend in better here.”

We start to walk across when Lucas brings up a good point.

“Do you have any money?” he asks.

I hadn’t thought about that. Of course, I don’t actually need to pay for anything. I could easily kill the people inside the shop and take whatever I want. It’s not as if I haven’t done something similar before. When we reach the other side of the street, I look down at Lucas. He looks up at me with his innocent doe eyes.

Damn it.

I can’t kill people while he’s watching me. Anna would have a conniption fit if she ever found out I tarnished his childhood in such a blatant way. It would be hypocritical of her, though. Considering how many rebellion angels she's killed in front of him, a few humans shouldn't be that big a deal, but I know my sister's odd sense of what's right and what's wrong.

"I don't suppose you have some I could borrow," I say.

"No. I've never had to buy anything for myself."

"Ahh, yes. I should have known someone as privileged as you doesn't have to deal with something as petty as money."

"I'm not privileged," Lucas says defensively.

"Don't even try to defend yourself; you know you are. There's nothing wrong with having rich parents. I can assure you that almost any child living in the down-world would change places with you in a heartbeat. It's not your fault your parents spoil you rotten."

"I'm not spoiled either," Lucas is quick to inform me. "I always share with others."

"Eh, your philanthropy is the least of my worries right now," I say. "How are we going to get enough money to buy me some new clothes?"

"We could put on a show," Lucas suggests. "I saw a man in New Orleans once make money by singing in Jackson Square."

"Do I look like a street performer to you?" I ask, inwardly cringing at the idea of public humiliation. "Or has inter-dimensional travel thoroughly scrambled your brain?"

"Do you have a better suggestion?"

"Well, no, but begging is out of the question."

"Excuse me, Miss," I hear a female say from behind me.

I turn to find a rather plain-looking redhead with pale skin and freckles dotting both cheeks. She's wearing a white sleeveless shirt and matching slacks.

"Yes?" I ask as she stands there and continues to stare at me. Well, in point of fact, she's not looking at my face. She seems mesmerized by my dress. "Speak up. What do you want?"

"I'm sorry if this sounds forward, but I was wondering if you would be willing to sell your dress to me. I can't say I've ever seen anything like it before. I know some people who would be very interested in purchasing a vintage outfit like yours. This is my store," she says, turning her head and nodding to the shop we're standing in front of. Through the window, I can see a plethora of stylish garments for both men and women. The color scheme of the clothing seems to match what everyone else is wearing in the city.

"I tell you what," I say. "I would be willing to do a trade. You can have this dress in exchange for some clothing from your store."

"Absolutely!" the woman says excitedly, jumping at my offer.

I look down at Lucas and ask, "Do you have anything in there that would fit him, too?"

"I don't," the woman admits, biting her lower lip as she thinks, "but there is a children's store just up the street. I know the owner personally. I'm sure I can make an arrangement with him for some new clothes. Would you like for me to go there now and pick out some things for your son to choose from?"

I almost tell her that Lucas is not my son, but I think better of it. It might send up a red flag that would hinder our cause.

“Yes. That would save us a great deal of time.”

“Please feel free to take as long as you need to find an outfit you like,” the redhead says. “I’ll be back in a jiffy with some clothes for your boy.”

The woman scurries down the street as Lucas and I enter her shop.

The style of clothing within the store seems to suit me. The dresses are dramatic but not over the top.

I pick up one black dress that’s practically sheer all the way through, except for some strategically placed appliqués.

“What do you think about this one?” I ask Lucas, holding it up in front of me.

He scrunches up his face, immediately telling me he does not approve of my choice.

“Only women who work at the Ladies in Waiting would wear something like that,” he informs me.

“How in the world do you even know about an establishment like that?” I ask, aghast at his knowledge of the brothel in Cirrus.

“Oh, I hear things,” Lucas says with an air of knowledge well beyond his young years. “Especially when Xander is around. From what I’ve heard, he gets in trouble there a lot. The last time he did, my mom had to go straighten him out.”

“Have you ever been there yourself?”

Lucas begins to laugh like I’ve said the funniest thing in the world.

When he catches his breath, he says, “Nope! My mom would kill me if I stepped foot inside a place like that. She doesn’t even know that I know about it.”

"Well, if I were you I would stay clear of such places, even when you get older."

"I doubt Bai would talk to me again if I ever went somewhere like that."

"Oh, yes. I know who you're talking about," I say, recognizing exactly to whom Lucas is referring. From what I remember, Lucifer pegged her as being the reincarnation of JoJo Armand, Gabe's wife. It was sickeningly sweet that the two of them would choose to come back from the dead to have a second chance at an earthly life together. Why that seemed so important to them, I have no idea.

"You stay away from her," Lucas tells me.

When I turn to face him, there's something in his eyes that wasn't there before. The childlike quality is missing for some reason.

"Gabriel?" I dare ask. "Is that you coming out to play with me?"

After a slight hesitation, Lucas answers, "Yes, but I'm not here to play with you, Helena. I'm here to deliver a warning."

"Oh, really? And what exactly does the Archangel Gabriel want to warn me about?"

"You can't trust the Lucifer of this world."

I have to admit I wasn't expecting that from him. I thought for sure he was going to threaten me with some sort of Heavenly punishment if I interfered with Gabe and JoJo's planned happily-ever-after.

"Why are you warning me, Gabriel?" I ask. "You almost sound as if you care what happens to me."

Lucas' expression loses its hard edge, and I see the innocence return to his eyes.

"Why wouldn't I care?" he asks. "I need you to help me find my mom."

How strange. Why did Gabriel feel the need to take over Lucas' body to deliver his message to me? His meaning was cryptic, but he seemed to be implying that the Lucifer on this Earth might harm me in some way. Did God tell Gabriel to deliver that message to me? If He did, why would He do it?

"Is there something wrong with you?" Lucas asks. "You look upset."

"I'm fine," I lie, not wanting to admit I'm a bit shaken up. "Everything is fine."

I turn back to the rack of clothing I'm standing in front of, privately mulling over Gabriel's words. I have to admit that I'm curious to meet this reality's Lucifer now. Gabriel's warning begs a couple of question, though. Does this Earth's Lucifer already know I'm here? And if he does, will he seek me out?

It's not often I'm involved in a mystery not of my own making.

I smile, wondering what unexpected adventures the future here will bring.

CHAPTER SIXTEEN

I decide to let Lucas pick out what I should wear. Apparently, everything I like looks whorish to him. Unsurprisingly, he selects the tamest dress in the shop. It's ivory in color and made out of a thick stretchy material with a hem that goes just below my knees. It's tight-fitting and has a décolletage that curves around the tops of my breasts and ventures all the way down to the band of fabric around my waist. The shoulders are embellished with a mixture of bronze and gold beads stitched into the fabric in an asymmetric pattern.

The shop owner keeps true to her promise to bring Lucas some new clothes. What he's wearing is functional, but not very fashionable. I can't have people thinking he's some beggar child I picked up off the street. We pick a grey ensemble for him to wear, replete with a simple grey cotton T-shirt underneath a stylish leather jacket. A matching pair of pants with boots completes his outfit. As we stand in front of a full-length mirror in the main show room, I have to admit that we look rather good together. Lucas is the best accessory I've ever had.

A man enters the store behind me. I catch a glimpse of his reflection in the mirror and instantly know who he is: this reality's Lucifer. However, he doesn't look anything like my father anymore. This world's Lucifer has a brand-spanking-new body. His facial features are finely chiseled, giving him the appearance of a Greek god. His six-foot frame fills out the grey suit he's wearing rather nicely, and offers a striking contrast to his tan skin and brown hair.

When his hazel eyes lock with mine in the mirror, a slow smile stretches his lips and I'm certain he already knows exactly who and what I am.

"Lucian Forester?" the shopkeeper says, her mouth agape in utter shock as she stares at this world's Lucifer.

Lucian doesn't even acknowledge the poor girl's presence, much to her chagrin.

"Hello," he says to me as our eyes remain steadfast on one another. "I thought I might find you here."

I turn around to face him.

"Well, it took you long enough," I reply condescendingly. He needs to know upfront that I'm not impressed by him. "I was wondering if you were paying any attention to what happens in your world."

"I knew you were here," he assures me with a cocky grin, unshaken by my contemptuous words and attitude. "I wanted to give you some time to get acclimated to your new surroundings before I introduced myself."

"Who are you?" Lucas asks, looking at Lucian and me in confusion.

Lucian considers him for a moment before he begins to chuckle softly.

"I can't say I ever thought you would come back here," Lucian declares.

"Back here?" Lucas asks, looking even more puzzled. "I've never been here before."

I quickly clamp my hands over his ears and stare daggers at Lucian.

"Don't you dare say another word to him about that," I order in a terse whisper. "He doesn't remember anything, and I need to keep it that way for now."

Lucian sighs his disappointment.

"Very well," he agrees with a small shrug of his shoulders. "It's water under the bridge now anyway. I'm evolved enough to let bygones be bygones."

Hesitantly, I lower my hands from Lucas' head. I don't trust Lucian to keep his word. I know I'll have to remain vigilant while he's around Lucas.

"What did you do that for?" Lucas asks, obviously annoyed by my handling of him as he rubs his ears.

"Well, if I told you that, it would defeat the purpose of me doing it in the first place," I say with a roll of my eyes.

"Why is he with you?" Lucian asks. "Is he your son in some weird cosmic way only my father would understand?"

"I seriously doubt this body can conceive children," I reply.

"But you told me he was your son," the shopkeeper says, drawing our attention to her.

"You really shouldn't interrupt the grownups while they're talking," Lucian chastises her. "It's bad manners."

He lifts his right arm and quickly twists his hand at the wrist as he looks at the woman. I hear the shopkeeper's neck snap. As her dead body falls to the floor, Lucas grabs me around the waist and buries his face against my stomach. I automatically place a comforting hand on his back, faintly wondering why I feel the need to soothe him.

"Seriously?" I say to Lucian in aggravation. "A little bit of warning would have gone a long way in this particular situation. Now look what you've done! He's scared of you."

"He *should* be scared of me," Lucian counters unapologetic. "I *am* the devil, after all."

"Well, I hate to be the one who bursts your narcissistic bubble, but you're not the only devil in town today."

"Oh? Has the Origin's Lucifer decided to grace us with his uninspiring presence again? I really don't see why he bothered to come back. He wasn't at all helpful the last time he was on my Earth. In fact, he actually colluded with those people to tear down everything I was trying to accomplish here. Now look at my world." Lucian looks out the front window of the shop in disgust. "Everyone is so *peaceful* and *happy*. It's sickening."

"I've been wondering about that. Why is it so nice here?" I ask. "When Lucifer left, this Earth was in shambles."

"I know," Lucian sighs as his eyes become unfocused. He looks as if he's remembering his time in the sun as the orchestrator of the End of Days. "Once they ruined my plans, the surviving humans and Watchers started working together to rebuild this Earth. It was a true Renaissance era. It took them hundreds of years to make things even better than they were before the Apocalypse, but they persevered and made a world to be envied by others."

"Why didn't you do anything to stop them?"

"All of this peace, love, and joy have weakened me." Lucian looks in my direction. "Hell isn't what it used to be. Without enough new souls to energize it, I'm left virtually powerless."

"That certainly sucks for you," I admit, feeling zero pity for him. "I suppose my counterpart here is as feeble as you are."

"Obviously," Lucian replies patronizingly with a raised eyebrow. "Why do you think I'm here?"

"I have no idea why you're here." A warning bell goes off in my head, and Gabriel's words of caution come back to haunt me. *You can't trust the Lucifer of this world,* he told me.

"She wants to meet you. You give her hope that better days will be just around the corner. We all know this supposed peace and prosperity mumbo jumbo can't last forever here. Humans are wired to destroy themselves. It's just a matter of time before they start making the same mistakes again. The odds are stacked in our favor. We just have to wait it out."

"She?" I ask, finding his use of a pronoun for Hell curious. "Has your creation taken on a physical persona as well?"

"Yes, but she's not nearly as strong as you. She can't maintain a body for very long, and she certainly isn't capable of leaving Hell, much less travel through a wormhole between realities. I have to admit you're quite remarkable."

"I know." I see no reason to feign modesty. "It took a lot of hard work on my part to get where I am today."

"Your Lucifer must be very proud of you," Lucian says, sounding envious of my father's good fortune.

"Not really. He wanted me to remain in Hell. He seems to think that's the only place I belong."

"It's a pity he doesn't appreciate what you can do for him in your current state."

"Oh," I say, realizing Lucian is in the dark about my father's status. "You probably don't know that Lucifer found redemption."

Almost every muscle in Lucian's face goes slack after hearing my revelation.

He slowly begins to shake his head in denial. "That isn't possible. God could never forgive us for the things we've done."

"That might be true in your case," I concede, finding a small bit of joy by rubbing my father's heavenly state in Lucian's face. "I mean, you did start the Apocalypse here, after all. Lucifer never went that far in the Origin. It probably earned him at least a few brownie points with the man upstairs. I guess you should have thought about that if you were hoping to ask for forgiveness one day."

"I will never ask my Father for forgiveness," Lucian says stubbornly. His defiant expression makes me feel forlorn for the Lucifer I used to know. He would frequently profess the same thing to me. Then Jess entered his life and made him soft by giving him hope God would allow him to atone for his sins one day.

"You should keep thinking that way," I tell Lucian. "I'm sure Heaven isn't all it's cracked up to be."

"You have no idea what it's like there." He turns his gaze away from me to stare at something outside the shop.

I don't think he's actually looking at anything. He just doesn't want me to see the longing he has in his eyes to return to Heaven. I know that's what he's thinking. Lucifer would get the same look sometimes. I mean, I guess I can see the appeal. Anyone can imagine almost anything into existence in Heaven. There's probably a certain attraction due to that fact alone. I know I love being able to do it in my own domain.

Lucas lifts his face to look up at me and whispers, "I want to go now, Helena. I don't like him."

Lucian looks back at us. "Do you need somewhere to stay while you're here? I have a place you can use."

"Will you be staying there with us?" I ask.

He shakes his head. "No. You and the boy can have it while you're on my world. I have another apartment in town I can use."

"Why are you being so generous to us?" I ask, suspicious of his motives.

"I want to know more about your Earth. It *is* the Origin, after all. I'm curious to know what's transpired there during the last thousand years."

It seems like a logical explanation, but I'm certain he has another agenda he isn't being forthcoming about.

"You might as well take us to the apartment now," I say. "I think Lucas could use some rest."

"Would you mind if I showed you something first?" Lucian asks. "Ivy thought you might enjoy seeing the last remaining remnant of the Apocalypse on this Earth."

"Ivy?" I ask a second before it dawns on me to whom he is referring. "Oh, is that the name your version of Hell has chosen for herself?"

"Yes, sorry." He smiles self-consciously. "I should have told you that already. I'm so used to calling her by name I didn't even think about it. My apologies."

"What does she believe will interest me?" I ask, curious to know if Ivy and I share the same predilections.

Lucian smiles beguilingly. "Come with me and I'll show you. I promise you won't be disappointed."

"Helena," Lucas says urgently, lightly tugging on my dress with both hands to regain my attention.

I look down at him.

"What?" I say irritably.

"I don't like him," he says again, more urgently this time. "We shouldn't be going places with him."

Lucas' insistence is annoying me. I realize I need to take care of him, but I also want to know what it is my counterpart on this Earth wants me to see.

"I need you to stop whining," I tell him as gently as I can without sounding like an ogre. "Let's go see whatever it is Lucian wants to show me first. Then, we'll go to his apartment and I'll make him leave us alone. It's the best deal you're going to get from me; take it or leave it."

Lucas huffs his disappointment. "Fine."

I take one of his hands with mine and walk us over to Lucian.

"Ready?" he asks, looking excited about our little excursion.

"Yes," I reply, wondering if I really should have said no.

Lucian places his hand on my shoulder and phases us to the top of a circular stacked rock formation within a cavernous depression. I feel as though I've traveled back to a time in Earth's history when humans didn't even exist yet. I look straight up and see the sky, noticing that the area we're standing in is actually the result of a sinkhole. Flowstone formations drape the rocky interior walls like curtains, while moss and other low-growing vegetation make a carpet of green on the concave floor of the chasm. It's morning wherever we are, and the rays of the sun flow through the opening above us like a spotlight.

"Where are we?" I ask Lucian as I continue to look around the isolated area.

"Vietnam," he answers. "This is the Son Doong cave system. It's been called an infinite cave because the chambers within it are so enormous. You could fit a block of 40-story buildings within most of them."

"And this is what Ivy wanted you to show me?" I ask, underwhelmed by what my counterpart here thinks will impress me.

And then I hear it.

My attention is immediately drawn by the low growl of one of my most precious creations.

"What was that?" Lucas asks, his fear causing him to clutch me even tighter around the waist.

"A leviathan," I answer breathlessly, briefly remembering the time Levi and I spent designing them in Hell together. It was the only time I ever found that particular prince of Hell interesting.

I look down at the large hole directly across from us within the chasm and watch in amazement as the leviathan emerges from the mouth of the cave. My breath catches in my throat as it floats towards us. My whole body begins to tingle with a mixture of emotions, the most predominant one being pride.

"Why is it still here?" I ask. "I thought Jess and that other vessel, Leah, destroyed all of the ones that were sent here."

"They missed this one," Lucian replies. He holds out a hand and runs it lovingly along the translucent belly of the leviathan as it floats over our heads. "It's been trapped on Earth since then."

"How has it survived this long?"

"I bring it humans to feed upon every once in a while," he tells me. "I think it's so comfortable in these caves because they remind it of Hell. It seems content to stay hidden here. Ivy loves knowing that one of her favorite creations is still able to roam freely on Earth."

I remember wishing, not so long ago, that I could make a fissure large enough for my leviathans to roam the Origin's Earth. Leviathans are majestic creatures born to terrorize and consume the bodies and souls of the living. Only here, on this alternate Earth, were they given a chance to live up to their full potential. The leviathan eventually makes its way back down into the cave. I feel Lucas tremble against me as he continues to hold onto my waist.

"Thank you for showing me this," I tell Lucian. "And tell Ivy she was right: I did want to see a leviathan on Earth. You should probably phase us to the place we'll be staying while we're here."

"Of course." Lucian places a hand on my shoulder and phases us.

I instantly find myself standing in an apartment on a high floor in one of the buildings in New York. All of the exterior walls are made of glass and the furnishings are minimalistic in color and detail, but everything looks functional enough.

"This is a penthouse suite," Lucian tells me as he drops his hand away from my shoulder, "so you're welcome to access the roof in case you want to sit outside for some fresh air. There's a pool up there and a seating area as well. If you're hungry, the kitchen is fully-stocked, but if you need something in particular just call down to the front desk and tell them to get whatever you need. I normally use this apartment for special lady friends who visit me in the city, so no one will question your stay here."

"Are you famous on this Earth?" I ask. "The shopkeeper acted like you were someone important here."

"That's because Lucian Forester is an actor," Lucian grins cockily. "I'm currently starring in the number-one movie playing in theaters, and I'm the star of a very popular Broadway show, which is why I'm in New York right now. I suppose fate wanted to make sure I would be close by during your visit."

"I suppose," I say, even though I've never believed in coincidences. "Well, thank you for letting us use your home. I think we could use some time alone, if you don't mind."

"Of course." Lucian's gaze briefly lowers to look at Lucas, who is still clinging to my waist. "I'll come back tomorrow. As I told you before, Ivy wants to meet you. I can take you to her in the morning if you think you'll be up for it."

"We'll see," I say apathetically.

Lucian doesn't look pleased with my response, but he says, "Very well. Take your time to think about it. Have a good evening."

After Lucian leaves, I pry Lucas' arms from around my waist.

"You're safe now," I gripe. "For someone so young, you sure do have a strong grip."

"I was scared," Lucas confesses, taking a step back from me.

"I wouldn't have let him hurt you," I say. "Like I told you before, I need to keep you alive if we're ever going to get back to our own Earth."

"Are you always so selfish?" he asks, not being judgmental, exactly. He looks more curious to know the answer than anything else.

"Yes," I say truthfully. "I'm the most important person to myself. Why wouldn't I be selfish?"

"That's just weird to me. My parents always tell me I need to think about other people's feelings."

"What's the point in doing that?"

"To be nice."

"Being nice is overrated. Most humans like people who take charge of situations, not constantly asking them what they would like. A good leader tells other people what they should do and the way they should think."

"That's not true."

"You're six years old! How would you know what traits a good leader should have? Plus, you've been sheltered all your life. You know absolutely nothing about the world or the people in it."

"I know you should treat others the way you want them to treat you."

"Oh, good grief, did you really just spout the Golden Rule to me? If ever there was a rule that needs to be broken as often as possible, it's that one."

"Why are you so mad all the time?"

"Because humans like you aggravate me beyond all reason. You think if you treat someone the way you want to be treated, it will make everything all right. Well, I hate to break it to you, my little angel, but it does not. There are people in this world who will take advantage of your kindness. They would just as soon use you for their own purposes and toss you aside once they've gotten what they want from you. You need to learn how to look out for the most important person in your life: yourself. If you don't, every beggar in the world will come knocking at your door asking for a handout."

"You're supposed to help people who are less fortunate," Lucas tells me. "My dad is always saying that most people are willing to work for a better life. You just have to give them the chance."

"No. Most people want a handout," I reply. "They don't want to work to make their lives better. They want you to do all the work and give them what they feel entitled to. One of these days, you'll understand the fundamental truth that most humans are naturally lazy. That laziness will eventually lead to their downfall."

"There's just no talking to you," Lucas says with a shake of his head, as if I'm a lost cause.

"Are you hungry?" I ask, deciding to change the subject before I become angry. "I'm feeling a bit peckish. Let's see what's in the kitchen to eat."

I walk out of the living room to the adjoining kitchen area. I have to say, I don't like how modern everything is in Lucian's abode. It feels sterile and lacks a certain *je ne sais quoi*. Most everything is white and steel. It's not a style I can appreciate.

We find a stack of flat silver packets in the refrigerator that are labelled with what food they contain. We choose a few and place them into the rehydrating oven one at a time. The contents of each packet only take a few seconds to transform into the desired food. Within a few minutes, we have roasted chicken, baked potatoes, and yeast rolls.

For whatever reason, traveling to this Earth has made me extremely hungry. I begin to wonder if perhaps the food that was inside my stomach just didn't make the trip with me. The way Lucas attacks his plate of food seems to indicate that he's just as ravenous as I am. Then again, maybe it's simply the excitement of it all that's causing my appetite to peak.

Once we're through eating, Lucas takes my plate and cleans it in the sink for me.

"Thank you," I tell him as I watch him wash my dish.

"You're welcome," he replies. "Can I ask you something?"

"Go ahead," I say cautiously.

"How are we going to find my mom and the others?"

Lucas glances away from his task to look at me when I don't answer him right away.

"I'm not sure," I reply. "They could be anywhere."

"Maybe Lucian will help us. He seems to like you."

"Do you really want him to find your mother, or even know that she's here?"

He thinks about this for a moment and finally says, "No. He might hurt her."

"My thoughts exactly. That's why I only told him about Lucifer being here. I'm sure Lucian is looking for him as we speak. All we need to do is wait for him to find Lucifer for us."

"What if Lucifer doesn't know where the others are either?"

"It doesn't matter. If we have him, we can team up to find Anna and Jess. I suggest we give Lucian some time to prove his usefulness to us. He won't be able to stop himself from looking for Lucifer."

"Why is that?"

"Because he's going to want to know if what I said is true."

"That Lucifer asked God for forgiveness?"

"Yes. I'm not sure if he believed me when I told him that little gem. He'll want to confirm it with Lucifer himself."

"Do you think Lucian wants to ask God for forgiveness?"

"I'm sure there's a part of him that wants to return to Heaven. I know Lucifer lived with the yearning since he was cast out by his Father. I don't see why this version of him would be any different."

"This Lucifer isn't like ours, though," Lucas says. His words come out sounding oddly grown up for someone so young. I begin to wonder if Gabriel's consciousness is beginning to blend with his.

"I agree. He's very unstable. Lucifer may have lost all his marbles there at the end by asking his Father for forgiveness, but he normally kept a level head. Lucian seems unbalanced, and I know I can't trust him."

Once Lucas places the clean dishes back on the shelf, he lets out a big yawn.

"Come on," I tell him, walking out of the kitchen and back towards the living room. "Let's find the bedrooms. I think we could both use some rest."

It wasn't hard to find the bedrooms. There were three of them down the main hallway leading off from the living room.

We find one with a large bed, but very little in the way of other furnishings. While I turn down the bedding, Lucas removes his jacket and boots. He crawls underneath the covers, and I begin to walk away.

"Helena?" he calls out.

I turn back around and say, “Yes?”

“Would you sleep in here with me? I don’t want to be alone.”

“Nothing will harm you here.”

“How can you be so sure about that?”

It’s a good question. I can’t be sure Lucian won’t return and try to snatch Lucas away from me, or, even worse, try to kill him for retribution. Gabe irrevocably destroyed his plans for this Earth. I’m sure he’s still holding a grudge about that. As I told Lucas earlier, Lucian doesn’t seem to think before he acts. It’s quite possible he would seek his revenge by ending Lucas’ life.

Without saying a word, I walk over to the other side of the bed, remove my shoes, and lie down on top of the comforter.

“Go to sleep,” I tell him. “I’m not sure what we’ll need to do tomorrow.”

Lucas doesn’t make a verbal reply. He simply closes his eyes and smiles.

He’s such an odd child. Who else would ask me to lie in bed with them for protection? I’m not exactly the mothering type. I don’t believe anyone would accuse me of being a nurturer.

I watch Lucas sleep for a while before I allow myself to close my eyes and try to sleep, too.

As I told him, I have no idea what the next day will bring on this alternate Earth. All I want to do is find the others and go back home. When the word ‘home’ flashes through my mind, a picture of Cade forms in my thoughts. I instantly make it disperse, because thinking about him is a distraction I don’t need right now. Unfortunately, my plan doesn’t work. I begin to worry that he's fallen into the purple veil surrounding the castle by now. To be honest, I'm not even sure if the fight is still progressing without me being there to control my minions. I've noticed that they sometimes need my unique power of persuasion to do their jobs effectively.

I turn over onto my back and force my mind to go blank. The less I worry about Cade the better. He's a War Angel, for goodness' sake. He should be able to take care of himself.

"Hello."

I quickly sit up and look at the woman now standing in the doorway. The bedroom is dark, with the only light coming from the city through the large windows in the room, but I can see the woman clear enough in the dim lighting.

"Who are you?" I ask.

"I've gone by a lot of names in my life," she says with an air of mystery. "I think the one you've probably heard before is Ravan Drake."

I swing my legs over the bed's edge and stand up. I walk over to the woman claiming to be Ravan until I'm only inches away from her. She's young, possibly twenty-five, with pale skin and long strawberry-blonde hair parted to the side. Her large blue-grey eyes watch me cautiously.

"How do I know you're really her?" I ask. "You definitely don't look the same."

"It's been a thousand years," she answers with a small shrug. "I've occupied a lot of new bodies during that time."

"I thought the Watchers here had you locked away in that prison cell of theirs. You know, the one you can't phase out of."

"They did for a time, but humans are weak-willed. I was able to talk one of them into letting me out."

"I'm surprised the Watchers here haven't hunted you down and killed you by now."

"I'm sure they would have if they had been able to catch me."

"You still haven't answered my question. How do I know you're the real Ravan Drake? Or, should I call you Lilith, since that's the original name God gave you?"

The woman claiming to be Ravan smiles. "Why would I lie about who I am?"

"Oh, I don't know. To make a fool out of me?"

Before I can stop her, the woman grabs my arm and phases me somewhere I thought I would never be allowed to go.

Heaven.

CHAPTER SEVENTEEN

I'm rarely at a loss for words, but, as I stand in Heaven beside Ravan, my mind goes totally blank. My heart begins to pound against the walls of my chest as if it's trying to escape its boney confines. My breathing becomes rapid, making me feel as though I might pass out at any moment. I take in gulps of Heaven's sweet air, finding its scent unlike anything I've ever smelled before. After spending so much time in my own acrid domain, the untainted air of the saints provides a stark contrast to what I'm used to.

As I absorb my surroundings, I know exactly where we're standing.

It's a recreation of a setting I used for one of the scenes I showed Anna from her past as Seraphina. This is where she and Lucifer danced for the last time before he started the war. The hill I'm standing on is covered with long green grass. The blades are so soft against my bare feet I feel like I'm standing on a carpet of velvet. The sound of the rustling leaves on the tree we're standing underneath is rhythmic and soothing. As I look out across a large body of water that seems to reach well into the horizon, I see a classic sunset that divides the upper blue sky from the lower red-orange hues.

I look over at Ravan and notice how beautiful she looks in the glow of the setting sun. Her pale skin is luminescent, giving it an otherworldly quality, while her hair shines as if each strand is lit from within.

"I don't understand," I say to her. "How was I allowed to even come here?"

"He said you would be able to breach the veil in the body you made for yourself," Ravan tells me, looking me up and down but not in a judgmental way. "Apparently it isn't human, or you wouldn't have been allowed to come here, but you're not angelic either. To be honest, I'm not sure you can be classified as anything known."

"Why have you brought me here?" I ask.

"He wants to speak with you," she replies with a wistful smile.

I know the 'He' she is referring to without having to ask her to explain, but I still don't understand why I've been allowed to breach the hallowed halls of Heaven.

"You may leave now, Ravan," I hear God say behind me.

Ravan looks over her shoulder and smiles at Him just before she disappears.

From Lucifer's memories and from the other memories of the angels I've met, I've always known what being in the presence of God is supposed to feel like. Now, as I actually stand before Him, I understand why they all treasured the sensation so much. Even after all the sin Lucifer perpetuated on Earth, he always yearned to be close to his Father again. I have to admit the warmth of acceptance God emits is rather addictive. If I thought I was a sinner, I can see how such a thing would call a person to Him.

I turn around to face God for the first time in my life, and find Him in His usual guise. He chose this form when he first met Lilly and has used it ever since.

"Hello, Helena," He says as His eyes bore into mine, as if He's searching for some particular truth. "I thought it was time we had a talk."

"What could you and I possibly have to talk about?" I ask. "And why was Ravan the one who brought me here? I thought she hated You."

"Ravan is attempting to atone for her many sins," God informs me. "She came to Me not too long ago and asked for My forgiveness."

"Well, I hope you don't expect the same hero-worship from me," I reply defiantly.

"I have no expectations where you're concerned," God replies.

To be honest, I'm not sure if I should be happy or offended by His statement.

"Then why am I here?" I demand.

"I thought it was time I met Lucifer's second-born," He tells me.

I swallow hard after hearing His reason. I feel a yearning in my heart to hear Him say it again.

"Lucifer doesn't see me that way," I reply, feeling as though God has touched upon the one thing in my life that has always bothered me.

"No, he doesn't," God agrees. "Do you know why he refuses to acknowledge you as his child?"

Having God state for a fact my true relationship to Lucifer crumbles a wall I've sustained all of my life. It's a wall I've used to protect myself from my father's cruel denials of who I am to him. I try to blink back unwanted tears, but one escapes anyway and slides down my right cheek. I shake my head, silently telling Him that I don't know the answer to His question. I fear if I try to speak it might come out as a weak sob.

"It's because you were born from Lucifer's hate," God starts to explain to me, "and in his mind, that makes you nothing more than a tool he used to find a way to hurt Me."

"Why does he continue to deny who I am to him?" I ask, desperate to finally find out the truth.

"Because you're a reminder of everything that went wrong in his life," God answers honestly. "He made you to give him comfort in his darkest days, and he fed you so much of his hate and loathing that he can't imagine you as anything but a repository of the worst parts of his own soul. Now that he's come back to Me, he doesn't want to acknowledge what he did to make you what you are today."

"And what am I?"

"Only you can decide that, Helena, and in order to do that you have to face some truths about yourself."

Confused, I ask, "What do you mean by that?"

The tranquil scenery surrounding us fades, to be replaced by another scene I conjured to show Anna.

We're standing in the replica of the dark Guf in Hell. Behind God, I see myself appear to Lucifer as an eight-year-old Anna. The scene is frozen in the moment Lucifer first saw me. The expression of horror and disgust on his face is one I will never forget.

"Why are You showing me this?" I ask, unable to tear my eyes away from Lucifer's face.

"When you presented this scene to Anna, you embellished it to gain her sympathy," God says, unmasking my little deception. I don't feel an ounce of surprise. He is God, after all. Of course He knows what I did.

"So?" I ask defensively. "I manipulate people's emotions all the time."

"Yes. And you're very good at what you do," God says disappointedly. "You're so good at it that you even deceive yourself sometimes."

"You're not going to start talking to me in riddles like You do everyone else, are You?" I ask, already becoming annoyed. "I really hate that. Why don't You just say what You mean if You're trying to teach me some sort of life lesson here?"

"I shouldn't have to spell it out for you, Helena," God says patiently. "You already know what I'm talking about."

I remain mute and just stare at Him.

"Very well," He says, "if you refuse to recognize what you did, then let Me make it plain."

God unfreezes the scene and allows it to play out just as I did for Anna. When Lucifer throws me to the ground and I begin to sob, He freezes the scene again.

"I still don't see Your point," I say. "The way I showed this moment to Anna worked in my favor. She feels pity for me now when she didn't before."

"True," God concedes. "Your plan did work well, but do you fully understand why it worked so well?"

"Because Anna is too soft-hearted."

"You're missing the point, Helena," He says disappointedly.

"Then why don't You tell me what the point to all of this is?" I yell in aggravation.

"The scene worked so well because you showed Anna how you truly felt when Lucifer denied who you are to him. You try to hide from others how much he's hurt you over the years, but I know the truth. You can't hide your thoughts from Me."

“What I *can* do is blame You for making him hate me so much,” I say viciously. “He only created me because he wanted to make You suffer for what You did to him. If You hadn’t cast him out of Heaven, maybe I would have been made like Seraphina and been lavished with his attention and love, but the maybes of this world are a waste of time to think about. Nothing can change my life or who I’ve become. Not even You.”

“You’re right,” God agrees. “There is nothing I can do to change who you are. Only you can do that.”

“I don’t want to change. I love myself just the way I am.”

“In a way, I know you’re right, but I also know there is a part of you that wonders if you could have another kind of life.”

Our surroundings change once again to Anna’s chambers in the palace in Cirrus. God fades from my sight as I feel a pair of warm hands curl around my waist from behind, tugging me back against a firm body. I don’t have to turn around to know who’s behind me.

“You seem lost in your thoughts,” Cade whispers in my ear. “Do you want to share what you’re thinking about with me?”

I close my eyes and allow myself to soak in the moment. I know it’s only an illusion, but a part of me wishes it was real.

I hear the cry of a baby from the adjacent bedroom.

I quickly open my eyes and ask, “What was that?”

I feel Cade’s body tremble as he begins to laugh at my question.

“That would be our son, or have you forgotten about him already?”

“Son?” I ask in shock. “That’s impossible.”

“Come on,” he pulls his arms away from my waist and takes one of my hands with his. “I’ll bet he’s hungry.”

I allow imaginary Cade to escort me to the bedroom where I see a white bassinet. Lying within its safe confines, I see a baby with blue eyes staring back up at me. When he sees me, he begins to gurgle and smile as if I've just made his day brighter. I feel a deep, primal emotion well up from somewhere within my soul. Before it has a chance to overwhelm me, I wrench my hand out of Cade's and run back into the living room.

"Stop this!" I scream. "Stop this now!"

My surroundings fade away, replaced with the original one, and I find myself standing on the grassy knoll once again. God reappears in front of me.

"Why did You show me that?" I demand to know.

"Because it's what your heart truly desires," He says. "You want the love and peace a family of your own can bring into your life, but you don't feel as though you deserve it."

"Is that why You made Cade my soul mate? To torture me with the possibility of love when You know I can't accept it? Are You trying to punish me for being the way I am?"

"You are the only one holding yourself back from such a life, Helena. Everything you need to have the life you want has been given to you. Whether or not you accept it is your decision. As I said before, only you can decide your fate."

"I don't want to be here anymore," I tell him. "Send me back to Earth."

"You can leave at any time," God tells me. "I'm not holding you prisoner here."

"And if I ever want to come back?"

"You know what has to be done in order for that to happen."

"What? Bow down to You and ask for forgiveness? No thanks. I don't have anything to be forgiven for. Everything I have done or will do has been to serve my own purpose. Anyway, why would I want to live here in Your realm when I already have one of my own to rule over? I'm not the servant type, and I definitely don't intend to serve You."

God lets out a disappointed sigh. "I fear Lucifer made you too well. I'm sorry."

"I'm not," I retort before phasing back down to Earth.

When I return to the bedroom where Lucas is still sleeping, I find Ravan standing by one of the windows, looking out at the city she once helped destroy.

"Why are you here?" I ask her curtly.

Ravan turns around to face me. "I didn't want to leave Lucas here all alone. I wasn't sure if Lucian would try to take him while you were away."

"You can leave now. He's safe with me."

Ravan considers me for a moment before saying, "Why are you protecting him? It seems to go against your nature."

"He's my sister's son. She would expect me to keep him safe for her."

"Do you love Anna that much?"

"I'm not sure I can love," I admit. "It's not something I was made to do."

"You could learn to love if you tried. It took me a long time to figure that out, but I finally did."

"What made you change?" I have to ask. "From what I remember, you were a real bitch during the Apocalypse."

"You definitely say what's on your mind," Ravan says with an embarrassed smile. "And yes, I was selfish and cruel back then."

"So what happened to you? Why has your attitude changed so much?"

"I guess you could say that I saw the error of my ways and decided I wanted to be a better person."

"But what made you *want* to change? Something must have happened for this epiphany of yours to occur."

"I'm not sure exactly," she begins. "After living for so long with so much hate, it finally dawned on me that I'd only been living a half-life. I started thinking about all the people I'd wronged in my time, and the guilt of what I did to them began to weigh so heavily on my soul that I felt as though I couldn't breathe anymore."

"So you asked God for forgiveness and He granted your wish," I say sarcastically, with a touch of meanness.

"To put it simply, yes," Ravan answers.

"There was a time I wanted to meet you in person," I admit. "I even fashioned a body to look like yours because I thought you were someone I could identify with. I wish I could have known you back then because, frankly, the way you are now sickens me. You're pathetic and you're weak. Get out of here before I tear your head off and spit down your throat for being such a great disappointment to meet in the flesh."

"I see your talk with God hasn't changed you yet," she replies, unaffected by my threat to do her bodily harm. "Maybe in time His words will sink in, and you'll decide to choose another path for your life."

"Don't count on it. I like myself just the way I am. Now leave," I say threateningly.

Ravan phases out of the room and I go to lie down on the bed again.

Lucas is still fast asleep. He seems to be able to sleep through almost anything that goes on around him.

I close my eyes, but find sleep unattainable. My mind keeps going back to how sweet and fresh the air in Heaven smelled. Why did God feel the need to have Ravan take me there? Did He really believe His little pep talk would work a miracle on me? Obviously, He doesn't know me as well as He thinks He does. Or, does He know something about me that even I don't understand? He *is* God, after all. He isn't one to waste time on lost causes.

I groan in frustration and roll over onto my side, away from Lucas.

I may not know what God's true agenda is, but I do know one thing: I'm ready to go back home to my own domain. The sooner I make that happen, the better.

Apparently, I fall asleep at some point during the night. When I wake up the next morning, I turn over to check on Lucas and find him missing from the bed. I quickly stand up and phase to the living room but find it empty of his presence, too.

"Lucas?" I call out, feeling a sense of panic set in.

"I'm in the kitchen," I hear him reply.

I walk over to the entrance of the kitchen and see him pull some silver packets from the refrigerator.

"You scared me to death," I admonish. "I thought someone kidnapped you."

"No, I just got hungry," he tells me. "Would you like some breakfast?"

My stomach growls, answering Lucas' question.

We eat a simple meal of eggs, bacon, and buttered toast. While I'm sipping coffee, he says, "I had a dream about God last night."

"Really?" I set my coffee cup down on the table and give him my full attention. "That's interesting, because I had a nightmare about Him."

"A nightmare?" Lucas asks, baffled as to how I could have such an experience with the Almighty.

"Don't think about it too hard," I advise. "You might hurt that tiny human brain of yours. In your dream, did He happen to tell you where your mother is?"

"No," Lucas says, looking dejected by the lack of help God provided. "He just told me not to be afraid no matter what happens. He said I would make it back home to see my dad again."

No matter what happens? What was that supposed to mean? Why didn't God just say what He meant?

"Is that all God told you?" I ask.

"Yeah," Lucas replies with a small shrug of his shoulders. "That's all He said."

"He's not a very helpful deity."

"Well, He can't tell you everything," Lucas tells me. "I don't think He always knows what's going to happen either."

"Why wouldn't He know?"

"Everyone has free will. He doesn't control that. He might think you're going to turn right on a street when you decide you want to go left instead. I bet He has to adjust things a lot because we don't always do what He expects us to."

"You could be right about that," I admit, amazed yet again by Lucas' ability to reason the obvious from the obtuse.

"I'm pretty sure I am," Lucas says confidently.

"Sure about what, exactly?" I hear Lucian say from the kitchen's entryway.

I turn to watch him as he strides into the kitchen and up to the dining table.

"Have you found Lucifer yet?" I ask him, choosing to ignore his question to Lucas.

"No, I haven't, but Ivy thinks she knows where he is."

"So where is he?"

"I'm afraid she wouldn't tell me," Lucian says regretfully, almost sounding like he meant it. "She said the two of you would have to come to her if you wanted the information."

"Why is she so interested in meeting me?" I ask, suspicious of my counterpart's motives.

"You probably know the answer to that better than I do. You and Ivy are basically the same person, after all. You're just more powerful than she is. If I were to wager a guess, I think she wants to know how you're able to keep your physical form outside of Hell. I know I'm curious to understand that as well."

I smile tight-lipped at Lucian. If I don't have to, I'm not about to tell him that I absorbed five of the seven seals to gain my ability. It's very possible Ivy will discover that information when I enter into her realm, but if Ivy is as weak from the lack of new souls entering Hell as Lucian claims, she may not have the power to read my mind. I can't find Lucifer on my own, and I'm sure he's aimlessly roaming the city streets trying to find Lucas for Anna. I'm not deluded enough to think that he cares what happens to me. His only reason for concern over my welfare would be the fact that they know I'm needed to get us all back home.

"When can we meet her?" I inquire, desiring to find Lucifer and leave this Earth as quickly as possible.

"If you're ready, we can go now."

I stand from my chair. "Come on, Lucas. Let's go see what the Hell of this Earth looks like."

"Do I have to go?" Lucas whines.

"Apparently so," I say. "Ivy wants to meet you, too."

"I don't see why. I'm nothing special."

If only he knew just how special he was. Lucian knows who Lucas really is, and if he knows, Ivy knows, too.

"Stay close to me, Lucas," I say, holding out my hand to him.

He doesn't question my request. He simply walks over and firmly takes hold of my hand.

I look back at Lucian and say, "Let's go."

Lucian touches my arm and phases us to alternate Earth's Hell.

We enter into an almost pitch-black construct. The only thing present is a large oak tree devoid of leaves. Attached to one of the larger limbs is a rope and wood-plank swing. Sitting on the swing is a girl who looks about nine years old. She has pale white skin with brown freckles that run from cheek to cheek. Her long black hair is tied into ponytails that lay past her shoulders. She's wearing a sleeveless black dress cinched in at the waist by a ruby red ribbon.

"Hello," Ivy says to us as she sits on the swing. It continues to sway back and forth by some invisible force.

"Hello," I reply as I quickly size Ivy up in a glance. I don't feel much power emanating from her. I suppose Lucian was telling me the truth about Hell starving for power. As far as I can surmise, she isn't a threat to either Lucas or me.

When the swing pushes forward, Ivy jumps off it effortlessly and skips over to us like any normal little girl would.

"Thank you for coming," she says in a voice that has a highborn British accent.

"You're welcome," I say, squeezing Lucas' hand a little tighter to make sure he understands not to let go of me while we're here. Even though she seems powerless, I don't trust her. If she's anything like me, no one in their right mind would trust her fully.

"Lucian says you know where Lucifer is," I say, getting to the point of my visit. "Where is he?"

"Around," Ivy says, tilting her head as she studies me. "How did you become powerful enough to leave your Hell?"

"A lot of hard work," I reply tersely. "Did you honestly believe I would tell you my secret?"

Ivy smiles, but it's a perfunctory one. "No. I didn't. I wouldn't tell you, either."

"Then why am I here?" I ask, becoming annoyed. "Are you going to tell me where Lucifer is or not?"

Ivy wipes the smile off her face as her features become pinched. "You're being rude to me. I don't like it."

"And how exactly did you expect me to treat you? Like a long-lost alternate Earth sister?"

"I expect you to treat me with the respect I deserve!" Ivy's face becomes so red with rage her head looks like it might shoot off her shoulders at any moment.

I knew there was a temper hiding behind that childlike façade.

"Why would I respect someone with so little power?" I ask scathingly.

Ivy continues to study me for a little while longer without saying a word. Just as I'm becoming bored with her, it finally dawns on me what she's doing.

"Stop it," I order. "Who's the one being rude now?"

"Too late," she tells me with an evil little smile. "I already have everything I want to know."

I knew there was a possibility she had enough power to look inside my mind and find the answers she was seeking, but I had to take the chance in order to find out where Lucifer is.

"If I had known the seals were the key to my freedom, I never would have let my Lucifer open them on this Earth."

"She has the seals?" Lucian asks in disbelief. "How did you get them?"

"She didn't retrieve them herself," Ivy answers for me. "Her sister absorbed them from all of the princes, even from the Origin's Lucifer, but Helena took them away from her. Or, at least some of them. Her sister still has two of the seals, but they're being used as the souls of the babies Anna carries."

I try to phase out of Hell to get away from Ivy, but apparently, she has enough power to prevent me from leaving.

“Her sister?” Lucian questions. “How can she have a sister?”

Ivy tilts her head as she looks at him. “Anna is Seraphina born in human form. She’s also Lucifer’s natural-born child with his human soul mate in the Origin.”

Lucian’s face goes entirely slack from shock.

“That can’t be true,” he whispers, shaking his head to deny what Ivy has told him.

“I’m afraid it is true. Anna is the one who helped the Origin’s Lucifer find redemption,” Ivy tells him. There’s a certain amount of joy on Ivy’s face as she watches Lucian’s reaction to her words.

“Oh, that’s right,” I say, looking over at him as I remember an important piece of information Lucifer discovered on his last visit to this reality. “I seem to remember you telling Lucifer that you killed your Seraphina before you were exiled from Heaven. What a pity. You killed the one person who could have helped you find forgiveness from your Father.”

“I don’t need to be forgiven,” Lucian replies testily.

“Yeah, keep telling yourself that,” I say, unconvinced. “Lucifer used to say that, too, but look what happened to him.”

Lucian looks at Ivy meaningfully. Before I can react, Ivy throws a ball of energy, hitting me square in the stomach. As I’m propelled backwards a few feet, I lose my grip on Lucas’ hand and fall flat on my back. Ivy quickly runs over to me before I’m able to recover from the physical pain of her attack.

"Give me the seals!" she screams irately as she continues to pummel me with ball after ball of energy. The madness in her eyes tells me she's gone past the point of simple madness. Starving from the lack of new souls has driven her insane from hunger.

I really don't have time for this.

I lift my right hand and aim a charge of electricity right at her chest, preventing her from throwing any more of her energy balls at me. I let my charge build up in intensity before releasing it. The force of my power propels her little body off me, and her flight through the air doesn't stop until her back hits the trunk of the oak tree.

I quickly sit up and look around for Lucas, but he's already gone.

"Where has Lucian taken Lucas?" I demand as I regain my feet.

Ivy begins to laugh hysterically as she lies on the ground in a broken heap.

"Far, far away," she says in a sing-song voice.

"I need him back," I say angrily.

"Then I guess you'll have to go find him. I'm sure Lucian will be willing to trade you something for him. I just hope he doesn't take his anger out on that little angel of yours."

"Don't call him that," I snap. "He hates it."

I try to phase, but Ivy is still preventing me. I hear her cackle again at my attempt.

"How am I supposed to go see what he wants when you're keeping me here?" I fume.

"Well, I can't let you go until I give Lucian enough time to find somewhere to hide. You should know that."

I growl in frustration.

Ivy is silent for a few minutes, but then she asks, "What's it like?"

I watch as she reassembles her body and stands up from where she fell. She walks back over to her swing and sits down, looking at me expectantly as she waits for my answer.

"What is what like?" I ask in aggravation.

"Loving someone," she says, looking truly curious. "I saw him in your mind, you know. Cade."

"I don't love Cade."

"You don't have to lie to me," she says. "In fact, I'm probably the only person you can tell the truth to."

Ivy looks at me with more understanding than I would expect.

"It's confusing," I finally admit. "And I don't like being confused."

"Me neither." She tilts her head at me. "What are you going to do about him?"

I don't answer because I don't have one to give.

"You'll figure it out," Ivy tells me. "I can tell you what I would do, if you want to know."

"I have no desire to take advice from a lunatic like you," I say derisively.

Ivy shrugs her shoulders, unfazed. "Just trying to help out."

"I don't want your help except to get out of here!"

"Go."

I phase back to the living room of Lucian's apartment. I look in the kitchen but see no one there. I phase into the bedroom Lucas and I slept in, and discover a sheet of paper lying on Lucas' side of the bed. I grab it and quickly read Lucian's demands for Lucas' safe return. Apparently, neither he nor Ivy actually knows where Lucifer is, but he tells me where to begin my search for him. After I find Lucifer, he and Anna are supposed to meet Lucian at his other apartment in town by noon today, but there isn't an address for this mystery apartment.

Wonderful.

I read the letter once again to confirm where I'm supposed to start my search for Lucifer and ask myself, "How the hell am I supposed to get to Boldt Castle?"

CHAPTER EIGHTEEN
(Anna's Point of View)

Xavier and I talk for hours. Jess does bring me the tea she and Ava made, but she doesn't linger in the room with us. I think she understands his need to know all about my life with Malcolm, and that he will be more comfortable if she isn't there, listening to our conversation. Knowing that Jess trusts him enough to leave me in his care also helps me open up to him in a way I normally wouldn't with a complete stranger. Although, I guess he isn't exactly a stranger. There are small similarities that Xavier shares with my husband. The sound of his laughter and the way his eyes sparkle while he listens to me talk reminds me so much of Malcolm that I have to remind myself he isn't my husband.

By the time I tell him everything he needs to know about my situation, it is well into the wee hours of the morning. He tucks me underneath the covers of his bed and tells me to get some rest. Before he leaves, he leans down, kisses me on the forehead, and wishes me sweet dreams, as if it is the most natural thing in the world for him to do. Only after Xavier leaves the room do I allow myself to cry. I cry over my worry for Lucas' safety, and I cry because I desperately need my husband's arms around me. I wish he had been the one to kiss me goodnight just now and reassure me that everything will turn out all right.

What was happening to Malcolm in Hell? Since Helena wasn't there anymore, was he able to leave? Even if his ability to phase out of Hell was restored after we left, I wasn't sure he would go since my release had been contingent on him winning Helena's sadistic little game. I eventually fall asleep from exhaustion, and don't wake up until I hear a knock on the bedroom door the next morning.

"Anna, are you awake?" I hear Xavier ask from the other side of the door.

"I am now," I grumble groggily as I push myself into a sitting position on the bed. I don't want to make him feel bad for waking me up, so I say, "Yes, I'm awake. You can come in."

Xavier opens the door and walks in with a wooden folding bed tray in his hands.

"I thought you might be hungry," he tells me as he stands the tray over my lap.

There is a large plate filled to almost overflowing with scrambled eggs, sausage, buttered toast, and strawberries mixed with blueberries. A tall glass of cold milk stands in one corner of the tray while a small pink vase with a single, perfect yellow rose decorates the other.

"Jess said it might be too much food," Xavier says, "but since you're eating for three, I thought you might need it."

I can't help but smile at his thoughtfulness.

"It's fine," I tell him. "I do feel like I haven't eaten in days."

I pick up the fork that is lying on a perfectly folded white cloth napkin beside the plate, and begin to eat.

Xavier sits down on the corner of the bed and asks, "Did you sleep well? I hope I didn't wake you up, but I thought you would want some breakfast and to know that Lucifer is back."

"Does he have Lucas?" I immediately ask, but fear I already know the answer. If my son were here, he would be in my arms right now.

"No," he reluctantly replies, confirming what I already suspected. "He hasn't been able to locate him or Helena yet. I think I might try something to find them, though."

"What are you thinking?" I ask, forcing myself to start eating the eggs on the plate, even though Xavier's news has made me lose my appetite.

"I'm going to see if the Lucifer in this world has them."

I swallow what's in my mouth before I ask, "Even if he does, do you think he'll tell you something like that?"

"I don't know. As you might have already guessed, we're not exactly on friendly terms with one another, but he might let something slip inadvertently. Lucifer seems to think that our version of Hell may have felt Helena enter this reality. If that's the case, Lucian has probably tracked Helena down by now, and if Lucas is with her, well, then he knows about both of them."

"He'll be able to tell that Lucas is Gabe reincarnated, won't he?" I ask, fearful for my son's safety. "Lucifer was able to see it right away."

"If he could sense it, I'm sure Lucian can, too."

"Why do you call your Lucifer Lucian?"

"He's used the name Lucian for a long time on this Earth. At the moment, his name is Lucian Forester. I know he's living in New York City right now because he's starring in a popular Broadway play there."

"He's an actor?" I ask, finding it hard to believe the devil is actually working for a living.

"Yes. He's always liked being the center of attention. Personally, I think he just craves hearing people scream his name. Ever since we started setting our world right, he lost a lot of the power he accumulated during the Apocalypse."

"Why?"

"Fewer souls are being sent to Hell nowadays. Without an influx of energy, neither he nor Hell has much power anymore. He's basically been neutered. Every time Ava and I see him, all we can do is laugh at how pitiful he's become. This acting hobby of his just seems to be a desperate ploy to regain some of his former glory. All he's really doing is feeding his ego so he doesn't feel so powerless."

"I meant to ask you last night where the other Watchers of this world are. You've only mentioned you and Ava."

"We're the last two left."

"Why only the two of you?" I ask, finding it odd. "Where are the others?"

"After we set the world back on track, a lot of them asked our Father to make them human and allow them to live out normal lives. Brand was the first one to do it. He wanted to marry the Empress of China, Jai Lin. They ended up having a happy life together and had three little girls. He and Jai Lin led the people of the world to unite and work hard to make it a better place than it was before the Apocalypse."

"Why have you and Ava stayed behind?"

Xavier grins sheepishly and looks down at his hands resting on his lap. I get the distinct impression he doesn't want to admit his motivation to me.

"I'll tell you my reason for staying, but I would rather you didn't say anything to anyone else. Only Ava knows why I haven't asked to become human yet, and as far as her reason for staying goes, I think she just doesn't want to leave me here all alone."

"Your secret is safe with me," I promise, setting my fork down to give Xavier my full attention.

"I've been hoping to find someone I can build a life with before I leave this world. I just haven't found her yet. I may never find her."

"If that's what you really want, you shouldn't give up on it," I tell him in earnest. "Malcolm had to wait a very long time for me. Maybe the woman you're waiting for will show up soon, too."

"I hope you're right. To be honest, ever since you arrived I can't shake the feeling that maybe this deep-set desire I've had to find a love of my own is something my Father instilled in me to make sure I remained here."

"What do you mean?"

"I need to show you something," Xavier says as he stands up. "I'll be right back."

He phases but returns less than a minute later with a sword that looks exactly like mine. In actuality, my sword originally belonged to Jess. I did notice that she was wearing my baldric, with the sword safely housed in its sheath on her back, but I didn't say anything to her about it. After all, both items were originally hers. I simply inherited them from a long line of descendants. Plus, she needed a weapon in Hell to protect herself with.

"Is that the sword Jess pulled out of the Tree of Knowledge from this reality's Garden of Eden?" I ask, remembering the story Malcolm told me. I knew Jess used this sword when the original one found its way into the hands of Ravan Drake. Thankfully, Jess was able to retrieve her sword from that madwoman, and she gave Xavier the sword he's holding now for safekeeping.

"Yes. This is Jophiel's sword. I think I'm meant to give it to you." He reverently lays the sword down beside me on the bed.

As I run my hand over its hilt, I feel the cold metal grow warm against my skin as if it's welcoming me as its new owner.

"I think you're right," I reply, feeling a strange, cosmic connection to the weapon. "I think I'm meant to take it back home with me."

"Do you know why?" Xavier questions.

"Not exactly, but I might have an idea," I admit as my mind races with the possibilities.

I hear him sigh in relief. "Good. Maybe this means my journey is almost complete."

"And maybe," I say with an encouraging smile, "this means you'll find true love soon."

"I guess she won't be my soul mate, though," Xavier says disappointedly. "I'm still not sure why the Origin has them and we don't."

"I think I can answer that question for you."

Xavier and I both look towards the open doorway, and see Lucifer standing there now.

"You think you can guess the reason why?" I ask as he walks in to stand near the foot of the bed.

"I don't have to guess," he tells me. "I know the reason. I didn't know it when I first came here, but now I understand why no one has ever felt that sort of connection to someone else in this world." Lucifer looks at me meaningfully. "It's because the Lucifer of this reality killed Seraphina before she was able to ask the Guardians of the Guf to remake her soul into a human one. When you did that in our reality, it produced soul mates, but since she never got the chance to do it here, they weren't created."

"I never knew your counterpart in this world killed his Seraphina," I say, wondering why my husband neglected to tell me that part of the story.

"I'm sure Malcolm didn't say anything to you about it because he didn't want to upset you," Lucifer says, as if he just read my mind.

It's upsetting to learn of Seraphina's fate in this world, but it also goes to show just how different my father is from his doppelgänger.

"Have you told Lucifer about your plan?" I ask Xavier.

"No. I thought I would tell you first."

"What plan?" my father asks.

"I want to see if Lucian knows where Lucas and Helena are. He has two apartments in New York City. I figured I would start there."

"Then I'm coming with you," Lucifer declares.

"I want to go, too," I say.

"No," the men say in unison, and rather forcefully.

"Well, that didn't make me feel very loved," I tell them, a bit miffed at their automatic refusal of my help.

"If we're lucky, Lucian doesn't know about you yet," Lucifer explains. "I would like to keep it that way for as long as possible. It's for your own safety, Anna."

"And I simply don't want you anywhere near that lunatic," Xavier says, justifying his response. "Lucifer's right. We have no idea what Lucian might try to do to you once he learns who you really are. He killed his own daughter without feeling any remorse afterwards. He wouldn't have any qualms about killing you, too. In fact, he would probably do it just to watch your father suffer."

"But why?" I ask. "What would that gain him?"

"Revenge," Lucifer answers without hesitation. "If Helena is with him, I'm sure she's told him that I've been granted forgiveness by our Father. If he isn't already insane, that knowledge will certainly drive him over the edge. Please don't argue with us about this, Anna. I need for you to stay here where it's safe."

"Even if he does try to kill me, you know I can kill him first," I counter.

"Yes," my father says, "I'm fully aware of how powerful you are. Look. I have no love for Lucian, but I would rather not kill him if we don't have to."

"Why not?" Xavier asks, obviously not having a problem with my countermeasure. "I certainly wouldn't miss him."

"I don't want to doom him to an eternity in the Void," Lucifer responds, looking disappointed in Xavier for not showing an ounce of compassion for Lucian. "I may not like him, but deep down inside I know he still harbors a desire to return to Heaven and be with our Father."

"Are you sure about that?" I ask doubtfully. "To me, it sounds like killing Seraphina placed him on an entirely different path from yours. I'm not sure how you can defend him after everything he's done."

"I'm not defending what he did to her or for him starting the Apocalypse here, but I'm trying to give him the benefit of the doubt. People can change, Anna. I think I'm proof of that."

He was right. I couldn't argue against what he was saying, and a part of me felt guilty for trying to justify killing Lucian.

"If he does have Lucas and won't give him back to us," I say, "I'm going to do whatever I have to in order to rescue my son."

"And I won't stop you,' Lucifer promises. "All I ask is that you use restraint where your powers are concerned."

I nod my agreement, and pray Lucian doesn't harm Lucas so I'm not forced to take his life. It seems important to Lucifer for his counterpart here to have a chance at redemption. Personally, I believe Lucian is a lost cause, and I think, somewhere deep down inside, Lucifer knows that, too. I can understand his need to give his alternate self a chance to change the course of his life, but I'm afraid Lucian killed his only chance to do that when he murdered Seraphina.

Lucifer turns to Xavier. "Where should we start looking for him?"

"I think we should go to one of his apartments in New York first. If he isn't at either one of those, we can try the theater on Broadway. He might be there, rehearsing for his play."

"Let's say you find him, and you don't see Helena or Lucas with him. How are you going to make him tell you whether or not he has them?" I ask.

"We could always try to beat the information out of him," Xavier says rather enthusiastically. "I still have the talisman JoJo made to protect against an archangel's power. He won't be able to kill me."

"It doesn't seem like the most effective way to get him to talk." I turn my attention to Lucifer. "If he proves to be uncooperative, you'll need to come back and get me. I'm the only one who can actually threaten his life. Do you promise to do that?"

“Yes, I will,” he declares. “Lucas’ safety takes first priority.”

“What’s going on?” Jess says as she and Ava walk into the room.

My father briefly tells her what he and Xavier are planning to do.

“Do you need back-up?” Ava asks Xavier.

“I think we’ve got it handled,” he answers. “Plus, we have a secret weapon in Anna if Lucian is less than forthcoming.”

“What’s that supposed to mean?” Ava asks, looking between Xavier and me.

“I’ll let her explain it to you,” he says. “We’ll be back as soon as we can. It won’t take us very long to search for Lucian in the three places I know about.”

Xavier walks over to Lucifer and places a hand on my father’s shoulder.

Once they phase Ava looks at me questioningly, and I know she wants an answer to her previous question. After I tell her about my power to kill archangels, she looks at me in awe.

“Wow,” she says, her eyes wide in shock. “I’m not even sure what to say about that. Have you had to use your power often?”

“A few times,” I admit, not going into any details. How do I tell her I killed my own father with my power? Obviously, everything turned out for the best for Lucifer, but the memory of having to make that decision still stings.

Ava notices the sword Xavier entrusted into my care laying beside me on the bed.

“He’s been carrying that sword around for years,” she tells Jess and me. “He did exactly what you told him to do with it, Jess, and he’s kept it safe all this time.”

“Xavier thinks he was meant to stay here just so he could give it to me now,” I tell them both. “And to be honest, I think he’s right.”

“I wonder why you need it,” Jess muses.

“I have a theory,” I say hesitantly. “And it might be one of the reasons the babies brought us here.”

“You make it sound like the babies can reason on their own,” Ava says jokingly, with a small laugh. When neither Jess nor I join in her mirth, she looks between us and asks warily, “*Are* the babies thinking on their own?”

“They appear to be,” I answer, even though I know such a phenomenon sounds crazy. “It seems like the closer they get to being born the more they understand what’s going on in the world around them. I can’t explain why that appears to be the case, but there’s no other explanation for the things they’ve been able to do together. They’re the ones who opened the vortex to this Earth, and I think they did that so that I could come here and retrieve this sword.”

“So what’s your theory?” Jess asks. “What’s the sword for?”

“I think I can use it to hurt Helena,” I reveal. “I’ve already tried to use our sword on her,” I say, pointedly looking at the weapon strapped to Jess’ back. “It went through her but it didn’t do any permanent damage. Maybe this one will,” I say, patting the sword’s hilt. “Since it’s of this world and not ours, it might work.”

"So, are you going to try to kill her with it?" Ava asks, looking unconvinced about my plan.

"Not until we get back home," I answer. "I know it might sound heartless to say such a thing, but I can't allow her to remain on our Earth. She's causing too many problems there."

"But even if you kill the body she made for herself, won't she just create herself a new one and come back?" Jess points out.

"Maybe," I concede, "but we won't know if we don't try, and I need to do something, Jess."

"Agreed," she says. "It's worth a shot."

Xavier and Lucifer phase back into the room. I'm surprised that they've returned so soon from their search for Lucian. My surprise diminishes somewhat when I see who is standing between them.

"Hello, sister," Helena says as she meets my gaze. "I'm afraid we have a little problem."

CHAPTER NINETEEN

"Where is Lucas?" I demand harshly. "What have you done with my son, Helena?"

She lifts her hands in the air, looking frustrated by my question. "How many times do I have to say that I didn't do anything to your perfect little angel? These two," Helena points at Lucifer and Xavier, who are standing on either side of her, "didn't believe me either until I showed them the letter."

"What letter?" I ask as my blood runs cold with dread.

Xavier walks over and hands me a sheet of paper. I quickly read what's written on it.

"How did Lucian know she would find Lucifer here at the castle?" I ask him.

"I don't think he did," he replies. "It was probably an educated guess on his part since he knows Ava and I still live here. Since we used this place as our headquarters during the Apocalypse, I'm sure he assumed this would be one of the places Lucifer would come to search for help."

"What time is it?" I ask. "The note says we're supposed to meet him at noon."

Xavier looks at a clock mounted on the wall by the bedroom door. I hadn't noticed its existence until now. From the position of the clock's hands, I see that it's ten minutes after eleven.

"Should we go to the apartment he mentions in the letter now to see if he's already there?" I ask.

"He won't be," Lucifer says with certainty. "If I were him, I wouldn't show up until exactly noon."

"Then should we go there to set up an ambush for him?" I suggest, desperate to do whatever it takes to get Lucas back safely.

"I don't believe he intends to hurt Lucas," Lucifer states, his tone insinuating that my son's safety is the last thing I should be worrying about. "Lucian is using Lucas to make sure you come to him. He's curious about you. I doubt he believes what Helena has told him concerning the closeness of our relationship to one another. If I were him, I would want to see us in person to judge whether or not the story of my redemption and how you helped me find it is true."

"Why does everyone I talk to have such a hard time believing what I tell them?" Helena asks, sounding offended by Lucian's lack of faith in her words.

None of us says anything. We just look at her as if she should know the answer to her own question.

"I don't lie that much," Helena defends.

"You lie when it suits your purposes," I tell her. "We all know that. Now be quiet so we can figure out what to do before the meeting."

"If you would let me, I could help you," Helena retorts defensively. "Lucian is weak. You or I could easily overpower him."

"Does he know Anna can kill him?" Lucifer is quick to ask her, obviously worried she might have let that important detail slip during her time with Lucian.

"No. I saw no reason for him to know that much about her."

"Well, at least you were smart enough not to tell him everything." Lucifer's sarcastic tone isn't lost on Helena. It certainly doesn't help her already-defensive mood.

"You've never given me enough credit for my intelligence," she tells him. "And guess what, Father? Lucian isn't the only one I've spent time with since we traveled here. Ravan took me to Heaven to have a little heart-to-heart with the Almighty."

"What?" Jess explodes. "You're lying."

"As a matter of fact, I'm not," Helena replies, looking rather smug about her trip to Heaven.

"Ravan Drake took you to Heaven?" Lucifer questions, openly stunned by Ravan's help in such a matter and the fact that God let Helena into Heaven.

"Ravan isn't the way she used to be," Ava tells us, "but that's a recent development. She's on a mission to atone for all the terrible things she's done in her life. I assume that's going to take her a while."

Lucifer looks unconvinced about Ravan's apparent change of heart.

"I know. It's hard to believe," Jess says, reading my father's expression. "I had a hard time believing it, too, when Ava told me about it last night, but apparently it's true." Jess focuses her attention back on Helena. "I'm more interested in learning why God wanted to talk to you."

"He basically agreed with me that Lucifer is being an idiot by not recognizing me as his daughter," Helena answers, giving him a scathing sideways glance to gauge his reaction to her words.

"No, He doesn't," Lucifer says with certainty.

Helena turns her head to look at him without attempting to hide her contempt. “I’m not going to argue about my paternity with you again. Ask God the next time you see Him if you don’t believe me.”

“Don’t worry,” Lucifer says derisively. “I will.”

“In fact, right after I met God, I was introduced to this reality’s version of me as well. She isn’t as impressive as I am, but that was to be expected considering her current circumstances. Nevertheless, it was interesting to meet her. She looked inside my mind while I was with her, and found out about Anna’s existence. I wasn’t the one who told Lucian I had a sister. In fact, I’m a little surprised she didn’t warn Lucian herself about the strength of Anna’s powers.”

“She?” I ask. “Has Hell taken on a physical form here, too?”

“Yes. Her name is Ivy,” Helena informs me. “She can’t leave her domain like I can, but she has assumed the form of a young girl. Personally, I think she’s gone a bit insane from the lack of new souls entering Hell.”

“At least the two of you have one thing in common,” Lucifer quips.

“I’m in full control of all my faculties, thank you very much,” Helena informs him tersely.

“I’m just glad she isn’t able to leave Hell,” I say in relief. “We don’t have to worry about the two of you running around together and causing trouble.”

“You make me sound like I’m a child,” Helena says, sounding offended by my words.

“Well, if you didn’t act like one,” I reply, “I wouldn’t treat you like one.”

I hear Ava give a single dry laugh. When I look at her, she explains herself.

"I'm sorry, but the two of you *do* sound a lot like sisters, bickering with one another."

"No, we don't," I refute.

"Thank you," Helena replies, choosing to accept Ava's words as a compliment instead.

"What should we do?" Jess asks Lucifer. "Do we just sit around here and wait until noon?"

"It would be pointless to do anything else," he answers with a sigh. "Lucian will stay hidden until the appointed time."

I lean back on the bed pillows. My half-eaten breakfast is still sitting over my lap on the foldout tray.

"I'm sorry, Xavier. I've suddenly lost my appetite. I won't be able to finish the meal you made for me."

Xavier walks over and lifts the tray from my lap.

"It's understandable," he tells me. "Do you need anything else?"

"Just my son," I reply despondently.

"You know I would move Heaven and Earth to get him back for you."

I try to muster up a smile for him. "I know."

Jess slips the letter out of my hand to read it.

"Um, so it only mentions Lucifer and Anna going to the meeting. We're not doing that, right?" she asks. "Surely he knows we wouldn't let you meet him without having back-up present."

"I think we have to abide by his rules," Lucifer says. "If it were me, I wouldn't want to feel like I was being ganged up on."

"I can take care of myself, Jess," I reassure her.

"If he lays one hand on you, kill him," she practically orders. "Don't take any chances. I don't give a rat's ass about his soul. You protect yourself and your babies by any means necessary."

"I will," I promise.

"Since I'm not needed or wanted here," Helena says, looking at us all with complete disdain, "I think I'll take a look around New York City while we wait."

"You need to be back here by noon," I tell her. "As soon as we have Lucas, I want to try to leave this Earth and go back home."

"That's not really up to you, though, is it?" Helena asks, looking pointedly at my belly. "It seems like the twins have all the control."

"I think they'll want to leave," I say confidently.

"Whatever," she shrugs, not seeming to care one way or the other. "I'll be back later."

After Helena phases, I breathe a sigh of relief and look at Xavier. "I need you to wrap this sword up for me," I tell him. "Thankfully Helena didn't notice it while she was here, but she'll definitely see it if it's not camouflaged in some way when we go back home."

"Let me wrap it up for you," Ava says, walking over to pick up the sword. "I've got a box it will fit into."

"Thank you."

I push the comforter off me and swing my legs over the edge of the mattress.

"You should rest, Anna," Lucifer tells me.

"I've rested enough. I want to go stretch my legs and get some fresh air."

Seeing that I'm not going to take his advice, my father walks over and bends down to slip my shoes back onto my feet for me. He then lends me a hand to help me stand up. When he tries to pull his hand away from mine, I tighten my grip so as to prevent him from leaving my side.

"I would really like it if you and I could take a walk together," I tell him. "We haven't had time to talk since your return."

Lucifer smiles. "I would like that very much."

"Ok, the two of you together are just too cute," Jess says, smiling at us. "Go have your father-daughter time. Who knows if you'll get another chance once we return to our Earth? I'm not sure how long God will let us stay there once we get back home."

Lucifer phases us out to the front of the castle. The sun is so bright I automatically shade my eyes with a hand. When I chance a glance up at the sky, I see that it's a beautiful deep blue color with puffy white clouds drifting on a light breeze. The ambient temperature here on this Earth is so much cooler than it is on our own. I take a deep breath of the clean, crisp air to clear my lungs and calm my troubled mind.

Lucifer keeps hold of my hand as we begin to walk around the island.

"Your mother wanted me to tell you how much she loves you," my dad says.

I smile. "She just saw me not that long ago."

"I know, but she's your mother. She'll never get tired of telling you how much she loves you. Neither will I, even though I might not say it as often or in so many words. I'm still getting accustomed to 'using my words', as your mother puts it."

"You came back to help me. That tells me more than any words could about how much you love me."

"I still can't believe Jess kept me in the dark about what was going on with you before she and Mason left Heaven."

"She didn't want you to jeopardize your soul by going back to Hell," I say. "Honestly, I wouldn't have told you either. You shouldn't have taken the risk, but I'm glad you did. I've missed you."

"I've missed you, too."

We walk in a comfortable silence for a moment before I ask, "Does it feel odd to be back on Earth? I know when I go to Heaven I don't feel like I belong there."

"I have to admit it does feel strange, but it's also very familiar. I don't think I could live on Earth full time again, but it would be nice to come back and visit every once in a while. Maybe I can talk my Father into letting me do that on special occasions."

I feel a slight twinge in my lower abdomen and have to stop walking. Lucifer holds my hand as I feel a contraction begin. I concentrate on my breathing until it subsides. It's the first one I've felt since the doctor injected me with the medicine the night before.

"Do you need to go back in?" Lucifer asks worriedly. "Have you taken any of the medication the doctor gave you today?"

"I forgot to take it this morning," I confess. "I'm all right. I'll take a dose of it when we go back inside. I would rather keep walking for a little while longer. The movement seems to ease the ache in my lower back."

"Do you want me to neuter your husband when we return home so he doesn't put you in this condition again?" Lucifer asks a little too eagerly.

I just laugh. "Absolutely not. I like my husband with all of his parts firmly attached to his body and functional."

"Ugh… I'm already sorry I asked the question."

"Will you ever be able to accept Malcolm as my husband?"

"Oh, I accept him," Lucifer assures me. "I actually have more admiration for him now than I did while I was alive, but don't you dare tell him that. I will deny I ever said it. I don't want to add to his already-over-inflated ego."

"Malcolm came to Hell to get us," I remind him. "You know how hard that was for him to do."

"I'm aware. I remember what being there was like for him the last time. I may never like Malcolm, just because I'm hardwired not to, but I do respect him, especially when it comes to his love for you and for his family and friends."

I feel another twinge occur, but this time it's even more painful.

"That's it. You're going back inside," Lucifer says. Before I can even think about arguing, he phases us back to Xavier's bedroom.

After my dad helps me back into bed he seeks Xavier out, since he's the one who knows where my medicine is located. Everyone comes back up to the room while Xavier administers another dose of the treatment Marie gave me to slow my labor. When fifteen minutes pass and the contractions don't stop, Ava leaves to find the doctor again. Within a few short seconds, the doctor is standing at my bedside. She shoos everyone but Jess out of the room so she can do a quick examination of me.

"I'm sorry," Marie tells me, "but your babies want to come out, Anna. I thought the medicine I gave you would buy you some time, but whatever you were given is something I've never seen before. Without knowing exactly what chemicals were introduced into your system, I'm afraid I can't do anything but help you deliver these babies."

I shake my head resolutely. "I refuse to have them until I'm back home."

"Then I suggest you leave as soon as possible because, considering how far along your dilation is, they'll be coming within the next hour."

I look over at the clock on the wall and see that it's close to twelve. I just need to make it a little while longer. As soon as we have Lucas, I'm sure the babies will take us back home.

"Thank you for coming," I tell her. "But I don't think we'll need you here anymore. I'll have my own doctor deliver the babies when I get home."

"Do you want some medication to dull the pain?"

"Will it affect me in any way?"

"It may make you drowsy."

"Then, no. I need to be able to think. I appreciate everything you've done for me, doctor. I'm sure Ava can take you back to where you were before she brought you here."

"Well, if your circumstances change, don't hesitate to have Ava come and get me." Marie stands from her seat on the bed and heads for the bedroom door as she says, "I wish you the best of luck, Anna."

"Thank you," I grimace as another contraction strikes.

After she leaves the room, Xavier and Lucifer walk back in to learn what the doctor had to say.

“I don’t see how you can go to the meeting while you’re in the middle of labor,” my father declares, clearly showing his anxiety over the matter.

“I have no choice,” I try to explain. “Lucas is depending on his mother to rescue him. I won’t let him down, not even if I have to drag myself there on my hands and knees.”

“Maybe we can use this situation to our advantage,” Xavier suggests. “If we explain what’s happening, Lucian might be more willing to let me stay with you. I have to phase you there anyway. We can just say that my presence is required in case you need to be rushed to the hospital.”

“That might actually work,” Lucifer agrees. “It won’t hurt to try, and I would feel better having you there with us in case things do go south.”

“We need to get going,” I say, attempting to stand up on my own, but finding the task difficult given my current condition.

Both Xavier and Lucifer come to help me stand up. They each grab one of my arms, making me feel like an invalid. However, I don’t complain about their assistance. I need all the help I can get at the moment.

“Are you ready?” Xavier asks, unable to stop himself from looking concerned over my welfare.

I nod. “Yes. Let’s go get my son.”

“Good luck,” I hear Jess say behind me.

With both men still holding me up with gentle hands on my arms, Xavier phases us to the rendezvous point: Lucian’s apartments in New York City. I faintly register all the glass and steel in the room, but I immediately focus all of my attention on Lucian, who is holding one of my son’s arms in a tight grip and keeping him firmly by his side.

"Mommy!" Lucas says excitedly when he sees me. He attempts to tug his arm out of Lucian's hold, but all that does is make him tighten his grasp on Lucas.

"Don't you dare hurt him," I warn, on the verge of losing the little bit of self-control I have left that's preventing me from rushing over to my son.

"I won't as long as he behaves himself," Lucian replies curtly. "All I want to do is talk to you."

I look at Lucas and try to give him a reassuring smile, hoping it doesn't look like a grimace instead. "He won't hurt you. Just stay put and we'll be able to go home soon."

"Ok," Lucas says reluctantly, visibly relaxing a little bit after my promise. He knows I would never lie to him.

I return my attention to Lucian. In any other circumstance, I would have considered the body Lucian inhabits to be handsome. With his tanned skin and finely chiseled facial features, he reminds me of the men who live in Bianca's cloud city of Alto above South America.

Lucian narrows his eyes as he takes in my appearance. "Are you in labor?"

"Yes, she is," Xavier answers for me. "And I need to stay here in case she needs to go to the hospital quickly."

"Whatever," Lucian says off-handedly. "I don't care if you stay, Xavier."

"What do you want, Lucian?" my dad asks, unable to hide his irritation at the whole situation. "As you can see, we don't have a lot of time for small talk. What will it take for you to let the boy go so we can leave?"

"I want to know if it's true," Lucian says to Lucifer. "Have you been redeemed by our Father?"

"Yes," Lucifer says simply. "Can we go now?"

"But how?" Lucian inquires, looking mystified by my father's answer. "How were you able to ask for forgiveness and truly mean it? I just don't understand how you could humble yourself in front of Him after everything you've done in the Origin."

"It's not like my redemption happened overnight," Lucifer replies impatiently. "I found my soul mate and had Anna. My wife and my daughter helped me learn how to love again. The explanation is that simple. If you hadn't killed Seraphina during your war, it might have happened to you, too, but I guess we'll never know."

"No, we won't," Lucian agrees. "Even if I had left her alive, I don't think I could act as weak as you. To be the original, you sure act like a pathetic copy."

"It takes strength to admit when you're wrong," I tell Lucian, trying to make him grasp what he refuses to understand. "That's what my father learned in the end, but I think you're a little too pigheaded to do something so noble."

Lucas whimpers slightly as Lucian tightens his hold on my son's arm.

"Don't hurt him!" I order vehemently. "You said you wouldn't if we came here to talk to you!"

"And what exactly are you going to do to me if I do?" Lucian asks snidely. "None of you brought weapons. Although, I'm sure my counterpart can probably conjure up his sword if he needs it. I doubt our Father sent you back to Earth defenseless."

"No, He most certainly did not," Lucifer states. "Let the boy go, Lucian. He hasn't done anything to you."

"Hasn't done anything to me?" He asks, a crazed look in his eyes. "He ruined my party! I should snap his fragile little neck and end his life again for what he did."

"What are you talking about?" my son asks, looking at Lucian in bewilderment. "Why do you keep saying things about me being here before?"

"He's crazy, Lucas," I say, in an attempt to deflect Lucian's anger away from him. "Don't listen to anything he says. He's a liar."

"Well, if that isn't the pot calling the kettle black, I don't know what is," Lucian says spitefully. "Who is lying to whom exactly? I'm willing to tell the boy the truth. If you're supposed to be his mother, then you should stop lying to him about who he really is."

I let out a gasp in pain as another contraction begins. However, this time my water breaks, spilling clear amniotic fluid all over Lucian's white-tiled floor.

"Eh," he says in disgust, "thanks for the mess I'll have to clean up later."

"Mommy, are you ok?" Lucas asks. I truly love my son. Even when he's the one in mortal danger, he worries about me instead of himself.

"I'm fine, sweetie," I reassure him before he tries to run over to me again. "The babies just want to come a little earlier than I want them to, but we'll all be okay."

"So I guess you're all just one big *happy* family," Lucian sneers. "How wonderful for you."

"Jealousy isn't a very attractive look for you, Lucian," Xavier chides. "If I were you, I would just let them go back to their Earth. All you're doing here is torturing yourself because you'll never be able to ask for forgiveness and mean it."

"I don't need forgiveness!" He roughly pushes Lucas forward onto the floor, finally letting go of his arm. "All I need is revenge."

Lucian phases and I instantly feel his hand underneath my chin.

I don't think.

I simply react on a primal level, knowing that if I don't do something, he will snap my neck and end not only my life but also the lives of my children. I'm faintly aware of Lucifer calling his black sword to his hand and of Xavier turning to face Lucian as he stands directly behind me.

In less time than it takes to blink, I wrench my arms out of my protectors' hold and call upon a power only I possess: the ability to end an archangel's life. Within the short window of time I have to make a decision, I know I don't have any other choice. I never wanted it to come down to this, but Lucian has forced my hand. I have to wonder if there is some small part of him that knew this was the way things would play out if he attacked me. I remember my promise to Lucifer that I would do my best not to take Lucian's life and exile him to the Void for all eternity, but I also made a promise to Jess that I would do whatever it took to keep myself and my babies safe.

With our only point of contact being his hand beneath my chin, I unleash my power, instantly reducing Lucian to a pile of black ash behind me. I hear both Xavier and Lucifer let out gasps of surprise. I'm not sure if they're truly shocked by what I did or if it's an involuntary reaction on their part. I feel no guilt over what just happened. As far as I'm concerned Lucian deserved what he got, not only for threatening me but also the lives of my unborn children.

As another contraction begins, I end up doubled over by the pain and say, "We need to go! I refuse to have these babies on this Earth."

Lucas runs over to us and takes hold of my father's hand.

"Let's get my mom home," he says.

We immediately phase back to the living room in Boldt Castle, leaving what remains of this Earth's Lucifer on the floor of his apartment.

Ava, Jess, and Helena are waiting in the room for us.

"Oh, thank goodness," Jess says, walking over to Lucas and kneeling to give him a fierce hug. "We were so worried about you, Lucas."

"I'm okay," he says, returning her hug. "But we need to go back home so my mom can have the babies."

Jess stands up to look between Lucifer and me. "So Lucian didn't give you any trouble?"

"He's dead," my father informs her quickly. "He won't be hurting anyone again. We need to go, Jess. Anna needs to have these babies back home."

Xavier gives me a quick hug. "I'm grateful I was given the chance to meet you," he says to me. "Tell Malcolm I think he's a lucky man and to take care of you."

"I will," I promise as he lets me go.

Ava hands Jess a long brown box without saying a word about what's inside it.

"I wish you all a safe trip home," she tells us as we all reach for each other.

"Well, I can't say it hasn't been an interesting visit, but I'm ready to go back to our own problems," Helena says, coming to stand with us. "I just hope the babies aren't too preoccupied with being born to open the vortex for us."

I grab one of her hands to complete our connection.

As if they heard her statement, which they probably did, the twins kick me hard in unison and the lavender vortex of stars reappears above my head. With my free hand, I reach up to touch the brightest one, which seems to be calling me home.

As we travel back to our own Earth, I pray to God that we don't ever have to venture this way ever again. The pain is excruciating, to say the least.

I end up finding myself lying flat on my back in a grassy field, groaning in pain.

A cool hand rests on my brow. "There, there, sister. I'm here for you."

I open my eyes and see Helena's smiling face hovering only inches above mine. I've never seen her look so peaceful.

The sweltering heat surrounding us practically suffocates me, but it's a clear indication that we are definitely back on our own Earth. With the midday sun high in the sky, I feel as though my skin is being roasted slowly. I hastily take in our surroundings and see that we're in the same place Jess, Lucifer, and I were deposited on alternate Earth: the park at the center of New York City. It's where Cirrus is situated above, but the usual white mist from my cloud city's propulsion system is nowhere to be seen. In fact, I don't see my home in the sky at all.

"Where is Cirrus?" I ask as I continue to stare up at the sky.

"Oh, yes, that," Helena says, as if I've reminded her about something. She glances skyward and says, "I'm afraid those pesky rebellion angels tore it from the sky out of spite. I'm sure it's sitting safely at the bottom of the Atlantic Ocean by now."

"What?" I say, feeling my heart sink at the thought of my beautiful city and home forever lost to me.

A severe contraction causes me to cry out in pain, temporarily causing me to forget about Cirrus' fate.

"Oh, you poor thing," Helena croons, attempting to sound sympathetic about the pain I'm experiencing, but she can't hide the underlying happiness I hear in her voice.

"You need to get me to a doctor, Helena," I practically beg, desperately trying to reach any shred of decency she might possess.

"Oh, I'm sorry, but I'm afraid I can't risk taking you anywhere just yet."

Frantically I turn my head from side to side, searching for Jess, Lucifer, and Lucas.

"Where are the others?" I ask.

"I have no idea," Helena replies with a small shrug of her shoulders. "I'm afraid it's just the two of us, dear sister. But don't you worry your pretty little head. I won't let anything happen to your babies."

Helena crawls over to my feet, grabs my ankles, and bends my legs up. She lifts the hem of my dress and lays it over my raised knees.

Unceremoniously, she rips my underwear away with more physical strength than I thought she possessed.

"I see the top of a head, sister!" Helena says with glee. "I had no idea you were this close to giving birth. How exciting!"

I have another strong contraction and automatically begin to push.

"That's it. Keep pushing," she urges excitedly. "The little head is almost out now. Don't stop!"

When the next contraction comes, I try to resist the urge to push but can't seem to. My body feels like it's acting of its own accord. I scream out in pain as I feel the baby slip out of my body.

I sigh with relief when I hear Liana's sweet cry as she takes in her very first breath. I have no doubt it's Liana because every descendant has had a female child as her first born.

"Is she all right?" I ask anxiously, lowering my legs so I can see my baby.

"Yes," Helena says, picking Liana up from the ground and cradling her in her arms. "She's absolute perfection."

I feel another strong contraction and know that Liam is ready to come into the world to join his sister.

"Liam is coming, Helena," I warn.

I watch in confusion as Helena stands to her feet, cradling Liana in her arms. The possessive way she looks at my daughter sends an icy dagger of panic straight through my heart.

Helena looks down at me and smiles. "I have no need for your son. I already have my prize… your first-born child."

"No!" I cry, holding out my arms. "Give her to me, Helena. You can't have her!"

"I'm sorry, sister, but you're the one who forfeited the game when you transported us to alternate Earth. Liana is mine by right."

Without allowing me to argue for my daughter's life, Helena phases straight to Hell, taking Liana with her.

I feel as though Helena has just ripped my rapidly-beating heart out of my chest with her bare hands as I dissolve into inconsolable tears. I attempt to phase and follow her, even though I'm in no condition to fight anyone for anything, but even with just Liam left inside my womb I'm unable to work that simple miracle.

All I can do as my heart breaks is scream, "Malcolm!"

CHAPTER TWENTY

(Malcolm's Point of View)

When the pain from my guilt instantly vanishes, I know something is very wrong in Hell. Helena wouldn't ease my suffering unless she had something even worse planned. Cautiously I stand to my feet, wondering what to expect from her next. Slade and Jered also rise, warily looking around us, assuming the worst just like me.

"What's happening?" Mason asks as the thick fog which has hampered our search for Anna and Lucas begins to dissipate. It's almost like it's being sucked away by some unseen force.

"I'm not sure," I admit as I take in our surroundings.

With the fog gone, I can see the children of the Watchers who have been hampering our search for the castle with their random attacks and taunting howls. There are ten of them, standing in random positions around us. Those who were close to us scurry away from our location before they all begin to transform back into their human forms.

"Something is definitely wrong here," Jered says as he and Slade come to stand with Mason and me. "Do you feel it?"

I look away from the Watcher children to Jered. "I'm not sure I feel anything."

"Exactly," he says, as if I've confirmed his suspicion. "This place is normally filled with an oppressive hate. Now, it feels empty of it."

"He's right," Slade confirms. "It's never felt so peaceful here."

Jered looks around us until his gaze finds Silas. His son stands fully naked in his human form, only twenty feet away. His brooding hazel eyes are filled with a deep-set animosity as he stares back at his father. It's been a very long time since I last saw Jered's son. I'd almost forgotten how much he favors his dad.

"Silas!" Jered calls out. "What's happening here?"

Silas stands motionless, just staring at his father as if he doesn't intend to answer, but finally he does.

"I don't know," he replies, his bitterness towards Jered not forgotten but at least pushed aside for the moment. "If I didn't know any better, I would say Helena is dead."

"What makes you say that?" I immediately ask, wondering if Anna has found a way to end Helena's life and free us all from her ruthlessness.

"My connection to her has been broken. I can't feel her anymore," Silas replies, clearly confused by what he senses. "That's the best way I can describe it."

Now that the fog has dissipated, I can clearly see the black castle in the far distance where Anna is supposed to be trapped. Not only do I see the castle, but I also see where Helena sent the War Angels when she separated them from us.

"Am I hallucinating, or do the War Angels have wings on their backs?" I ask those around me. The War Angels are embroiled in aerial combat with creatures that look angelic in form, with wings of their own, but I'm sure they are minions of Hell.

"You're not seeing things. They do have wings for some reason," Mason replies, confirming that my eyes aren't just playing tricks on me.

"Whatever is happening here," Slade says, "I suggest we take advantage of it and get to the castle before everything has a chance to change back."

We start to run across the hard-packed earth towards the castle, but I instantly notice Jered isn't following us. I stop to look behind me, and see him standing motionless as he continues to stare at his only child. I can tell he wants to go to Silas, but his window of opportunity is suddenly lost when the other Watcher children surround his son, urging him to follow them into the darkness, away from us.

"Jered!" I call out to gain his attention.

With Silas lost to him again, Jered seems to come back to his senses and begins to run after us. We travel as far as we can until we come to a large chasm that separates us from the castle. As I look over the ragged edge into the depths of the gorge, all I see is darkness.

There's no way for us to cross over to help the War Angels with their fight, but I'm not sure we could have aided them much anyway. Without having wings, we can't join the battle.

I hear a ferocious growl come from close by. We all turn around and see a pack of at least forty hellhounds standing behind us. Unfortunately, they're not alone. Hellspawn stand directly behind them, as far as the eye can see. We're already on the edge of the chasm. There's nowhere for us to go.

"Need a ride?" I hear above me.

When I look up, I see Ethan, Roan, Xander, and Alex swooping down towards us. Just as the hellhounds begin to charge forward, the War Angels lift us up and fly us across the chasm. As we reach the castle side of the ravine, the purple barrier protecting it disappears, as do the wings on the War Angels and Helena's minions. We all end up tumbling out of the air onto the ground directly in front of the castle.

"I actually kind of liked the wings," Ethan grumbles disappointedly, grabbing his black and gold sword up from the ground as he stands.

We all pick up our weapons and join the fray on the stone steps of the castle to help the other War Angels. Now that no one has wings, including Helena's creatures, we're able to help. I have to restrain myself from just running into the palace to begin my search for Anna and Lucas. I know they wouldn't want me to leave the middle of a fight just for them. Thankfully, we're able to win the battle swiftly and make it inside the castle to seek out my family.

None of us waste any time after we enter Helena's dark replica of our home in Cirrus. I head straight up the grand staircase. I'm faintly aware of Ethan giving orders about where the others should start their search. I run from room to room, shouting Anna and Lucas' names, but there's no response. The castle feels empty, and I fear that's exactly what it is. Just as Hell feels empty of Helena, this castle feels empty of my family.

As I run down a long hallway, checking every room. I hear a soft yelp come from down the corridor. When I look, I see Luna running straight towards me.

I bend down on one knee when she reaches my location.

"How did you get here, girl?" I ask, but I don't expect to get an answer from her. She may be a creature of Hell, but she wasn't given the power to speak like a human. I assume Lucifer probably brought her here to help search for Anna and Lucas. Perhaps that's why she kept pawing at me before we left to come down here. If I had been thinking straight at the time, I might have figured out her non-verbal communication.

"Something's not right here, Malcolm," Cade says as he walks down the hallway towards me. "It's like they just disappeared."

"Do you think Helena phased them somewhere?" I ask, standing back up.

Cade shakes his head.

"I don't think it's that simple," he tells me grimly. "There's an emptiness to this place, and I'm not just talking about the inside of this castle. Hell doesn't feel like it did when we first entered. Can't you feel the difference?"

"Yes," I sigh. "I know what you're talking about. We all feel it, but I don't understand what it means. Do you?" I ask, hoping Cade's connection to Helena lends him a unique perspective to what's happening that the rest of us don't have access to.

"If I didn't know any better," he begins, "I would say Helena has disappeared from existence, but that doesn't make any sense."

"No, it doesn't," I agree. "Yet that's exactly what it feels like."

"I found Luna standing alone in an odd-looking bedroom at the other end of the hallway," Cade informs me. "Considering what I saw inside of it, I think it's where Helena was keeping Anna and Lucas."

"Show me," I tell him.

Cade touches my shoulder and phases Luna and me to a room that does look decidedly strange. I can well imagine Helena choosing the furnishings and decor with her morbid taste for all things dark. I immediately notice the two baby cribs on either wall, across from the large four-poster bed in the room. I also notice the small, round dining table with three dirty plates still set on top of it. My eyes are instantly drawn to the solitary window in the room, with Anna's chair sitting in front of it. I walk over and run my right hand along the top of its wooden frame.

I need my wife back. I can't even take in a real breath without her near.

I feel like my entire existence has been a series of trials. Some I passed by sheer luck or cunning, but most of them I failed miserably either due to my own ego or stubbornness. Anna has centered me like no other person ever has in my life, not even Lilly. I know in my heart that I will find her, because my life has no meaning without her and our children being in it.

Other than the remnants of food left on the table, there are no additional signs that Anna and Lucas stayed here.

"What do we do now?" Cade asks me.

"I don't know," I say, feeling adrift without a specific goal to reach anymore. "Staying here seems pointless, though. It's obvious they're somewhere else, but I don't even know where to start searching for them."

"I don't either."

I turn to look at Cade. "Before Helena left us, she said Lucifer was here. Somehow he and Jess made it to Anna and Lucas."

"We didn't see them," he replies, looking thoughtful about this new piece of information, "but I'm sure there are multiple entrances into this place. They must have found a way in from the back side of the castle."

"Since they obviously had Luna with them, maybe she found a way in," I reason. "What bothers me is that if Lucifer is still with them, he would have found a way to notify us where they are by now."

"What do you think it means that he hasn't?"

"I don't know. I don't know anything at this point."

"We should probably regroup and discuss things with everyone else."

Cade and I return to the entrance of the castle to rejoin the others. As soon as we all phase back to the living room in my New Orleans home, I'm surprised to see an unexpected visitor standing there waiting for us.

"Father?" I ask. God ceases his conversation with Desmond and Andre to turn around and face me. "What are you doing here?"

I instantly assume that His presence doesn't bode well for Anna and Lucas' safety.

"Your family is fine, Malcolm," my Father reassures me, instantly allaying my fears. "Jess and Lucifer are looking after them. I wanted to come here in person and tell you that before your imagination begins to cause you worry unnecessarily."

"Then where are they?" I plead, walking over to stand in front of Him.

"They needed to go somewhere before they could return to you."

"Don't do that to me!" I bellow at Him out of frustration. "Stop talking in riddles and just tell me where they are! For once, Father, tell me what I need to know!"

I can feel the others around me physically tense up after my heated outburst towards my Father. Only God remains relaxed in the face of my open resentment. I know I should apologize, but I can't bring myself to do it. I need to know where my family is, and I'm not in any mood to play His games.

"They're on alternate Earth," my Father tells me unexpectedly. I'm shocked not only by His words, but also because He gave me a real answer.

"Alternate Earth?" Mason asks, as if needing confirmation that he heard our Father correctly. When God nods in response to his question, Mason says, "Why in the world would You send them there? Didn't Jess suffer enough the last time she went?"

"There were things that needed to be done there," He tells us, returning to His cryptic form of answering direct questions. "But rest assured, they will all be coming back to this Earth. I came here to alleviate any fears you have concerning their safety and current whereabouts, especially you, Malcolm. You've been through enough lately, and I believe Anna would be very vexed with Me if I let you suffer any more than you already have."

"Since You're in the mood to give real answers," I say, hoping my Father's openness continues, "did Anna really walk away from me after she saw what I almost did to Sebastian, or was that one of Helena's tricks?"

God doesn't say anything right away. He seems to be weighing His response to my question.

"What does your heart tell you?" he asks. "If you listen to it, you already know the answer to that question without Me having to say it."

I sigh in relief, because I don't believe Anna would turn her back on me. Instead, she would have taken me in her arms and helped me cope with reliving such a terrible moment from my past.

"Thank you," I tell my Father.

"You're welcome." God smiles at me. "She loves you just as much as you love her. If there were ever two souls meant to be together, it's yours and Anna's. She will return to you, Malcolm. You just need to be patient a little while longer."

"Can you tell me how long I'll have to wait? When will I know she's back on our Earth?" I ask urgently.

"You will be the first person to know when that occurs. All I can say is that you won't have to wait much longer. Have a little more patience, My son."

"You know that really isn't my strong suit."

My Father's smile grows wider. "I'm acutely aware of that fact."

Vala walks over to Luna and me.

"I'm glad to see you made it back unharmed, Luna," she tells her.

Once Vala gets close enough, Luna nuzzles her snout against hers.

"When Lucifer came here to ask if he could borrow Luna," Vala tells me, "I didn't think you would mind."

"No, I didn't mind," I assure her. "I wish I had thought to do it, but I'm glad she helped him find her."

Brutus phases into the room.

"Where are Anna and Lucas?" he asks, looking around the room at all of us. He rightly assumes we wouldn't have left Hell unless we had them with us.

"According to our Father, they're on alternate Earth," I tell him.

"What in the world are they doing there?" he asks, thrown for a loop by my answer.

"We're not sure yet," I tell him, briefly glancing in our Father's direction.

"Ahh," Brutus replies, understanding God's penchant for not answering our questions most of the time. Though, He's been exceedingly helpful in this situation. It was more than I could have ever hoped from Him.

"Are the rumors about Cirrus true?" Andre asks Brutus, changing the subject.

"Yes," he replies, looking dejected to have to give his answer. "I'm afraid they are."

"What rumors?" I ask. "What are you talking about?"

Brutus looks over at Desmond and Andre, as if asking if he should answer my question.

"We were informed that Cirrus is lying at the bottom of the Atlantic Ocean," Andre tells me. "Brutus went to confirm that what we were told is true."

"Let me guess," I say. "The rebellion angels did it?"

"That's what we think," Desmond tells me. "No one else would be foolish enough to go there with so many hellspawn roaming around."

"I can report one good thing," Brutus says. "The force-field that surrounds Cirrus is still in place. Apparently, they didn't think about disabling it. Besides a few collapsed buildings, it looks like the majority of the city is still intact. Of course, my perspective was limited since I had to view it from a shuttle in the air. I don't think any of us can actually phase inside. Unless one of you has been swimming in that particular spot in the Atlantic, none of us can phase into Cirrus."

"What about the teleporters?" I ask, knowing that Cirrus has various public ones stationed around the city. "Are they still operational?"

"No," Brutus answers. "Everything is offline in Cirrus. Not even the personal transporters will work until everything is brought back online."

"I will take you there," God offers, once again dumbfounding me with His helpfulness.

He looks at me and grins. “I do have my moments, Malcolm. I’m not always the curmudgeon you all make Me out to be.”

“I’m not complaining, Father,” I say, holding up my hands. “I’m just surprised is all.”

And who could blame me for being amazed? This was the most helpful my Father had been to any of us in years. All I could assume was that He felt extremely sorry for me. I would take what I could get, no matter the reason.

I turn to my fellow angels and say, “The force-field around the city should hold until we can repair the propulsion system and get Cirrus back into the air. We should go there and start work on it now. Maybe we can get it back into the sky before Anna comes home.”

I’m just thankful to have a new project to work on to keep my mind busy until Anna and Lucas return.

“We’ll go with you to watch your back,” Ethan tells me, speaking for his brother War Angels.

“I’m going, too,” Andre says.

“Count me in” Desmond volunteers.

“I wish I could go with you all,” Brutus says regretfully, “but I need to take care of a problem that’s cropped up with the Cirrun refugees.”

“What problem?” I ask. “Do you need my help?”

“I can handle it,” Brutus assures me. “Levi is trying to buy Catherine some votes by offering to house people in Nimbo. I’ve basically told those considering his offer that if they go, they will temporarily lose their Cirrun citizenship and will have to reapply for it after the election takes place.”

"That should certainly make them think twice before abandoning their own city," Desmond says.

"It's brilliant, Brutus," I praise. "I'll leave things in your hands for now. I don't think I'll be able to think straight until my family is back home anyway."

"Then go repair Cirrus and busy your mind with that for a while," Brutus tells me. "I've got things handled here."

I turn to my Father. "We're ready when You are."

God phases us all to the castle in Cirrus. I'm thankful my Father phased us to the balcony just outside my chambers. The vantage point from here allows us to assess the damage done to the city. I already expected to have to face a ruined metropolis with hellspawn roaming all over it, but what I didn't expect to find was beauty.

The only light to see by comes from the few fires that seem to be contained within the city. As Brutus told us, the force-field is keeping the ocean waters at bay, at least for the time being. When I look up, I see dolphins pecking at the shield out of curiosity and fish swimming over it, as if it's just another obstacle that they have to navigate around. When a pod of whales pass by, one of their tails hits the force-field, causing it to glow green momentarily from the impact.

"We need to get the propulsion system back online as quickly as possible," I say to the others. "There's no way of knowing what kind of damage might have been done to the force- field generator. If that goes out, the whole city will be lost. The marine life isn't exactly helping matters either if they keep testing its strength like that."

I turn to my Father and say, "Thank You for coming to me and letting me know where they are. You know how much I appreciate You doing that."

"As I said, I couldn't allow you to suffer through wondering what had become of them. Have faith that things will work out the way they should, Malcolm. They almost always do." God turns to look at the War Angels. "For My last bit of helpful advice, I want to also tell you that the fissures between Hell and Earth have been sealed. When Helena left, the energy keeping them open also disappeared."

"Does that mean we can get rid of the hellspawn in the city?" Ethan asks eagerly.

"Yes," God answers. "No more of them can come here. Helena's promise that two hellspawn would replace every one you kill can no longer be fulfilled. I suggest you get to work and start clearing out the ones roaming the city."

"That's the best news I've heard in a very long time," Gideon says with a smile as he happily spins his Warhammer in his hand.

"Then I will leave you all so you can get to work repairing Anna's city for her."

God phases away.

"I don't know about the rest of you," I say to my angelic brethren, "but I'm ready to get these things the hell out of my city."

I lead the way out of the castle, which is conspicuously empty of hellspawn. Once we reach the castle's exterior, we're met by a horde of the stinky beasts. We immediately begin to blaze a path through their numbers to reach the area beneath the city where the propulsion system is housed. It takes us a while to kill our way down there, but once we're below street level, the hellspawn stop pursuing us. The only reason I can come up with to explain their odd behavior is that Helena gave them specific orders to leave certain areas of the city alone.

Ethan and the other War Angels stay topside to clear out the rest of the hellspawn while Desmond, Andre, and I begin making repairs to the propulsion system. I hope to have things repaired by the time Anna and Lucas return home. I want to be able to give my wife her city back. I focus all of my energy on that one goal and let everything else fall to the wayside.

Hours pass while we work. I don't even attempt to keep track of time. I know if I do it will drive me crazy. I let the physical labor of repairing the propulsions consume my thoughts so I don't dwell on what's happening to Anna and Lucas on alternate Earth. It's a place I've tried my best to forget, but, for whatever reason, I'm constantly reminded of it. Having my son there worries me. Will someone who was alive during the Apocalypse say something to cause memories from his life as Gabe to resurface? Ever since I learned that Lucas was Gabe reincarnated, I've done everything I can not to mention alternate Earth in his presence. I assumed that the less he knew about that place the better. Was I wrong to keep the information from him? Even knowing what I do now, I still don't believe I should have told him anything. Gabe came back to Earth to have a second chance at a new life with JoJo. I didn't want to do anything to jeopardize their future together or their happiness.

"I think we're almost finished," Andre says, wiping the sweat from his brow as he leans back from the control panel he's been working on for the past few hours.

"You might need to take a break, old man," Desmond teases. "You're not as young or as angelic as you used to be."

"Ha ha," Andre retorts. "Your jealousy is showing, Desmond. Maybe you should just give up on finding your soul mate and join me in the human race."

"I've waited this long. I think I'll wait a little while longer before throwing in the towel," Desmond says, replacing the panel over the oxygen system he was working on. He walks over to a set of controls and begins to bring the system back online. "Here goes nothing."

A few seconds later, a gust of fresh air fills the room.

"It's about time," Atticus complains as he, the other War Angels, and Slade come to join us in the engineering room. He inhales deeply, relishing the fresh, clean air. "It smells like dead fish in this city."

"It's because the hellspawn were inside it for so long," Slade tells him. "They're not the most hygienic of creatures."

I stand away from my work area and let myself enjoy the fresh air, too. It's grown increasingly stuffy where we are because the system that circulates the air in the city was knocked offline. I have to agree with Atticus' assessment: Cirrus was beginning to smell like dead fish.

"I never thought…" I begin before I feel overwhelming, unimaginable grief strike my soul.

"Anna…" I whisper just as the connection between our souls tells me exactly where I need to phase to find her.

When I arrive, I find Anna lying on the ground in the center of Central Park in New York City. The bottom half of her dress is soaked with blood.

She's sobbing uncontrollably as I immediately fall to my knees on the ground beside her.

"She has her!" Anna screams at me between sobs. "Helena took Liana to Hell!"

Everyone who was with me in Cirrus phases in behind me, having followed my phase trail.

"Go get our daughter, Malcolm!" Anna orders hysterically.

Knowing Anna will be in good hands if I leave, I try to phase down to Hell, but instantly find that Helena has closed the doors to her domain once again.

"She won't let me phase there," I tell Anna distraughtly, not knowing what else to do.

"I'll go," I hear Cade say behind me. "She'll let me in."

Anna looks behind me with fire in her eyes. "Get my daughter *back*, Cade. I don't care what you have to do. Just bring her back to me!"

"The next time you see me, I'll have her," Cade promises before phasing.

I look back at this phase trail and see that Helena has indeed let her soul mate join her in Hell.

Anna screams out in pain as she experiences a contraction. I instantly pick her up and phase us to our bedroom in New Orleans.

Desmond phases in with Andre, but the others wisely don't follow.

"Desmond," Anna pants, "Liam is coming."

"Get the things we need for the babe, Andre," Desmond says as he comes around to Anna's side of the bed and sits down to lift the hem of her skirt so he can get a better look at the situation.

Andre rushes out of the room to get the necessary supplies.

Anna grabs one of my hands and squeezes hard. When I look into her eyes, she says, "I'm sorry. I'm so sorry, Malcolm. I couldn't protect her. I couldn't keep Helena from taking our baby."

"Now you listen to me," I tell her, brushing away the long strands of white hair from her sweat-soaked face. "You have nothing to apologize for. You weren't in any condition to prevent Helena from taking her. Cade will bring our daughter back to us. I know he will."

"But what if she won't give her to him?" Anna asks frantically. "What if she tries to keep her?"

"Then we'll find another way to get our baby back," I vow vehemently. "I won't allow her to keep our daughter, Anna. Do you trust me enough to believe that?"

"Yes," she says without hesitation. "You know I do."

"Good," I say, feeling as though I could pry the doors of Hell open with my bare hands as long as she has faith in me. "We *will* get her back. You have my word."

"Well, the two of you are about to have another child in just a minute who will need you, too," Desmond informs us.

When Andre walks back into the bedroom carrying a bowl of water, a knife, and a couple of fresh towels, he isn't alone.

"Mommy?"

I turn to face the doorway to the room and see Lucas standing there with Jess, Lucifer, Vala, and Luna directly behind him.

"Lucas!" Anna cries in a mixture of pain and happiness.

He runs over to us, grabbing me around the hips with one arm and using his other hand to hold onto his mother's outstretched arm. Luna stays close to his side while Vala leaps up onto the other side of the bed to be near Anna.

"Am I finally going to become a brother?" Lucas asks excitedly.

Anna begins to cry even harder at the reminder that Lucas is already a big brother. We just don't have Liana with us to prove it.

I move my son's arm slightly so I can kneel down on one knee and give him a proper hug. He uses both of his arms to squeeze me tightly around the neck.

I kiss one of his cheeks and tell him, "Why don't you crawl up onto the other side of the bed so you can hold onto your mother's hand? I think she needs us both right now."

Lucas runs around me to crawl onto the bed as I instructed. As he sits cross-legged beside Vala, he gently takes Anna's left hand while I take her right one.

"Ok, Anna," Desmond says. "On your next big contraction, I need you to push as hard as you can."

Anna nods that she understands his instructions, but she's unable to speak because the simple act of breathing is taking top priority right now.

"Can you give her something for the pain?" I ask Desmond.

"Afterwards, yes," Desmond replies. "But she's about to have Liam in just a few seconds. One big push, Anna, and you'll have the newest little Devereaux in your arms."

Anna squeezes down on my hand, but I know she isn't using her full strength. Otherwise, she would have ripped my hand off at the wrist. She screams out in pain as she pushes one final time before allowing herself to collapse from exhaustion. When I hear the first cry from my son, it's a bittersweet moment instead of a joyous one. The absence of his sister leaves me feeling hollow inside, and I know our lives won't be complete until she's with us.

After Desmond cuts and ties off the umbilical cord, Andre quickly wipes Liam's face with a wet washcloth and bundles him in one of the white towels he brought in earlier. He then walks over and hands my son to me.

"Congratulation, Malcolm," he says as I take Liam from his arms. Andre leans over Anna and kisses her brow. "You have a healthy baby boy, cherub."

Andre begins to take a step back, but stops abruptly.

I look away from Liam's face to see if something is wrong and notice what's caught his attention.

As I stare at my wife, I watch as her white hair and blue eyes turn back to their natural brown color.

"What's wrong?" Anna asks as she notices we're all staring at her.

"Your hair isn't white anymore," Vala tells her in amazement.

"And your eyes are brown again, too," Lucas says, smiling at his mother's physical transformation.

"I suppose it makes sense," Andre says as he contemplates this new development. "The seals were probably how Helena was able to make a connection to you in the first place. Now that you're not carrying them at all, your connection to her has been broken."

Anna sighs in relief. She's always hated the white hair and blue eyes. She runs the fingers of her right hand through her hair and brings up a handful in front of her face so she can see it for herself. She smiles, but it's a faint one. I know neither of us will be able to feel pure joy over anything until Liana is with us.

When Andre steps fully away, I immediately place Liam in his mother's arms. I hope having at least one of her babies close will ease a small portion of her heartache over Liana's absence.

"He's simply gorgeous, Anna," Vala says, her voice filled with pride and joy.

"But where is Liana?" Lucas asks, innocent of the situation concerning his little sister.

"Cade's bringing her," Anna tells him, attempting unsuccessfully to hide her tears.

"Oh," Lucas replies, as understanding comes into his eyes, "Helena took her, didn't she?"

"Yes," I tell him, seeing no reason to lie about Liana's whereabouts. "But Cade will make Helena give her back to us."

"She won't do it for nothing," Lucas says with certainty. "She's gonna want something in return."

I know Lucas is right. Helena won't just give away her prize without requesting something of equal or greater value to replace it.

I have no idea what she might want, but I know I'll pay whatever price she asks for to get my daughter out of Hell.

CHAPTER TWENTY-ONE

(Cade's Point of View)

I don't have to think very hard to know where Helena has taken Anna and Malcolm's baby. We've all been aware that she's had an unnatural desire to protect the children. We just haven't been able to figure out what it is she wants with them yet. Considering she only took Liana, it's apparent that the little girl was the one she was interested in possessing the most. I'm not sure why. I'm her soul mate, but it doesn't give me the power to read her thoughts or understand her motivations.

When I first came to Earth, I envied the love I saw Anna lavish on Malcolm. It wasn't because I wanted her to treat me the same way. I was jealous of the close connection they seemed to share. I quickly decided that I wouldn't enter into a relationship with anyone unless I felt that kind of love. I was fully aware that Malcolm had to wait thousands of years before Anna was born, but I didn't care. All I wanted was to feel that connected to someone else in my life. I was certain it would be worth the wait as long as I eventually found my soul mate.

When I first saw Helena, I couldn't believe she was the one I was destined to share that bond with. Our souls are nothing alike, yet fate matched them to one another a very long time ago. I'm not sure what God hopes to accomplish by bringing us together, but I have faith He knows what He's doing.

I phase into the bedroom with the cribs, where Helena kept Anna and Lucas. I find Helena there, leaning forward against the front of the crib nearest the window. She's humming Brahms' Lullaby as she watches Liana slumber peacefully.

"I wondered how long it would take Anna to send you to me," Helena says just before she looks up and over at me. "I suppose she wants her baby back."

"You know she does, Helena," I say, slowly making my way to her. "It was wrong of you to take her in the first place."

"I only took what was mine." Helena stands up straight as I come to stand beside her. "Anna lost her to me fair and square."

"We didn't get to finish your little game," I remind her. "How does that automatically make you the winner?"

"Because Anna transported us all to that alternate Earth! She forfeited the game when she did that."

"You make it sound like she knew that would happen," I point out. "Did she?"

"Well, no, but that's not the point."

"As I recall, all you told us was that we had to get into the castle and find Anna. We made it into the castle. It wasn't our fault that none of you were in here."

"Exactly my point! Anna is the one who messed up your chances to win. She also made a mess of my home by taking me away from it."

"Yes. We did notice that things didn't feel the same here while you were gone."

Helena smiles at me coquettishly. "Are you saying you missed me, Cade?"

"This place certainly did," I admit, knowing exactly what she wants me to say, but not giving in so easily. "I'm not here to flirt with you, Helena. I'm here to take Liana back to her parents."

"Admit it," she whispers, resting her right hand against the bare skin directly over my heart. "You missed me, didn't you?"

"You need to give Anna her baby back, Helena," I say. "Or this thing between us ends here and now."

She drops her hand away from me. When I look into her eyes, I see her anger, but I was prepared for her reaction.

"Do you think your threat is supposed to make me bend to your will?" she asks crossly. "I bow down to no one, much less you."

"I'm not asking you to bow down to me," I tell her in a calm voice. "I'm merely stating a fact. I can't be with someone who would keep a baby away from her family. You call Anna your sister, but you're not acting very sisterly at the moment, Helena. If you actually want her to see you like that, you need to give Liana back."

"But I won her fair and square," she replies, as if it's some sort of defense for her actions.

"Do you hear yourself?" I ask her in disbelief. "I mean, seriously, you need to start listening to your own words. How would you react if people talked to you the way you talk to others? If you truly want to be a part of Anna's life, you need to stop acting like a spoiled child, and you need to stop throwing a tantrum every time you don't get your way. Grow up, Helena. Start acting your age."

Helena's mouth puckers and I expect to hear a string of curses gush forth from her mouth, but surprisingly she remains silent except for a loud huff of frustration.

"Let me take Liana back to her mother," I implore. "It's not too late. If you give her back now, Anna may forgive you, but the longer you keep her away from her daughter, the more she will grow to hate you."

"I don't see how she can hate me any more than she already does," Helena scoffs.

"Trust me, she can," I assure her. "Humans are very protective of their young. I know I would hate you if you kept me away from my child."

Helena considers my words before saying, "All right. I'll make a deal with you. That is, if you're willing to give up something in return for Anna's little spawn."

"What kind of deal?" I ask cautiously.

"You can take Anna's baby back to her," she says, "but you have to return here and stay with me until I say you can leave."

"Is that all?"

Helena raises a questioning eyebrow at me. "Isn't that enough?"

I walk over to the crib and lift a slumbering Liana up into my arms. Helena has wrapped her in a pink baby blanket, which I find unsettling and endearing at the same time.

"Is that a yes?" she questions me as I turn to face her.

"Yes," I tell her. "It's a deal."

"You're not even going to fight for terms?" Helena asks, baffled by my simple acceptance of her bargain. "Most people would negotiate for more specific conditions, especially the length of their stay with me."

“I don’t think a time limit really matters, do you?”

She eyes me up and down. “No. I suppose not.”

“I’ll be back in a minute,” I tell her. “You have my word I’ll return to fulfill my end of the agreement.”

“I never thought you wouldn’t.”

I phase back to the living room of Anna and Malcolm’s New Orleans home and find my brother War Angels standing around. When Ethan sees me holding the swaddled baby, he says, “They’re in the bedroom.”

I phase up to the room’s door and knock.

“It’s me,” I say through the door. “I have her.”

Malcolm almost rips the door off its hinges in his rush to open it.

I carefully hand Liana over to Malcolm, and he immediately takes her to Anna, who is lying on the bed as she cradles Liam against her chest. She begins to cry when she sees her daughter, but I know her tears are happy ones this time.

“How did you convince Helena to give her up?” Malcolm asks me as he sits on the side of the bed, holding Liana in the crook of his arms next to her mother.

“I made a deal with her,” I tell them, not wanting to ruin their happy family moment but knowing I can’t lie to them either.

“What kind of deal?” Anna asks warily.

“We made an exchange,” I tell them, still standing just outside the door to their room. I feel like I need to keep my distance, or I’ll end up tainting their joy somehow. That’s the way being Helena’s soul mate makes me feel: tainted. I don’t want to spoil their perfect moment with my imperfection.

"She wants you to stay with her," Anna says, having deduced the terms of Helena's bargain with me all on her own. "For how long?"

"I'm not sure," I reply. "I didn't think it mattered, considering the circumstances."

"No, I suppose it doesn't," Anna agrees with a deep sense of regret.

"This isn't good-bye," I assure her. "I won't let her keep me as her prisoner, and when I see you again I would appreciate it if you didn't tell me any of your plans as far as countering her moves against you go. If I'm in Hell, she'll be privy to all my thoughts, and I don't want to inadvertently let her know what your plans are."

Neither Malcolm nor Anna says anything. I watch as Lucas scrambles off the bed and runs around it towards me. I bend down and hold my arms out to him as he throws his arms around my neck.

"Don't go, Cade," he begs. "Don't leave me. You're my best friend."

"I'm sorry, Lucas," I say, holding back my emotions because I know if I let them show it won't do either of us any good. "I have to do this. It was the only way to make sure Liana could meet her big brother." I gently make Lucas pull away from me. "It's your responsibility to take care of her and Liam now. Do you understand that?"

I almost lose control of my emotions when Lucas begins to cry. He tries his best to put on a brave face but he's only six years old, and the emotions of the young are strong and raw. He nods his head, letting me know he heard my words.

I bring Lucas back into my arms for another hug. I know it won't be the last one because I love him too much to stay away, but I'm certain it will be a while before I can visit him again.

“You take care of yourself,” I tell him. I hug him tightly one more time before I stand up. “Now go say hello to your sister.”

As Lucas walks away from me, I look at Malcolm and Anna once again before I phase to Helena to keep my part of our bargain. The worry I saw in their eyes tells me they’re both concerned about my safety. I can’t say I blame them. I’m not sure how safe I’ll be with Helena either.

I guess we’ll see…

CHAPTER TWENTY-TWO
(Anna's Point of View)

As Malcolm and I helplessly watch Cade phase back to Hell, I feel an emptiness form inside my heart. I'm so thankful to him for his sacrifice, but I feel an enormous sense of guilt that he had to make a deal like that with Helena in order to rescue my daughter from her clutches.

Malcolm looks at me with a worry in his eyes that has nothing to do with Cade going to Helena.

"What?" I ask him, seeking an explanation.

He shakes his head slightly and glances in Lucas' direction. It's obvious he doesn't want to say what's on his mind while our son is listening.

"We should probably give them both a quick bath," Malcolm tells me as he stands to fetch the bowl of water my papa left on his nightstand. Since Liana is still asleep, I let Lucas hold her while I unwrap Liam from the towel my papa swaddled around him. With the warm, wet cloth Malcolm hands me, I begin to wipe the front of Liam's little body down, removing the signs of his birth. When I flip him over to wash his backside, I can't help but marvel at how smooth and soft his sweet baby skin is to the touch.

Once he's clean, Malcolm swaddles him in part of a fleece blanket he just ripped into quarters with his hands.

"Ok, sleeping or not, you need a good wipe down, too, little Ms. Liana," I say, holding my arms out to Lucas. He scoots over and places her in my arms.

I unwrap her from the pink blanket Helena used. I notice that her umbilical cord is gone and that she has a perfectly healed belly button. I assume Helena probably did something to heal it so quickly. I remember her healing me after she snatched the seals away.

As I begin to wipe her with a clean wet cloth, her little eyes open to look directly at me. I suddenly find it very hard to breathe.

"What's wrong?" Malcolm asks, noticing my reaction.

"Her eyes," I say, staring at my daughter's face. "They're blue."

"Most babies are born with blue eyes," he says unconcerned. "They don't normally develop their natural color until their about six months old."

I slowly start to shake my head at him. "This isn't a normal blue, Malcolm. They're the same blue mine used to be."

Malcolm looks down at Liana and frowns, noticing the difference.

"Still," he says. "She'll probably outgrow the color in time."

I hope so, I think to myself, not wanting to alarm Lucas any more than I already have.

Once Liana's clean on her front side, I gently turn her over onto her stomach so I can wash her back.

I hear myself gasp and feel my blood run cold inside my veins when I see what's located at the base of her spine.

"Malcolm!" I involuntarily scream.

As I stare at the puckered skin on the lower portion of her back, all I can hear is my own ragged breathing. Faintly, I hear Malcolm ask, "How did she get a seal?"

I shake my head, rendered speechless as I stare at the shape of one of Helena's seals on Liana's back.

"What do you think it means, Anna?" Vala asks, looking up from Liana's back to me.

"I have no idea," I confess. My chest feels heavy with impending doom.

Why does my daughter possess a seal? Did Liana take it from Helena or did Helena give it to my daughter? If the latter is the case, what would make Helena give up some of her power so freely?

I don't have the answers to those questions yet, but I intend to find out what's really going on.

The only problem is, there's only one person who has the answers: Helena.

Author's Note

Thanks so much for reading *Reckoning*! The third book in this series will be titled *Enduring*. I plan to have it available by late summer or early fall of 2016. As always, you can follow my progress on the book every Sunday at either my Facebook page or my website.

Sincerely,
S.J. West

FB Book Page:
https://www.facebook.com/ReadTheWatchersTrilogy/timeline/
FB Author Page: https://www.facebook.com/sandra.west.585112
Website: www.sjwest.com
Email: sandrawest481@gmail.com
Newsletter Sign-up:
https://confirmsubscription.com/h/i/51B24C1DB7A7908B
Instagram: sandrawest481
Twitter: @SJWest2013

Made in the USA
Middletown, DE
09 April 2017